I0615790

ERROR
CODE::
LOVE

ERROR CODE:: **LOVE**

Not every story has a hero...

Suman Bhattacharya

Srishti
PUBLISHERS & DISTRIBUTORS

SRISHTI PUBLISHERS & DISTRIBUTORS
N-16, C. R. Park
New Delhi 110 019
editorial@srishtipublishers.com

First published by
Srishti Publishers & Distributors in 2014
Second impression 2014

Typeset by Eshu Graphic

To the compromising, yet fighting; traditional, yet rebellious; broken, yet optimistic; sleeping, yet awakening; struggling, yet surviving...

Indian Youth

CONTENTS

Acknowledgements   *ix*

Prologue   *xi*

Oops! Fasten Your Seatbelts!   1

The more IT, the less I see   10

A black Sunday – Face your damn fear   18

Dev's Journal Archives 1   31

    AUGUST 2004 - *When me and I met myself*

    NOVEMBER 2004 - *Money, Merit and other skills I lacked*

    FEBRUARY 2005 - *Jealousy, the first sign of love?*

Going back to hell   65

Choosing to remember- A journey   76

"Do you remember, my love?"   88

Love is blind; Friendship closes its eyes   98

Love one, trust none, do wrong to everyone   111

Dev's Journal Archives 2   **125**

    JULY 2006 - *Hearts are made to be broken*

    AUGUST 2006 - *Curing Evil with Evil*

    FEBRUARY 2007 - *A cheat code for Love*

The invisible scars   160

Forgive, but don't forget   170

Back to where it all started   178

Love and other irreversible mistake(s)   189

Dev's Journal Archives 3   203

       MARCH 2008 - *The final lie*

       APRIL 2008 - *Those 72 hours, an unforgivable sin*

The *first step to a thousand miles*   221

Friends- the family we earn   228

A bit like illness; a lot like love   243

The first touch, the last kiss?   254

I was holding on; I let it go   265

The formula of Love - there's none!   283

ACKNOWLEDGEMENTS

Every time we commence on a new journey, the first and final steps are taken by us. But on the way, there are hands that hold you, touches that comfort you and faces that give you courage and determination. A journey is a collective effort of numerous bodies and minds. People named herein helped me pledge, nurture and complete the journey of creating *Error Code Love*.

- My wife Karpur for her trust on this crazy software engineer who wouldn't socialize or sleep for months. For being patient and supportive while I pursued my wildest dream of penning my story. My parents for making me what I am today. I owe my love for literature completely to my mother. My sister Soma for being my book buddy, reviewer and very own critic.

- The entire Srishti team for their enthusiasm, creativity and support in every step of publishing. My first editor Manika Garg for adding sophistication to my rather colloquial English. Author, editor and friend R W

Jensen for her proficient editing bits on my manuscript.

- Author and cousin Sujata Massey for her encouraging feedback and priceless suggestions. My niece Sudatta for her blind faith on my manuscript. My friend and colleague Gautam Amin for being a friend who I can look up to.

- My cover designer Wasim Helal for an excellent cover design. Artist and friend Sakshi Garg for making my characters come alive through her illustrations.

- My company Adobe and my teammates for always being supportive and willing to help with anything. My college friends – this book is my humble tribute to those wonderful four years I spent with you. My Facebook page followers – thanks to each of you for inspiring me through all my ups and downs.

- Finally, thanks to you. Yes, you! The one who is reading this right now. You're generously gifting a few precious hours of your life to a young author's first creation. You're transforming his dream into reality. You're a true wizard, my friend. I hope you enjoy reading my book.

No more commercials. It's time. Sit back, relax and enjoy the ride! Welcome to the world of Dev.

PROLOGUE

I have been expelled from my college; a charge of sexual harassment.

Along with a year of college, I lost all my friends. My family is ashamed of me. All within the last seventy-two hours.

I pray I will wake up and it will just be a nightmare. Or I can use technology to build a time machine. I would give anything to reverse the clock and make it all right. But my Karma won't let me. I have to make amends for what I have done.

My mind replays the trauma, the mistake. I go through it again and again. Every time I close my eyes I am in a dark room sitting on the floor beside my bed. Mom opens the door and walks to me.

"What have you done?" she asks.

And every cell of body cries in pain, "I've made a terrible mistake Mom. It's all over. My life, my career, my education, my relationship, everything is over."

But that is not the beginning of my story. Once I was just like you. I wanted to be successful, a good son with a college degree. I wanted a happy and average life with a great girlfriend. I almost had it all. Almost.

But one day every thing changed. I messed up. I loved.

I'm not a hero ... and this is my story.

1

OOPS! FASTEN YOUR SEATBELTS!

The story of our life is about one perfect moment. That moment is something we strive for. A yes, a nod or an eye blink can make you run a thousand miles if it gets you to that. We rejoice, fight, laugh and cry, but through everything we still want to live that moment again and again. Whether you gain or miss it, you will try for yet another hundred years and make the same commitments and mistakes to get that one moment back.

"Sir? Sir? Can you please put your seat in the upright position? We'll be landing soon."

I stopped writing, "Sure." Not certain if she heard that. She had already moved on to the next passenger. I closed my journal and looked out of the window. What a beautiful sunny afternoon!

"Welcome to Bengaluru International Airport. The temperature outside..."

This part of a flight amuses me every time. I don't understand the hurry people are in to get off the plane. My thought process was interrupted as a man and a woman started pushing at me to gain a few precious seconds in getting off the plane. Most likely they didn't want to miss the fun the others were having all crammed up in the aisle. I made way for them and switched on my phone. Lots of missed call alerts and one message, all from the same number!

"Hey Champ! Welcome to Bengaluru. Sorry I couldn't come to airport. I have to complete some work today. I'll see you in the evening."

With my track record, only one person in the universe would call *me* 'champ.' That had to be Isha. Hearing from her sure felt good. I'd be meeting her today after a long time.

Coming out from the luggage area I tried to call Rishi. At least Isha remembered I was arriving today. That idiot didn't even bother to check with me. On the third try, he picked up.

"Hey Dev! I am off to lunch now. Let me call you later."

I couldn't find the appropriate foul language to scold this man, my best friend, who promised to meet me at the airport.

I controlled my anger. "What's your address? It's Jayanagar right? There was some main, cross, block, colony; lots of things. What should I tell the cabbie?"

There was a long pause on the other side. Yes, now he was downloading the data. "Hey Man! I am so sorry …Don't worry, I am coming in 15...no, 45 minutes."

"It's ok. You've already done enough. Just sms me the address." I kept my tone emotionless.

"Sure buddy. Sending right away! Take the key from the owner on the ground floor. Ours is on second. Welcome to..."

I disconnected. Enough of this drama! Time to get moving.

Airport cab facilities were non-happening at the Bengaluru Airport, unlike my hometown, Kolkata. There you would be immediately surrounded by cab drivers who would try to grab your attention by raising their voice. And if you were still undecided for more than a few minutes, they would try and help you with the luggage so you might end up playing a baggage tug-of-war with them.

This cab driver seemed pretty serious about his work. When I asked him about Jayanagar, he answered 'Jayanagar.' Nonplussed, I asked him a couple more questions. But I got the same answer, 'Jayanagar.' I understood either he was not that good with Hindi or he was like a RoboCab programmed only to help passengers reach their destination. No wonder Bengaluru is the hub of the Information Technology revolution in our country.

While entering the main city, I noticed a couple of things. The first was the attractive neighbourhood consisting of a perfect combo of multiple commercial, industrial setups and scenic parks. The second was the weather. The end of April is already peak summer in most parts of India, still I felt a perfect spring day on the breeze. I liked it already. This city might not come off as lively as other metro cities, but the 'Silicon Valley of India' had a charm of its own.

⊕⊕⊕

"Welcome buddy." Rishi shouted at me, "Have some vada & idlis. Try to get a taste of South India."

I looked up. Rishi looked exactly the same as I remembered; short hair cut, skinny boy from college with a smartass smile. Time didn't have any effect on his appearance. He had a big paper packet with him. The lady on the ground floor had offered me lunch, but I felt shy and refused. Over the next few hours I sorely regretted my decision. I desperately needed some food.

With swift hands I helped myself. "I thought you hated South Indian food?"

"People change man! Plus, it's the most economic food here. You can't afford Subway every day," Rishi explained.

"Tastes good! By the way, Isha messaged me and she wants to meet. I gave her your address. Are you guys in touch?"

"Not exactly. Not everyone is as lucky as you." Rishi smiled. I got the sarcastic bit but ignored it.

"You are joining your new work tomorrow, right?" Rishi asked. I nodded.

"Good. I'll give you a ride on my bike. Technoplaza is nearby."

I was already busy with my third idli, so I nodded again to concur.

Rishi sat near me. "It's really good to see you after such a long time."

We men are weak at expressing emotions. We hesitate to hug our best friend. We even hesitate to say we missed them. So all I could do for my best friend was to offer the last idli as a gesture that I had missed him too.

"You ate everything? You greedy monkey," Rishi laughed hard and jumped on me.

We started laughing and fighting. Funny, but that's how we express our affection. I really missed this psycho. My best friend.

⊕⊕⊕

"Am I ruining the party?"

Rishi and I were so preoccupied playing Multiplayer Football on Rishi's Xbox, we didn't realize we had a visitor.

I looked at the door and saw her. She had put on bit of weight in the last four years. Good, as she had been too thin back then. Her round face had an expert touch of makeup. She had done something with her hair too. It looked shorter, but nice. In college I had seen her only in Indian outfits; trendy stuff that she always carried off well. But this formal shirt and skirt and winning appearance reflected the corporate culture and she looked great! It took me some time to believe it was the same girl. Rishi's reaction was the same as mine.

"Is it a boy zone? Girls not allowed or what?" She smiled. Her smile was just as I remembered, 70% cute + 30% naughty=100% Isha.

I recovered, "You...you look so good." Rishi nodded. He was equally stunned with this version of Isha.

Isha smiled again, "You guys look good too. But look at you. You have put on weight." That last comment was definitely for me. Rishi was always in the underweight category. I remembered we used to buy jeans for him from the kid's section.

I wanted to make some small talk and ask how she was. But nothing came out. It's hard to believe how relationships change over time. After four years I was having trouble conversing with the person I spoke with the most in my entire college life.

Rishi saved me from further embarrassment, "Guys! Let's go out. The landlady is a bit conservative. She won't be happy with a girl up in here. There's a café nearby…"

Before he could finish Isha was already inside. "Wow! So you guys will be sharing the apartment. Oh look! Single bedroom! Interesting. Dev? I hope your taste hasn't changed." She started laughing at her own joke. Typical Isha.

Rishi's face turned red. I don't know why, but they never got along well. Before he could comment I barged in, "Very funny. Let's go. We can talk in the café."

"Roger that." Isha was already done with her survey of the apartment and gunning to go.

Rishi was a bit hesitant but I pulled him along. We walked to the nearest Cuppa.

"So guys, it's my treat," Isha declared.

I tried to protest, "Actually it should be mine; I am the one with the new job."

"Don't worry, Mr. Dev. I need a full-fledged dinner soon, you can pay for that. So it's decided, this is my treat and you pick up dinner for me soon. Ok Rishi?"

Rishi nodded. No surprise there. Rishi was always good with free food. With the first cup of coffee, sandwiches, and old friends, I was in Cuppa heaven. The good thing was Rishi and Isha started warming up to each other. Otherwise it would have been a nightmare for me staying in Bengaluru with two of my best friends not on talking terms.

Rishi got a call and went out in search of a better signal. That gave me a chance to speak to Isha alone. I had been carrying a burden for a long time and it was about time I expressed that to her. Time complicates things further. So many times I thought I would say this to her when I would see her next. But now, meeting her after all these years, I wasn't sure. I didn't have the courage to open old wounds.

"Well Divs. How are things?" Isha raised her eyebrows.

"You know it all, Ish. I am excited about this new job. It's so nice to have you guys back in my life. I…"

She didn't let me finish. "Oh, please stop boring me. Tell me about your love life. Are you seeing someone?"

"No!" I smiled.

"Stop it! You ask me to believe that?" She made a face at me.

"Yes, Ish. I am done with love," I said firmly. "Forget about me. What about you? How many guys are crazy about you?"

Girls dig compliments like that and Isha was no exception, "Shut up! I am single and not ready to mingle."

"Thank God. That'll save a few lives."

"What? You dirty..." she hit me softly and started laughing. It felt really nice to see her smiling. The last time I spoke to her, she was...

My thoughts were interrupted when Isha leaned in as if to share a secret. "Hey Divs, I think you should move to a separate house. Rishi's house is hardly big enough to be called a 1 BHK. I know how close you guys are, but think practically. I have some friends who can help you find a house near your office. Look, I am just concerned about your comfort and Rishi's. You understand, right?"

I smiled at her, "Of course I understand Ish. I know you wish only good for me. But as you rightly said, Rishi and I are close. We're like brothers. When I called and told him I was coming to Bengaluru, we didn't even talk about where I am going to stay. I can't leave him unless he wants me to. Don't worry, I'll be okay. My original house is not Buckingham Palace, you remember?"

"Okay. It's your call. But tell me if you need anything … deal?"

"Deal, ma'am!"

Rishi came back then, so we decided to go for a third round of coffee. Later we walked over to our house. I decided to stay back and help Isha find a ride to her apartment that she's sharing with colleagues. The lovely evening was about to end. Isha wished me luck for the next day.

"Get a local number tomorrow and call me. We'll meet this weekend." She sat in the auto.

"Yes Ish. But..." I hesitated, "I had something to say..."

"It's ok," she didn't seem to be curious. "I am not going anywhere. We'll talk some other time."

"Ok," I agreed. "Bye Ish. Take care."

"Hey! One second." She stopped me, holding on to my shirt. "Can I ask you something?"

I was surprised. "Shoot."

"You aren't here to meet Neera, right?"

There are some names, some incidents, and some memories which you want to keep in a dark, secret room; locked up with a lost key so that you couldn't go back even if you wanted.

I didn't know what to say. My face turned red. I tried to reply but my lips didn't cooperate. I wanted this conversation to be over right now. "No," I snapped. "Bye Ish."

I started walking without waiting for her to respond. I heard the sound of the auto fading away.

Neera. Thanks for bringing that up Ish. I took control over my emotions. Whatever is locked deep, deep inside should stay there. I have a big day coming up tomorrow.

2
THE MORE IT, THE LESS I SEE

"So you are Devo-sish Banerjee?"

"It's Devashish, Ma'am."

"That's what I said. You're late. Your starting time was 10 this morning."

I was speaking with Ms. Anita from the HR department. Honestly, I wasn't to blame for the delay, the culprits were Bengaluru auto drivers busy trying to rob my last penny in the name of fare. I could have shared my pitiful public transport experience with her but I doubted she cared. "Sorry for that. I got stuck in traffic."

"Get used to it. Bengaluru is infamous for traffic. It's not Delhi." She gave me a know-it-all look. Now how did Delhi enter the picture?

"Actually I am from Kolkata."

"Yeah I know. It's nearby. Right?" she said with an expression as if she jogged between Delhi and Kolkata every day.

Yeah, it's nearby, dumbo. Before your MBA, you should have read your grade four geography, I thought. Alas, we have freedom of thought but not speech in corporations, especially on the first day in a new company with your HR rep. Over the next 30 minutes, I gathered more evidence of the striking intelligence of the company's HR department. But every good thing comes to an end, and I was told to meet Mr. Hiten Shinde, my Project Manager.

Things were just getting interesting. I reached the third floor and moved to the last big room on the left.

"May I come in, Sir?" I knocked on the door.

"Yes!, Yes! Be my guest." The reply was slightly more dramatic than I expected. I entered the room.

Though I couldn't see him fully since he was sitting, calling him overweight was clearly an understatement. To my amazement, I saw a packet of chocolate and a box of cookies, both half-eaten, in front of him. He was sweating even with the air conditioning turned on full blast.

"So, you are that Bengali boy who joined today. Devo... Deva...what was your name...was it Devdas?"

"You can call me Dev, Sir." I put him out of his misery.

"That's better. You Bengalis like fancy names. Don't you?"

Now that's unfair. I agree some Bengali names can be complex and even the child named with one of those curses the parents when they start learning to write.

I tried to smile. "I don't know sir. For me, I prefer Dev."

"Ok. So Dev, why are you here?"

I started off with the 'Why do you want to join our company' speech I had mugged up for interviews.

"Sir, I really admire TTS as a company and a brand..."

"Oh, stop," he intervened, "I am asking why you are in South India? You know most people are vegetarian here. Can you imagine? Idli, dosa...what the hell? But you are from the land of fish. Wow! I love fish." He uttered those words with such intensity that I almost pictured him munching on a fish fry.

Poor fish, I thought. "So Sir, aren't you from here?"

His expression told me I had asked a dumb question. "Of course, not. I am from Pune." Then he continued, "So you can cook?"

Where was this conversation going? Not in my comfort zone at least. "Not exactly. Only Maggie and tea," I confessed.

"Hopeless." He seemed disheartened. "Ok, Dev. Let's talk work now. You are a Database Administrator? How is your expertise in Development?"

"Yes, sir. Though I have been mostly in Administration, I have done some hands-on scripting and development, especially on Microsoft Technologies."

"Good! I prefer all-rounders. Let me call Rajan. He will introduce you to the team. I have heard good feedback about you from the interview panel but you worked on a small project before. This is huge. You have to adjust to the work culture here. Watch how things are done and try to make your mark soon." He started dialling.

"I will Sir." Thank goodness. I was starting to doubt whether I was joining here as a software engineer or as a Master Chef.

⊕⊕⊕

My first day at the office was a mixed bag of experiences. After a 'mouthful' interaction with Hiten, I sat with Rajan, my team leader, for some time. The guy looked genuine and decent. He introduced me to the rest of the team.

Everyone seemed friendly, except a lady named Gayathri. I shook hands with everyone and went up to her and said, "Hi! I am Dev." She looked at me with an expression like I was a convicted criminal and walked away.

"What's her problem?" I asked Rajan.

"Don't worry, she is a bit unsocial. She doesn't talk much other than work stuff."

A bit? The word should be *anti*social, I thought. I liked the work part though. It should be more challenging than what I was used to and I would get exposure to new technologies.

At 6:30 I was looking to leave for the day, but hesitated since I didn't want to be marked as one who left early on his first day.

Rajan saved me, "Let's call it a day. Tomorrow you should get your desktop. The laptop will take longer. Take care of your personal things by the weekend and get settled in. Next week onwards I'll expect active contributions from you." He smiled.

"Sure. I am looking forward to it." I smiled back.

Going out of the quadrant I met Hiten.

"Hey Dev. How was your first day? No 'fishy' business, right?" *Snicker, snicker.*

What's the problem with this man? Why doesn't he leave his job and go fishing in the Amazon? I gave him a plastic smile and hurried off. That was end of day 1 at work.

⊕⊕⊕

Two days of continuous idli got me thinking; I need to find some kachoris and samosas pretty soon to survive in Bengaluru.

Rishi arrived home. "Hey Dev. How was the big first day?"

Don't get me started there, friend. I just gave a brief, "It was ok."

"Wow! You brought idlis. Here are some pakoras." I snatched at them.

"I'm sorry about this morning. I should have gotten up. But don't worry, I will definitely drop you off tomorrow." Rishi looked embarrassed.

I took advantage of the moment, "Actually, you should be sorry. But you can continue with your morning snooze. I have enrolled for office cab service. It's a bit costly but hassle free."

Rishi looked genuinely happy. It's amazing to see how much this man loves oversleeping. We finished snacking so I called him to help me unpack.

"So are you guys getting back together?" Rishi asked while pulling out my books from the airbag.

"What are you talking about?" I was confused.

"You know, I mean you and Isha."

"No, we're not."

"I don't like her much," Rishi said after a pause. "But she was good for you."

"Thanks Rishi. But we broke up long ago. So let's not talk about that. She's a great girl. If you spend more time with her you'll like her too."

"I doubt that. I overheard what she was suggesting to you yesterday." What! Was Rishi eavesdropping on our conversation? That's a clear invasion of privacy. We should give some personal space to our friends. I didn't express my anger though, "In that case, you must have listened to my answer too."

"Yeah, great job man!" Rishi laughed.

I stopped unpacking and looked at him. "Look Rishi, Isha has done a lot of things for me. Even this job. She is the one who got me referred through her friend. Whatever happens, she will always have an important place in my life…" I paused to take a breath, "…but as a friend. I am not comparing you guys, so just stop this silly fight."

"Yeah, I'm cool," Rishi made an irritating expression with his face, "But that great friend of yours dumped you four years back when you needed her the most. That bitch…"

"Enough Rishi!" I shouted, "It was not her fault." For a second I was amazed at the pitch of my voice. Needing some fresh air, I stormed out.

I don't understand why the people closest to me keep pushing me to talk about that phase of my life which I don't want to remember. When you don't know whom to talk to, mankind has only one saviour—mother. I called home from the nearest STD booth.

"Hey Babu! How are you? Why didn't you call me yesterday?"

"Stop calling me Babu, Mom. I am 26," I laughed.

"So how's Bengaluru? What are you eating? How is Rishi? You take care of your health, ok? Weather changes bring lots of diseases. You have a tendency to get a cough easily..."

Once a wise man said don't ignore your mother when she asks you whether you have eaten properly or not. When she is gone, there is no one in this world who will ask you the same question with the same degree of concern.

Five minutes of talking and I learned about the weather in Bengal, what my neighbours were doing, current prices of vegetables, and how the water problem affected our neighbourhood. Once I disconnected, I felt much more relaxed and walked back to my apartment.

Rishi was at the door smoking.

"Sorry. I overreacted." I smiled.

"It's ok man. I hit my limit too." Rishi threw the cigarette away.

"By the way, I found this in your backpack." He lifted something up.

"What?" I looked at him. Oh shit! One of my journals. Living with my best friend and his nature of poking his nose into everything was turning out to be a nightmare.

"Give it to me."

"You keep a diary? Seriously? Don't you think it's a bit girly?"

"It's a journal. Not a diary. Whatever, it's not your business Rishi. Give it back." I started tugging at the journal.

Rishi was more powerful than he looked. He pushed me away, ran to the bedroom, got to the other side of the bed and started reading out loud from a random page.

"*Something that keeps me going on a bad day is her smile... I never saw anything as stunning as this...* What the hell man? Were you on drugs writing this bullshit?" Rishi was laughing hard.

I tried to grab the journal, Rishi moved away. Suddenly he stopped. He looked shocked and confused, "Hey? You wrote all these things about her...not about Isha? What's going on man?" the journal dropped from his hand.

I picked it up and looked straight at him, "Rishi, if you want me to stay here with you, keep away from these journals and stop digging into my past. I mean it. This is my final warning." I put all the journals in my suitcase and locked it.

3
A BLACK SUNDAY – FACE YOUR DAMN FEAR

Boys, especially good friends, can't stay angry with each other for long. One good song, one good soccer match, one funny incident and we are back to normal. Rishi and I were no exception.

After the marathon 1st week at the office and constant 'foodle' with Hiten, I was looking forward to the weekend badly. It was my first weekend in Bengaluru. Normally Rishi would have made some plans. But we were under 'MTA' aka Minimum Talking Agreement. So I was not optimistic about the prospect of weekend fun.

Friday evening, the scene was different than what I'd expected. Rishi was already back and watching a match. Oh! I had forgotten all about India's one day series against South Africa.

"What's the score?" It came out naturally. Then I remembered about the MTA and acted as if I was not very interested.

"It's 45 for 1, 8 overs! We are chasing 295." Rishi answered. He acted quite normal as if we didn't have a World War III

18

mock drill a couple of days back. A peek at the kitchen told me Rishi had brought burgers. So clearly he wanted peace.

But I had to maintain my dignity, so I kept quiet. Rishi broke the ice, "C'mon Dev! Let's watch the match together, like old times." He called out, "Bring the packet from the kitchen. I got burgers for us."

I moved fast. In my life I have learned at least one thing, sticking to your ego in friendship and food just makes you a loser.

In India, cricket is a religion. As Sehwag started hitting more and more boundaries, the boundary wall created between us, two best friends, kept falling. When he reached 100, we were already hi-fiving together and when India won the match, I declared dinner was on me.

We walked over to a Punjabi restaurant.

Rishi asked, "So what's the plan for the weekend?"

"I was expecting you'd tell me."

"Ok, so let's plan. First thing is that I have to go to the office for a few hours tomorrow. Support projects suck, you know." He grimaced, "But the good news is I'll be back by early afternoon. We'll go out in the evening, maybe catch a movie. Then Sunday, we'll see. Unless you have any plans with your ex. Sorry. I mean Isha." After saying the last part Rishi made another classic expression.

I couldn't control my laughter. This guy is never going to change.

"Don't worry about my ex," I uttered the last word with extra stress. "She won't be here for a few days. She's travelling to Hyderabad for a recruitment drive."

"Ms. HR! Right. That's good actually." Rishi looked excited, "Then you should come with me for the party on Sunday."

"What party?" I felt suspicious.

Rishi was trying to get me into something he already had planned. He wanted to trap me and let me believe it all happened naturally. I've known this guy for the last eight years now and I had the feeling it was one of those ridiculous plans of his I definitely wouldn't want to be part of.

"It's no big deal. I am a member of this Bengali cultural association. We'll just go, enjoy poetry & music, have dinner and come back. You'll have a great time. Here comes the food … let's eat."

That's typical Rishi, he will decide things for you and before you can open your mouth to protest, he'll change the topic so his decision rules. That actually helps him skip the argument part.

"Wait! Are you telling me you are a member of some Bengali association where you go and listen to music and poetry? This is the same guy who was telling me writing a journal was girly? Huh?" I demanded.

"So?" Rishi started eating. Clearly he didn't want to talk about it. That raised my curiosity further. This was like a terrorist leader attending a seminar on world peace. Rishi could skip college classes for a soccer match or for a James Bond movie; but I couldn't take him to a single day of College Band Practice or get him to read a single novel I'd liked. Also, his childhood was spent mostly in Nagpur so this sudden secretion of Bengali hormone was just not digestible. There was something else beneath all this.

I decided to use my nuclear weapon, "You have two options. One, tell me the truth, or two, tomorrow I'll have to inform your soccer buddies about your latest self-discovery. They should know about the existence of this soft man hidden behind the tough Rishi who loves classical music and attends music parties. I am so excited to hear their feedback."

Rishi had this soccer group membership from college. These guys were supposedly toughies who made fun of me because I was interested in literature and music. Rishi acted macho in front of them for some stupid reason. This craze had him missing a Bollywood family drama which we saw in college. Instead, he chose to watch *The Matrix Reloaded*.

This was enough for Rishi to break down, "What? And you call yourself my friend? That's stabbing me in the back."

"Emotional blackmail won't help. I need the truth," I demanded.

"Ok fine, I'll tell you. Just don't do anything stupid. Deal?" He wanted confirmation. I nodded.

"Actually our company's regional head is one of those big shots in Bengaluru and a founder of this association. He has given the responsibility of running it to our manager. That guy is a freaking monster. He's obsessed about showing his boss and the advertisers that this organization is a big success. He forced us, all of his team members, to join and now we have to attend each damn party. Last time he even made us dance some drama bullshit as they were short of performers.

God! This is so humiliating. I just need another job offer. Then I will be gone like lightning."

I was trying to control my laughter but I couldn't, "That's what you're doing?" I just couldn't stop laughing, "What did you dance for your manager? Cabaret?"

"Look Dev, it's not funny," Rishi acted angry. "If you were in that position you would know I had no choice."

"Whatever, this is still funny man. And what did you tell me the other day? That you don't let your manager get out of line? Now I get it. You don't sing to his tune, you *dance*." I was laughing harder.

Rishi looked helpless but tried to save the day, "C'mon Dev. Stop it. Actually it's not that bad. You can see the best Bong beauties in Bengaluru there. Also, the food is delicious. This time you'll be there with me so it won't be that bad, right?"

I had to stop snickering after the last statement, what an anti-climax!

"What the hell? What makes you think I'll accompany you? Look, I have my own ways to die of boredom and humiliation."

Rishi was virtually on his knees, "Please Dev. I need you this time. At least come with me. If you don't like it, I won't force you the next time. Please?"

It got me thinking. Ideally, I just don't want to be part of this whole circus. But I have nothing to do this weekend. Also, Isha is not in Bengaluru. What could be worse than sitting alone at home on a Sunday evening? And there is also the free food.

I acted as if I was doing him a big favour, "All right. I'll go. But if I don't like the music and food, I'll not stick around."

"Done." Rishi's face was glowing, "I knew it. That's my buddy. Don't worry; I'll take care of you."

Let's see who takes care of whom, I thought. It sounded fun but I had a bad feeling about this whole party plan.

⊕ ⊕ ⊕

"I am not going to wear a Kurta!" I made myself crystal clear. First this man asked me to go with him to this Godforsaken party and now he was saying there is a dress code!

"C'mon. I have an extra pair," Rishi wheedled.

"What? Are you joking? You are a size 36 or 38 inches and I am 40," the idiot was getting on my nerves.

"Ok, leave it. Let's just go. Just try to wear something ethnic. Quick man! It's already 7."

"Yeah, whatever," I gave Rishi the dirtiest look possible and started looking for something 'ethnic' to meet the dress code.

The most ethnic thing I found was a short denim Kurta and jeans. I am sure Rishi wasn't happy with it but he didn't say anything. He was worried I would ditch him at the last moment.

We started out on Rishi's bike. That was a real visual treat. Rishi's Kurta flying in the air reminded me of Batman. I myself felt like the Joker though, sitting behind him and making sure I didn't fall off.

We reached Eastwood Hall in exactly 10 minutes. Eastwood Hall was pretty large with lots of folks inside. To one side there was a stage with a few chairs. Some people were sitting there and chatting. I couldn't see anyone performing on the stage. There was a game section with carom, cards and chess. Finally, I could see the most exciting part, the food section.

Rishi read my mind, "Wait, we'll go there later."

"You're the boss."

"Here comes the bloodsucker." Rishi pointed to a guy with specs, who looked like a typical geek with lots of good grades but boring as hell.

"What are you saying? This guy looks innocent," I tried to defend the nerd. "Are you telling me his real name is Bloodsucker?"

Rishi gave me a look like I'd just escaped from an asylum. "Don't go by the looks. He is a total menace. His name is Bala Subhash! B.S. aka Bloodsucker."

I simply couldn't believe this man was as terrible as Rishi was saying. "He looks quite mild to me."

Rishi fumed, "What? Mild? He's a loser who uses his power to screw with his team members. Can't believe this idiot got engaged last week. Poor girl! What? You don't believe me? Let me show you." Rishi pulled my hand.

"Hey Bala! How're you doing? Nice arrangements." Rishi offered to shake hands with his manager.

Bala ignored the outstretched hand. "Thanks. You're late. How many times do I have to remind you to be here before 6? I had to manage everything by myself. Venkat isn't going to like this much. Sometimes I wonder what happened to the recruiters nowadays. Every year the quality of engineers is decreasing. No commitment, no discipline."

The way Bala was putting it even I was feeling humiliated standing there.

"Who is with you?" Bala smelled new blood to suck.

"Oh! Dev, my friend. He is new in Bengaluru." Not daring to offer my hand to Bala, I waved.

Rishi continued, "He is Bengali and really interested in music. In fact, he sang a bit in college." What the hell is Rishi doing? Is he here to sell me to this vampire and gain a few extra plusses in appraisal? That's cheap.

Bala took over, "Friends are welcome. Make sure he joins first. Do remember the food is limited and we have guests coming who are actually invited. We don't want any shortage of food for them. The singing part I like. We can do with some extra singers. See you around Dev, and get membership quickly." Bala moved away.

"What the hell are you doing? Are you here to sell me out? And what was this singer bullshit? I did some chorus in college. So what? Everyone's a singer in college and the bathroom." I elbowed Rishi.

"Ouch! Behave Dev. Relax. I just wanted to end the conversation. I spoke with him only because of you, remember? You didn't believe this guy is a monster."

"You tried to end the conversation by almost starting a new singing career for me, that's very clever, Rishi." I tried to sound sarcastic. "The blood sucking part is definitely true. I would say he is a werewolf, vampire, and zombie all in one." I sighed.

Rishi started laughing. "Now you understand why I have to be here?"

"Sort of. Who is Venkat?" I asked.

"He's the regional head." Rishi explained, "and the founder of this association."

"Oh I see…" I tried to imagine Venkat, who had the ability to manage Bala. If the blood sucker is at this level, then what the hell is the limit for the Big Boss?

"By the way," another question haunted me, "This is a Bengali organization right? What is Bala doing here? Isn't this organization only for Bongs?"

"Not necessarily. But yes, it's difficult for others to enjoy these cultural activities as much as Bongs. There is a debate on why Venkat created a Bengali organization. I don't know for sure, maybe it's just one of his business ventures. About Bala, there's an interesting story. He has a mixed heritage. His father is Bengali and his mother is Kannadiga. This guy uses it whenever he can. He claims he is Bengali just to bank on Venkat's interest in Bengal. I heard there was a Kannadiga senior manager earlier and then Bala avowed he was basically from Karnataka. What a jerk." He made a face.

I took some time to digest all the information; this guy must be the next incarnation of Ravana or Kans from our mythology. I started pitying his fiancée.

"Screw Bala! Here are the girls," Rishi looked excited. "I told you about the best Bong beauties in Bengaluru." Rishi was not wrong; the sari-clad group of girls looked quite attractive. They were also giving us occasional glances.

"Let's go and meet them. I know a few. That's Rupali! Damn. She looks hot in a sari." Rishi couldn't hide his excitement. "C'mon Dev! Let me introduce you. Enjoy being a single man!"

"No thanks, Rishi. You go and chat with them; I'll have a soft drink." I am clueless about how to speak with girls I haven't met before and feeling uncomfortable is an understatement to express what I go through in those introductory meetings. Isha always used to make fun of me about this. Once I get to know them, it's a different ballgame though.

"Don't be shy Dev. They are very friendly. It's ok buddy."

"You go. I am here at the food section. Be quick and call me when you want to have dinner." I didn't give Rishi any chance to convince me further and walked over to the nearest snacks. Trying to be away from girls, I landed between more of them. I realized I was standing in front of the chaat counter; the second most important place for girls to gather after the beauty parlour.

I was thinking about moving away quickly but instead was ambushed with a question, "Is the Panipuri too spicy?" I looked at her, a sweet girl in a green sari.

"I…I don't know…I mean…" I stammered so badly as if she had asked me about my virginity.

"It's not spicy…madam." The Chaatwala saved me. I gave a thankful look to him but received an angry stare in return. Maybe he was not happy that the girls were asking me information about his prime ware.

"Thanks! Can I have one plate please?" Green Sari giggled. Why do young girls have to laugh at each and every small thing? What's so funny about panipuri not being spicy?

"Excuse me." My thought process was interrupted as the last statement was definitely for me. During my intellectual thinking I didn't notice I was blocking an important section of the counter.

"I...I...sorry," I moved away. I heard another giggle.

Making a fool out of myself in front of girls was one of my niche areas and I had lived up to my reputation. I definitely needed something to drink quickly. I started looking around.

"Have you seen a purse here?" I heard this behind me somewhere and wasn't sure if it was intended for me. I decided to ignore the voice. Some girl had lost her purse. What's the big deal? I need a drink.

"Anyone please? It's a black purse with a golden design on it. I must have dropped it somewhere here." I heard her again. To my surprise this time the voice sounded familiar and I could also relate this problem to someone I knew very well. I turned around this time, I couldn't stop myself.

Within a second my body froze, my blood circulation almost stopped and made it difficult to breathe.

The girl crossed in front of me but didn't notice me. After a few minutes I was able to move, but my brain didn't work well. I wanted to get away as fast as I could. I could clear my head standing in the parking lot. In the next few minutes I was able to think rationally. Maybe I was wrong, maybe I saw someone else, I tried to convince myself. In any case I needed to go back and get Rishi.

But while walking back hesitantly towards the hall

something inside told me, "You are not wrong Dev. After all these years you have seen her. It's no one else but Neera!"

⊕⊕⊕

When I stepped inside the hall, I heard clapping. I couldn't see anyone in the snack area or the game section. For some unknown reason everyone was gathered around the stage. I didn't bother about any cultural programmes going on, I just needed to find Rishi and get the hell out of there. I started walking towards the stage. Where did that idiot go?

The clapping started again and intensified my headache. I heard an announcement from the stage, "Let us congratulate Mr. Bala Subhash Roy, our beloved secretary of this association on his recent engagement and we are lucky to have the future Mrs. Roy with us today."

So that's the joke happening on stage. Bloodsucker's engagement celebration. Continue, you losers, I want to be out of here now. Where is Rishi? I didn't notice while searching for Rishi that I had ended up standing very close to the main stage. There I got a glimpse of Bala in his shiny suit and his future wife.

I saw the purse before her face. So she had found it. It was exactly like she had said. Black with golden geometric lines. Then I noticed the owner.

They say lightning doesn't strike twice. But 'they' are wrong. Am I dreaming? I tried pushing a couple of guys out of my way to see the stage clearer. They didn't take it very well and pushed me back. Maybe I had pushed them harder than I realised or they didn't want anyone coming between their fake cheer for Bala and a good performance rating.

I felt dizzy and was about to fall when two lean, firm hands held me up. "Take it easy guys! Let me take care of him," I heard a deep voice. Rishi's. My friend had found me, even though I couldn't find him. I was feeling seriously sick. Rishi helped me get out of the hall. I didn't protest, maybe I didn't have enough strength to do so.

Rishi left his bike there and called a cab. I was the patient and he was the attendant, so I didn't bother about that stuff. I spoke for the first time when the cab started moving.

"Rishi, I feel sick."

"I know buddy. I am here," Rishi assured me.

"Rishi…is Bala marrying a Bengali girl? I mean…" I searched for words.

Rishi never believed in sugar-coating his words. He always bats the truth right at your face. That's why I used to mock him, calling him my conscience. But today it wasn't very funny.

Rishi said, "Yes, Bala is marrying Neera!"

DEV'S JOURNAL ARCHIVES – 1
AUGUST 2004
When me and I met myself

The first day in an engineering college is a big and exciting day for all first year students. Teachers give you inspirational speeches.

It's all crap! Seniors are out there to rag the hell out of you and teachers are hesitant about your abilities as you must have screwed up your JEE ranking to end up in this private college.

Now these are the two extremes of what could happen to you on the first day of college. My experience ended up in between.

It didn't start well and finished the same way. My parents accompanied me the first day. I am not sure it was to give me moral support, more to check out where their son had managed to land in the Indian educational business. When we took the highway from the E M bypass, we saw boards advertising Oceanic Institute of Technology – *This Way 10 minute drive.*

Mom got a bit excited, "Look, it's a big college. They have billboards all around." Moms are made of a different material.

They will find a way to be proud of their child even if the loser ends up getting a rank which gets him no chance of admission in any of the reputed colleges.

Fathers are a more realistic type, "Whatever. No one has heard about this institute anyway. They must give directions."

Mom was already in love with my unseen college and about to say something in favour of it, but I gestured at her to stay quiet. I already had my share of scathing, extempore speeches from Dad on how I screwed up my ranking. I didn't need another one. After twenty minutes of driving, when I was starting to wonder if there was actually an engineering college somewhere in between these paddy fields, we saw a couple of buildings in white with a garden in the front.

No way could this be a 10 minute drive from the Bypass unless people are travelling by jets. But the college looked okay to me. It was quite a big area. The prospectus had shown a picture of a swimming pool. That I couldn't see, though there was a pond visible far away which could have gotten the marketing team excited about publishing it as a swimming pool. Other than a few white lies mentioned in the prospectus, overall the campus looked fine.

Time to bid goodbye to parents. Dad didn't look too impressed with the campus but thankfully he kept quiet. Mom was emotional as usual, "Take care of yourself, okay? Don't listen to those naughty seniors. They make you do things. Study hard. And eat your lunch on time." She touched my hair and tried to adjust it to give me the best look possible as per her fashion sense, which unfortunately was stuck in the '70s.

Someone giggled just behind us. There was another family, a girl in a pink suit accompanied by her parents. The girl was smiling and I understood the fun element was supplied by my mother. Maybe Mom realized that too. She gave the girl a dirty look and was about to start the second inning of valuable suggestions, but I intervened. "Mom! It's ok. I am not staying in a hostel. I am going to come back home in the evening, so keep some tips for tomorrow."

I entered the college along with that girl. I asked one of the boys standing near the stairs if he knew where the registrar's office was. In reply he asked, "Section C?" Was I supposed to know my section in advance? My puzzled look was an answer in itself so the guy asked me. "First day?" I nodded.

"Then you are section C. Go to the second floor and walk straight. End of the hallway you will find the registrar's office." I thanked him and took off. Then I noticed Pinky was following me. I tried to ignore her but she caught up while we were climbing the stairs.

"Hi, I am Isha! My first day too." As if I was interested.

It's not that she pissed me off by making fun of my mother's affection a few minutes back. I knew my mother could be too dramatic at times. The fact is, I don't feel comfortable with girls other than my family. I studied in a boy's school for the last 12 years and lived in a society where if you dared to speak with a girl of your age, the neighbours started gossiping and making marriage plans the same evening. So ignoring the primal instincts of my teenage life and avoiding girls had been the best choice for me for the last 18 years.

Still, in college I had to deal with girl students. So I tried to stammer as little as possible, "I am...um...Devashish."

"Hi Devashish, it's nice to meet you. Let's find the registrar's room together."

I could have just smiled and walked with her. Instead I produced a sound in my throat, "Uhhh." Sometimes I hate myself for being such a fool. We reached the second floor and walked down the hallway. I stole a few glances at her. She was not the most beautiful girl I had ever seen, but there was something attractive about her. Light make up perfectly complemented her light-olive complexion. Her shoulder-length hair was effortlessly arranged and her confidence was visible even in her silent lips. Her eyes were vivacious with a body language that screamed she was here to achieve something. Contrary to my loser self that just wanted to pass the day and watch television in the evening. I noticed lots of human eyes scanning us, mainly Pinky, aka Isha. I sincerely doubt if anyone was checking me out, a 5'7 average build mama's boy with a few extra pounds and a 70's haircut, wearing a grey half-shirt and boring trousers. Isha looked unmoved by all the attention. We reached the room with a sign: Raja Sen, Registrar, and were asked by an assistant to join a queue of at least 40 students.

The registration process was boring and time consuming, but I felt more comfortable as Isha found some girls to be friendly with. I was able to talk to some of the boys in the queue. Isha said bye and shook hands with me before leaving which had every guy turning around to look at me. I ignored all the attention and entered the room.

⊕ ⊕ ⊕

After receiving our ID cards and finishing other formalities, around 60 students gathered in the classroom. The door had a poster attached saying "Welcome Section C." So that guy was correct.

I joined my new boy 'gang' sitting in the class. The room was filled with enthusiastic voices as everyone was trying to guess what was going to happen next. Suddenly six boys and two girls entered the room. They were followed by some more students. Everyone stopped talking.

"Well, well. Rajiv. These guys need to learn some etiquette. Let's start by teaching them how to give seniors some respect. C'mon losers. Stand up now."

The program was clear to all of us. We were going to be ragged for the next few hours. I was comfortable with foul language, most boys are by this age. But still I felt nervous anticipating what was coming.

The boy referred to as Rajiv jumped right over the table portion of one of the benches. "Section C, I am Rajiv, Fourth Year Computer Science. These are my friends and your seniors. You are the last lot of students to join this year. We are already satisfied with sections A and B so it is your turn now. It's up to you whether you want to make it easy or painful. So rules first! Number 1, you guys will greet each senior in the morning and evening with a salute and call them sir or madam. No exceptions. Number 2, Section A and B joined before you and have better rankings which makes them superior to you. So you have to greet them with respect too."

That was something which definitely offended new students. Section C students started whispering. Rajiv raised his voice, "Silent fuckers! I didn't ask for your opinion. Keep your fucking opinion to yourself. I am the one to tell you what to do here."

There was silence again.

"Rule number 3, no belts for boys, no sunglasses and no watches. For girls, no extra makeup, no scarves and no nail polish. If we find anyone breaking the rules, the result will not be good."

Again a bit of whispering started which Rajiv silenced with his booming voice, "Silence!"

"You guys are little bastards. Aren't you? You have a problem with my rules? I want to know who has any issues. Raise your hand. Got guts? C'mon."

No one raised their hand. "What happened rebels? Peed in your pants? For the next 30 days you are ours, whenever we tell you to do something, you do it. Get it? Boys take off your belts and watches now and girls take off your hair bands and scarves."

"Sorry, I can't." Someone close to my bench declared in a hesitating voice. I looked at him. A fair, short haired, scrawny boy about my height, looking at least three-four years younger than the rest of us was standing there.

"Huh? What did you say?" Rajiv didn't expect anyone to contradict him so quickly after such a motivational speech.

"I said I can't undo my belt. My trousers are too loose. They will fall off." The skinny guy sounded more confident this time.

"Oh! I see you, milky boy. You sure are under developed. Why don't you ask your mother to give you Complan?" someone from Rajiv's gang commented. A wave of laughter filled the room.

The boy replied, "I did. Didn't help much, though." Another series of laughter filled the room.

The seniors didn't like the repartee much, "Answering back? You want to look tough, kid? We'll toughen you up. Undo your trousers and give us a walk in your undies. Do it now." the same guy behind Rajiv shouted. Pin-drop silence; this was going to a level beyond fun. I was feeling bad for the boy.

"Wait," Rajiv interfered, "Not now Kunal! I don't want nudity with the girls present. We'll take care of him later. What's your name?"

"Rishi, sir."

"Okay Rishi," Rajiv seemed satisfied since Rishi called him sir. "I don't give a damn if your mother didn't feed you enough or your trousers are loose. No belts tomorrow. Hold your pants while walking if you have to. Am I clear?"

Rishi nodded. Rajiv continued, "And boys? No flirting in our presence. All these girls are your sisters. One Casanova act and you will face my wrath."

"We already have one lover boy in the lot." someone commented.

"Who are you?" Rajiv asked the anonymous speaker. "I am Neel sir. Neeladri, CR from Section A." The speaker walked to the front of the room. That meant I could see him now. It was the same guy who had directed me to the registrar's room. What the hell? This guy looked so friendly and here he was trying to get someone from our section screwed just to get in the good books of the seniors.

"So are you saying we have a Casanova already in the group? Who is it?" Rajiv looked excited at the prospect to rag another so soon.

I didn't have any idea where this was heading. Before I could blink Neel pointed a finger at me. I was shocked. Me? Seriously? A Casanova? It's like giving the 100 meter sprinting gold medal to a sumo wrestler.

"This one? With the Rajesh Khanna hairstyle?" even Rajiv was hesitant to believe I was the one. "Girls have such bad taste nowadays. What did he do?"

It didn't really matter what I did or not. But at least one should have a decent conversation with a girl to deserve that fate. I hardly exchanged any words with Isha! What is Neel Armstrong's problem? If he wants to talk to Isha for 36 hours at a stretch he can be my guest. Why the hell is he dragging me into all this?

"I didn't do anything sir." I tried to protest but Neel was playing the perfect Manthara from Ramayana as he described my sins to Rajiv and the group. He kept his voice low so I couldn't hear much of what I was charged with. Perfect. A Kangaroo Court.

"Well ...well...Rajesh Khanna, you seem to be quite popular with the girls. Why don't you show us your lady-killer skills?" Everyone, including my newly made friends from Section C, started laughing. My face turned red. "Come here lover boy, show us your charms." Rajiv jumped down from the bench in excitement. I was amazed to see how everyone was cheering and having fun on my account.

"What the hell chicken? Are you going to come out here or do you want me to come there?" I preferred neither; but given the circumstances it seemed I had to choose. So I got up and with slow and shaky legs walked towards Rajiv. Seniors whistled and clapped.

Where I stood, I could see Isha sitting in the first row. All my anger moved from Neel to Isha. Why the hell did she have to talk to me?

I tried to see Isha's expression but she looked away. Maybe she was feeling bad for me or maybe she was afraid her name would also be dragged into this. Rajiv was ready to start his act.

"I need a girl from section A or B to come here. Hey girl, you! Come here," Rajiv called out to someone from the spectators at the door of the classroom.

I didn't care who was coming or who wasn't. I was looking at the floor. People cheered as the unknown girl from section A came and stood in front of me. Rajiv was happy to set up the stage for his big drama.

"Ok, Babumoshai. We have given you a heroine. Now let's see your magic. I want to see how you impress a girl. Dance, sing, strip, propose; do whatever you have to do but you will be up here till this girl is impressed."

Someone from the seniors shouted, "Strip, strip." I didn't feel that was required. With the umpteen numbers of eyes on me, I felt naked anyway. I was slowly going into a trance.

"Say something," someone standing very close to me whispered. That brought me out of the trance. I looked up and saw her for the first time. This must be my Section A heroine. Though my situation was screwed up to 9.99 on a scale of 10, I couldn't take my eyes off her. Her ponytailed hair framed a perfectly oval face. Agitated fair hands adjusted her wavy forelock. She was shaking a bit with all the eyes focused on us. Waiting for me to reply, finally she looked up. Damn! I hadn't seen anyone with such deep eyes ever. She could be a good psychiatrist, I thought. People could easily get hypnotized by those eyes. Then I realized it was a bad time to be poetic.

I had to say something. "What?" I whispered to her.

She clearly didn't expect me to ask for a suggestion. Her expression screamed 'Hopeless' at me. "How would I know? Say something and finish it. This is so humiliating for me."

Oh! So it was humiliating for her and I was receiving the Nobel Prize? Urgh, girls! I needed her by my side so I tried to be reasonable. "Please suggest something. I can't think of anything."

She looked confused, maybe she had never seen a loser like me before, "I don't know. Say something about me. Something you like about me, maybe my features …say you want to meet me at some place…just do it quickly… get it over with."

I listened to her and tried to form a few sentences in my mind, at least in the working part of my dysfunctional mind.

"What the …They already are whispering. I must admit this loser has something about him," Rajiv laughed very hard and his gang joined in.

"But we want to have fun too. So let's hear it loud and clear. Say it, you loser. Now!" He punched the bench and shouted so hard I almost peed in my pants. All sentence formation evaporated and the last working cell of my brain collapsed. Unfortunately my mouth still worked.

I said something like this, "I like…I like your features … Let's do it now…any place…get it over with quickly."

It sounded so damn horrible and everyone inside the room burst into laughter. I took a second to realize what I had actually said, and then I started to look at the reactions. Everyone around me was falling here and there in laughter, but to my surprise my partner in crime, the girl from section A, was laughing hard too. I just couldn't look away. I had never seen anyone express such emotions through laughter. Her smile was something that could bring cheer to the saddest of days. I started smiling too.

Before the seniors could get out of their laughter trauma, someone from their group announced, "Guys! Let's move. Prof. Vivek is coming." Prof. Vivek sounded like the police in Bollywood movies. They appear only after the murder has taken place and the villain is off at a safe distance.

My heroine didn't bother to say thanks after such a phenomenal proposal from my side, instead she just ran away. I was able to see her ID card hanging from her slim neck: Neera Sinha, ECE, I year - Section A.

We were let go early after the introduction speech from Vivek Joshi, our Electronics and Communications HOD.

The day took a lot out of me but somehow I didn't mind. I had some strange reason to be happy inside and I didn't realize what it was. I couldn't wait to reach college tomorrow.

⊕⊕⊕

NOVEMBER 2004
Money, Merit and other skills I lacked

For the last few weeks I hardly touched my journal. First semester examination is on the deck and we had to cover tons of pages of giant alien books on all possible engineering subjects. Though we all had our specific streams, for some strange reason, through the first year we also had to read mechanical, electrical and civil, basic electronics, C programming language... the list goes on.

Learning is a great idea but studying to pass exams is a big pain in the ass. The pain was more acute for Section C students, since we had started our class a month later than usual. All thanks to our fucked up ranking and the limited bank balances of our parents that kept us in the waiting list for most colleges for a long time. In today's educational system you need either of these two M's in an extreme amount: Merit or Money.

Long story short, we didn't get a chance to survive the ragging period properly but were hit badly as the mock tests began for the First Semester. I did terribly in the first set, but recovered in the second. The occasional declaration of Dad's downward spiralling financial status (my tuition fee being the prime reason) kept me awake for many nights. But I realized I am not star son material. After three sessions of late night studying, I just had to refresh with occasional porn and computer games for the next few nights.

The most important part of my recent college life is Rishi. We bonded very well and have become inseparable. Rishi is a fun person to be with and I liked him right from the first day's belt saga. I don't think I did anything likable in my 'indecent proposal' act, but he was the only guy who didn't mention it to me later.

He has something honest about him. Apart from his tendency to insult music artists and novelists which sometimes becomes intolerable, overall he is fun. He already knows everybody in college and is comfortable with everyone, including girls. I was shocked the other day to learn he had the numbers of many girls already, whereas I hardly recognize the faces of any students other than from my own section. Somehow he makes everyone comfortable around him.

I think I liked him and wanted to befriend him from that first day. He seems everything I am not. Smart, confident, and comfortable with girls. I like how he acts as a mirror to me and lets me see my own shades which I am unaware of or perhaps don't want to see at all. I don't know what he finds cool about a below average guy like me, but he seems to like spending time with me.

I also made peace with Isha recently. I really hated that girl and used as many foul adjectives as possible in my imaginary angry speeches to her. But it is difficult to stay mad at a girl who travels with you every day. We had pick up and drop off service from college buses at specific points of the city. Isha and I usually boarded a bus from the same stop and during our return we used to take the shared three-wheeler autos along the same route. I wanted to avoid being in the same auto with her, so I came up with a strategy. The first few days I waited and let her take the auto first. It worked initially but soon turned into a bit of pain for me as she joined a gossip-girls group who hung out at the stop after getting off the bus. They made fun of boys, teachers and other girls and sometimes their sessions ran for quite long. They didn't really care who was listening and even what they were talking about. After a regular interval I could only hear 'Ha Ha Ha Ha.'

Waiting for their sessions to be over and donating blood to the mosquitoes at the bus stand didn't seem great options. So I decided to change my timing. It worked for the next few days and when I started to believe that I had the perfect solution... it happened.

One evening I got into the auto and the driver was waiting for another passenger. These shared auto drivers would make perfect project managers. They believe in total resource utilization. They are never satisfied with less than six passengers. Till every inch of their auto is filled with human flesh, they just don't get enough motivation to start the vehicle.

"Can you move a bit please?"

We finally had our last passenger. All the passengers looked excited. They had almost lost hope the vehicle would ever start. However, I was in a bit of a dilemma since respecting the request would mean moving and the next movement of my body would take me onto the lap of the lady sitting beside me. I acted as if I was trying to shrink my body and make more room. She squeezed in beside me and said, "Thanks Devashish! That's your name right?" Holy shit!

All cryptic, I shot a Yes at her, keeping it brief intentionally. Already the driver, a couple of boys sitting in the front and that lady had given me an 'Ok so we can see what's cooking' look when Isha pronounced my name. What's wrong with our society? A girl can have a normal conversation with a boy in public. Sometimes it makes me feel we are still living in the Stone Age.

Then what Isha did shocked me and all the other people in the vehicle. She held my hand and said, "Hey sorry for the other day. It was my fault. I don't know what they were thinking. I can feel if someone is trying to flirt. You are not like that...I..."

The lady next to me had her eyes glued on our joined hands. I got rid of Isha's soft hands quickly, "Can we get down and talk please?"

"But..." Isha looked confused. Why can't girls see what's happening around them? "My stop is different than yours...I mean..."

"I'll get off with you," I assured her. When we got off at her place, the driver gave me an evil smile while taking our fare. I ignored him and walked away.

I already had enough fuel inside me all set to burn from the last couple of months and Isha's action here was the perfect matchstick.

Fire came in my words, "What's going on? You introduced yourself to me, followed me and then said good bye to me on the first day. Next thing I know, I was accused of being romantic with you. Today you are telling me you knew I was not flirting with you. Holy crap! I hardly spoke any words to you! Also in the entire wide world you choose to say sorry in a crowded auto while holding my hand? Don't you see people are staring? What's wrong with you?" I stopped to breathe and was shocked to see Isha was laughing merrily.

What an anti-climax, I wanted her to feel bad at my poisonous words and there she was enjoying my bitter blast.

"So you felt shy when I held your hand?" she was still smiling. Damn! Of my speech, she just filtered her own favourites. I was getting really worked up. "Bye." I started to walk.

"Hey! Dev! Chill. Please don't leave like that. Please! Let's start afresh okay? No more harsh words. Can I offer you our local golgappa? It's the best, you know. I owe you that."

"No thanks." I said, "I am late." Though I noticed she called me Dev.

"Please Dev. Look, I have never said 'please' so many times in such quick succession to anyone. So...c'mon buddy..."

When a pretty girl says sorry it's difficult to ignore her. Isha won me over with her feminine charm and I ended up having golgappas with her which were indeed very good. She didn't seem that bad as we talked. She is crazy of course and a bit self-obsessed, but I couldn't stay mad at her.

Though things with Isha are fixed now, I made another blunder in my engineering drawing mock test.

I never really liked the subject from day 1, and drawing with such a large T- square didn't seem to be my cup of tea. But I needed decent marks to secure a good internal score. We had our mock tests stream wise. So all the electronics students from three sections were randomly grouped in three batches and sat together for the test. Luckily Rishi and I were grouped in the same batch. Rishi came up with the news that a girl named Sapna in Section A was excellent at drawing and she was in our batch. So we planned to save our asses by arriving a bit earlier on the day of the test and grabbing seats next to her. When I entered the classroom I saw at least 30 students had beaten me to the exam room. I didn't know who Sapna was, so I started looking around for Rishi. I saw him at the end of the room fighting and pushing two other students. Amazingly, this clash was happening next to a gentle girl who seemed to be enjoying it.

That must be Sapna! So we had to fight hard to get a place near her. I saw Rishi literally battling for that goal. I was dumbfounded at the whole situation. Rishi was pissed off as I took far too much time to reach him. "What the hell are you doing, lingering at the door? Do you need an invitation?" Rishi shouted. I still stood transfixed.

"Throw me your bag." Rishi was losing ground fast.

"What?" My bag? Why? Does he need a weapon?

"I ...I can't ... Give me your bag...need to...block the place," Rishi muttered. He was almost on the verge of defeat.

In desperation I tried to throw the bag towards him and it got stuck on my hanging T.

Why does everything related to me end so disastrously? I pushed my bag far too hard to get rid of it and it shot off like a cannon ball. Rishi had lost the battle anyway and some random guy had won the place beside Sapna. But that was not the worst thing to happen. My bag flew in the *Matrix* style and hit a girl in the face.

A WOOOOOH sound filled the classroom. And then everyone was silent. As usual, I took some time to digest what I had done and when I got my senses back, I saw ten students gathered around the casualty. I couldn't see my actual victim. Someone shouted, "Take her to the restroom."

Considering that the best idea, the contingent paraded slowly out of the class. I was thinking I should go and check on her but the active members of the self-appointed nursing group gave me a 'get lost' look.

"What's wrong with you?" I didn't realize Rishi had walked towards me.

"The bag slipped from my hand."

"Whatever. It was a bit funny though. Let's hope she doesn't complain to the regulation committee." I kept mum. It was Rishi's idea to throw the bag. Smarty pants, why don't you shoulder some responsibility for the throw-away bag too?

Rishi was judgemental, "I don't know how you could throw so terribly almost in the opposite direction?"

"Should I go and say sorry to her?"

Rishi shook his head, "Not a good idea right now! She was

already pissed off with you and she might even kill you now." Rishi's wisdom wasn't comforting me.

"What do you mean she was pissed off with me earlier? I hit her for the first time." I was trying to analyse how damned my position was.

"Oh man! You didn't recognize her? It's the same girl you tried to impress on the first day with that unique proposal. Now you hit her in the eye. Have you heard of Dinesh Sinha, the advocate? Of course you haven't. But most of us have. He's a powerful man and a trustee here. Your bad luck, she's his daughter. You fucked up badly, my friend."

I started shivering. I was in the worst possible situation a human being could manage to be in. Trustee's daughter? Seriously? What next? How badly will my dad react if I have to go back to a degree college?

Suddenly everyone seemed in a hurry to get back to their seats as Professor Saha entered the room with a set of papers. "C'mon," Rishi called me. "Sit behind me. I can pass info from Sapna to you."

I nodded but was looking at the door; almost all the nurses and doctors had returned to the classroom but the patient was missing. Is she hurt badly? Does she need an artificial eye? Is she already complaining about me to her Trustee dad?

Prof. Saha announced, "Everyone settle down now. The test starts in five minutes."

Rishi pulled at my hand, "What are you thinking? C'mon. Pick up your bag and sit behind me."

I had to see how she was, and more importantly, what she was up to. I couldn't bear the suspense anymore.

I picked up the bag and gave it to Rishi, "Put this on the bench behind you. I'll be back in two minutes."

I rushed out to stand near the ladies toilet. I had absolutely no clue what to do next. I needed to see what was going on inside. Time was passing by and the exam would have already started. I was toying with the idea that maybe she was not in the restroom at all and had already returned to the classroom. As I was about to move back, the door opened and there she was; looking beautiful even with a black eye. I had just wanted to see how she was faring but she came and stood bang in front of me. I immediately regretted my decision to come checking on her. There was no chance I could come up with a decent sentence to show my concern or explain how sorry I was. I was back to the 'deaf and mute' Dev.

Luckily she spoke first, "Are you insane? Don't you understand how dangerous that could have been? I could have lost my eye."

I looked at the brighter side, at least she recognized me as the culprit; that meant she didn't need an artificial eye. I needed to say sorry and swiftly at that before I had to say it in front of the whole regulation committee. But before I could say anything she spoke again, "Because of you I am late for the exam too."

In desperation I announced my grief with the best possible intensity and the worst possible choice of words, "I am so sorry! Please! Please! Don't complain formally. Don't ask your father to suspend me. Please!"

I could have just said a simple sorry but I held my reputation up and spoke the exact words I shouldn't have.

"What do you know about Dad?" She turned back towards me and raised her eyebrows as high as she could.

"I…I have heard…" I mumbled.

She bit her lips thinking. I could not afford to let her think longer and get pissed off, so I intervened, "Look! I know what I said that day might offend you and today again I did something horrible. But trust me, I didn't mean any harm. That day I was out of my mind with the pressure of ragging, and today Rishi… my friend asked me to throw the bag. I am not good at throwing things. Believe me, the bag slipped from my hand. I know you are hurt but please don't get me suspended…" I was amazed I could speak so quickly to a girl. It's true that you explore your true potential only when it comes to survival.

She looked at me with one good eye. "What's your name?" Does she want to remember it to tell her father? Oh God!

I stammered, "D…Dev…"

"Look Dev… I don't know who told you about my father. But I don't want anyone to know. I am here on my own merit and I don't want to disturb my father for every small thing, especially not petty stuff…"

I had never felt so delighted to be referred to as petty before.

She continued, "…and about you. I didn't mind the other day. You were being ragged and I was pulled in too. It's supposed to be fun…right? Don't make things too serious when they are not. Today, you did something irresponsible. You are sorry about it. My eye will be better in a couple of days. That ends the matter. Can we go to class please? It's already 15 minutes into the exam."

"Yeah! Sure..." I was on cloud nine with my great escape and I really didn't give a damn about the test anymore. She looked like an angel to me, without wings of course, and with one black eye.

When we walked towards the classroom she looked at me, "Can I ask a favour?" I nodded. "Please don't discuss my father! I don't want to be treated as Daddy's girl for the next four years," I respected her more for that.

I rushed to assure her, "I am not going to bring it up again. I don't know how my friend figured it out but I'll tell him not to spread this further."

She looked more comfortable now. "Thanks! By the way, my name is Neera! Nice to meet you, Dev. Don't throw things at me in the future," she smiled.

I smiled back. Neera, I had read her name from her ID card on the first day but it had slipped my mind. I am not going to forget it again, that's for sure.

FEBRUARY 2005

Jealousy, the first sign of love?

If January was a horror show with first semester exams, February didn't provide much comfort either. I hate results more than exams. My performance wasn't really as per expectation but I did learn the rules of survival in the engineering college through it.

First rule, be born brilliant. I wasn't. The second rule is learning to mug up all semester. The third and last rule is learning to carry chits with you confidently in the safest place possible: your clothes. Alternatively, hide books and papers somewhere in the college bathroom—preferably in the dirtiest place possible. Don't bother about hygiene.

It is not that I didn't know cheating existed in school or colleges or I was born a saint and wanted to die as one. I peeked and even copied parts from my friends and returned the favour. But I hadn't carried chits, notes, or books in any of my exams earlier. I survived different exams but somehow I managed on my own.

Here I prepared for the semester with a similar mindset. However, I soon learned things are done a bit differently in private engineering colleges. The first day we had a paper on electrical engineering. I had two things to rely on, first all the mugging up I could do from 'B.L.Theraja' and second, all the exciting deals I offered to God in exchange for mere passing marks. I got my first shock when I entered the bathroom on our floor just before the exam.

"What are you doing?" Someone held me from the back before I could enter.

"Pissing …That's what we are supposed to do here." I tried to educate him.

"Not here bloody fool… Go somewhere else to pee."

"What if I have to go for number two?" I was getting curious about the actual motive behind his interest in where I should take a piss.

"What? Don't even think about doing it here. I have hidden my book in the commode." He finally revealed his secret mission, "It's taped inside. Don't flush it. Don't come near this toilet. Go to some other floor." He was really disturbed seeing my unawareness.

"What about the other toilets in here?" My curiosity was increasing, "I could use any of them."

"Are you mad? Next one is Sid's Xeroxes, and the next is Rita's reference book ...then..." he tried to remember the sources. Wow! I was impressed with his mind-mapping technique with commodes. But I was surprised too, "Rita? But this is a gents' toilet. How will she get her stuff?"

He smiled like a fox at my foolish question, "That one is just for backup. We shuffle the books later."

I was fascinated with the whole 'commode-knowledge-sharing-system', but had to respond to nature's call and ran towards the security urinals on the ground floor.

I met Rishi an hour later and we exchanged chits. Mine were dripping wet. I shuddered to think where it had been hidden. As the papers passed by I chose survival over morality and even hygiene, and copied more and more. But all said and done, I didn't do too well in the exams.

⊕ ⊕ ⊕

The results were out after three weeks. I got a 7.3 CGPA out of 10. It was not even close to the topper's grade of 9.3. Rishi was at par with me with 7.1. I didn't know how that had happened with all his master cheating plans. May be the material provided to him was not trustworthy. You just can't trust anyone nowadays, not even wet Xeroxes from the loo.

After the results, Rishi and I were mourning over cups of tea at a roadside shop. Both of us were used to getting 80% plus marks in school so we needed to make plans to convey the results in the mildest possible way to our parents so that we could avoid another 'look what you have become' speech. A couple of paper cups of tea didn't give much boost to the brain cells so we decided to go for a third round.

Rishi lit his second cigarette, "Look! Everyone is so damn happy. It's only us who screwed up."

I nodded though I knew he was not completely correct. We were not the ones with the lowest grades. Some had 6+ CGPA. But we were real unhappy with our grades. I had a strong reason too. All the students I was on talking terms with got grades better than me, except Rishi.

I didn't smoke normally but today I decided to make an exception to grieve properly and sought a puff from Rishi. He offered it without hesitation. That's what true friends are like. They don't hesitate in sharing their addiction with you.

Someone called out my name just as I was coughing out smoke. I looked in the direction of the voice, it was Neera! I immediately threw away the cigarette! Rishi gave me a dirty look which I ignored.

After my deadly encounter with Neera on the day of the mock test, we did talk a few times. I even helped her out with some math problems. I am not good at most subjects; math is one of the exceptions. I am not sure we could really be termed as friends, but we were on talking terms.

The final results didn't depict the teacher-student equation we shared. Neera was in the top 5 with a grade of 9.1.

"Hey Dev! There you are. What are you doing here?" She stressed the *here* part strongly.

Girls. What does one do sitting outside a tea corner? Anyway she was looking too cute to be hit with my sarcasm.

"Nothing. Just chatting. This is Rishi; he's in section C with me." It was a rare occasion when I had to introduce Rishi to someone. Normally it was the exact opposite.

"Yeah! Rishi. I met you earlier. By the way, Sapna speaks a lot about you!" Neera smiled at him.

Rishi smiled dutifully. I noticed earlier, Rishi doesn't really show any interest in Neera which is contrary to his normal instincts.

"By the way, I am here to invite you." She changed the focus to me. Invite me?

"My birthday is coming up shortly. Next week I am taking some friends for a treat. You should definitely come. And Rishi? You too. Sapna will be there." She smiled purposefully.

Is Rishi hooking up with Sapna behind my back? It's not that Rishi has to tell me everything. But because Rishi is my friend, I should know about his affair before Neera.

"I'll come," Rishi confirmed. I wasn't sure if I wanted to attend; I prefer to avoid these social gatherings. But now that Rishi's agreeing to go, if I refuse I'd appear impolite. I tried to show some interest, "Where is the party?"

"It's a new restaurant near Gariahat market, Neel recommended it. He says the food is excellent. You know Neel right?" I knew Neel very well from that first day. As if I am ever going to forget that cheapo. But why is he deciding the venue for Neera's birthday party? I didn't like it at all.

"So...Dev? You are coming, right?" Neera brought me back from my thoughts.

"I...I...don't know. That's in South Kolkata. My home is far away...I have to return, you know." I searched for an excuse.

"You can't return from South Kolkata in the evening?" Rishi intervened before Neera could say anything. I gave him a dirty look but he was on a roll, "Neera, he's coming. Don't worry kiddo! I will drop you off at your doorstep if it gets late." Rishi not only took the decision from me but also made fun of me in front of Neera! I really hated him at that moment.

Neera tried to control her laughter, "Thanks Rishi. And Dev, please come. See you. Ok? By the way, Happy V day!" She adjusted her hair.

I was still recovering from Rishi's insult and didn't respond. Just nodded foolishly.

She walked off. Rishi spoke first, "What's wrong with you? The girl wishes you Happy Valentine's Day and you stay quiet?"

Oh! Today is Valentine's Day?

But why the hell was Rishi yelling at me? "Forget about U-V-W day, what did you do just now? Who said you could make the decision for me? I am not interested in attending the party. You made a joke out of me in front of her."

"I didn't intend that." Rishi tried to justify himself, "One day you'll thank me. Only a donkey like you rejects a college trustee's daughter's invitation."

Great, so Rishi was just playing along because of Neera's father, huh? "Did you accept the invitation for the same reason?"

"Of course yes! Do you want to screw up with your college trustee and one of the biggest advocates in the city? I don't. I strongly believe a girl with a powerful father should be avoided for both friendship and enmity. But if she walks up to you and invites you and you still refuse, may God save you!"

I didn't believe in Rishi's philosophy but remained quiet. Whatever idea I have of Neera so far, she is not one to use her father. But I didn't say anything to Rishi because first, I am not good at convincing people, and second, my actual problem was a bit different. I just didn't feel comfortable going there with all the other friends of Neera, especially Neel. I feel a certain level of discomfort seeing them together. I don't understand the reason, or maybe I do. But frankly, I don't want to think about it. Sometimes it's better to keep certain feelings inside you hidden from your own self, let alone others.

Rishi screwed me badly and I had to attend Neera's birthday party now.

⊕⊕⊕

23rd February was The Day.

By the end of the day, I had forgotten about the party, that's what I kept telling myself. But I forgot Rishi was invited too.

Normally we had labs in the evenings. I used to sit on the stairs and wait for Rishi to join me after lab. Then we took our bus together. So, as usual I was sitting on the stairs and thinking Rishi was late. Rishi didn't show up for a long time but finally the birthday girl did.

"What are you doing here? We all are waiting for you at the south route bus." She looked a bit irritated at my casualness.

"I...I was waiting for Rishi." My plan was to avoid her somehow and get into my north route bus without her noticing. But now, as she already found me, it became difficult for me to say I wouldn't come.

"Rishi has been on our bus for the last half an hour. He had no clue where you were." She sounded a bit agitated at my lack of coordination with my friend.

"I...I am sorry..." I could not say anything to justify my actions.

"It's ok. Let's go. We're already late."

When I got into the bus, there was a mixed reaction. People were happy the host was back and the vehicle would finally move. At the same time they were not excited to see me, the loser who kept them waiting. I tried to sit somewhere but no one offered me a seat. I felt awful. Suddenly I saw Rishi. The asshole was sitting with Sapna and chatting away. He looked at me and said casually, "Hey Dev. What took you so long?"

I acted as if he didn't exist and walked over to the last seat. No one was sitting there, I plonked myself down. I wasn't feeling like talking to anyone so the last seat was a godsend. I could see Neera sitting on the front seat with Neel beside her. I closed my eyes. Oh God! Please fast forward this evening. I badly want it to be over fast.

The restaurant looked expensive from outside. Well, after all, we're talking about the trustee's daughter here. We entered and took up half of the restaurant. Rishi chose to sit with me instead of Sapna, maybe he felt bad about ignoring me earlier.

"You don't come to South Kolkata much, do you?" Rishi was trying to strike up a conversation but I ignored him. Each table was occupied by four. To our surprise Neera decided to join Rishi and me. And of course, not much of a surprise, Neel got up from his table and joined us too. God!

Rishi knew about my eternal 'love' for Neel, so he took care of the conversation, something he was good at. I love my friend. He could be a pain sometimes. But he takes care of me when I need him.

Neel realized I was rather silent. "What about you? It's Dev, right? Neera was telling me you are good at math?"

"I try to do my best." My tone was not what one can call friendly. Even Neera raised her eyes at me.

Neel didn't bother though, "Cool. I remember you. You were flirting with that girl on the first day. You got screwed. But it was fun." He laughed.

Salt on the wound? I tried to come up with a bloody reply, "Yes. Guys like you have a different definition of fun! You..."

Rishi didn't let me finish, "Neera, I heard you have a great DVD collection? Do you have all the Chaplin movies?" He almost shouted to make the last part of my statement inaudible. I had a full swing of my bat but Rishi bowled a wide ball deliberately. Maybe that was the best for everyone. I went back to my *maun-vrat* again.

Neera was slow to reply; maybe she could sense the silent tension between me and Neel, "Yeah! In fact I have all the Chaplin movies. I am a huge fan."

Rishi looked excited. I am not sure how fake it was, "Wow! I would definitely like to have a look at them. Can you bring them to college?"

Neera bit her lips; she does that when she is thinking about something. She looks adorable doing that. "It's a bit difficult you know. The cases are large. Why don't you come over to my home some day and have a look at them?"

"Sure. I'd love to. Here comes the food." Rishi changes the topic at will, it's a gift.

I ate silently and no one at my table tried to change that. Maybe they realized this psycho monk should be kept in 'Samadhi' only. When we were done everyone thanked Neera a thousand times for her treat. I didn't really feel like joining the fawning and came out of the restaurant. Then Neel and his group came out. Where the hell is Rishi? Is he is hooking up with Sapna again?

But Rishi came out with Neera, they were discussing something. "Hey Rishi. Let's go," I tried to remind him I was waiting.

"Dev, do you have ten minutes? I need to collect this Soccer DVD from Neera. Can you believe her dad has a collection of best goals of Maradona?"

Yes. I can believe that, you idiot! But I can't believe you are planning to collect it right now! "From where?" Why did he have to mess up every time I wanted to make a fast getaway?

"Neera's house. It's just a five minute walk from here. Ten minutes total. Promise! You can wait here." What was wrong with Rishi? I knew soccer was his biggest weakness. But collecting the DVD from Neera's house? Seriously? First he said he wanted to keep his distance from Neera because of her father and now he was walking straight into her house! And what was the crap about me waiting for him outside the restaurant?

I was about to tell Rishi I was leaving, but Neera spoke, "Rishi? Why should poor Dev wait here in the dark? Dev, come with us. You guys can get a bus from there. Come on, this way." This girl definitely had more grey matter than my friend.

Soon we walked into a hall as big as a basketball court with dreamy blue light. Looking at the decoration of the house and the number of guards standing outside; I thought Rishi had a point when he said we shouldn't do anything to get on the bad side of Neera's father.

Neera asked us to sit on the sofa. After a couple of minutes she came back and asked Rishi to come and choose from the DVDs. She didn't call me in so I stayed back.

I took some time looking around the drawing room. There were lots of pictures hanging on the wall. Divakar Sinha, Shashi Sinha; I got introduced to most of the Sinha family at short notice. Neera's father could be a top persona himself but clearly he had a great family heritage to follow.

I was looking for a picture of Neera but couldn't find any. Then I saw a small picture frame kept on a side shelf. Neera at her smiling best. That smile can make your day seem brighter. I picked up the frame and started looking closely when I heard someone speaking from behind.

"Who are you?" I saw a scary looking lady sitting in a wheelchair. She had some scars on her face. I was quite shaken at her sudden appearance and belligerent look and posture.

I answered hysterically, "I am Dev, ma'am. I study with Neera. She invited us to collect DVDs ...they are inside..." I knew I sounded foolish, I tried to brief the whole situation in five seconds.

"Why are you holding her picture?" she asked in a peculiar tone.

"I ...I ...I was just looking, ma'am!"

"Why did you stare at her for so long? Do you love her?"

Now that was a bombshell I never expected to land on me!

"I...I..." I stumbled as much as possible to avoid answering that. She was looking straight at me as if she could read my soul. Who is she anyway? God? Devil? RAW agent?

Neera came to my rescue. "Mom, what are you doing here? Raghu-da said you were sleeping."

I could see Rishi holding a bunch of DVD cases right behind her. The lady was silent. So that's her mom! What's wrong with her?

Neera guided the wheelchair out of the room. Fiery mom didn't say another word. Rishi and I were in statue mode for some time, trying to grasp what happened. Neera was back quickly. "I am sorry. Did she say anything offensive?"

I was about to reply 'no', but Neera continued as if she was talking to herself.

"She had this car accident a few years back. She can't move her lower body. It's difficult to accept that, you know. Doctors say she is not in a good mental condition. But she is perfectly fine. Just sometimes she says certain things which may sound rude to people."

"It's perfectly okay, Neera." I tried to calm her down, "She didn't say anything rude to me. She was just asking my name."

"Okay." She looked relieved and a bit shy about the emotional outburst. "Guys, you have to excuse me. I need to take care of her."

"Sure, we were just leaving." Rishi spoke for the first time.

We got out of the house and walked silently for a bit. Rishi spoke first, "What a day at the trustee's house, huh? Finished off in style too. Mad mother kicking your ass. She was saying something to you, wasn't she? We heard her voice. What was it?"

"I love her!" I said.

"What? Her mom? Freaking unbelievable!"

"No, not her mom, you moron!" I looked at Rishi and said calmly, "I love Neera."

4
GOING BACK TO HELL

Where exactly is this place? Why can't I remember how I ended up here? Is it a resort? Maybe. But what am I doing here? "Rishi," I call for my friend. Did he leave me here alone in this unknown place? Is that a garden? I walk into it. Wow! It's so scenic. I should get moving. Rishi must be waiting for me.

As I walk I can see an array of bird cages. Then there is an artificial fountain. How come there is no one here in such a stunning place? I am all alone here. No, wait. I can see someone. I can see a girl on a swing. Maybe she can help me with the way out.

I walk quickly towards her. She is just sitting there, unmoving. I call out, "Hello, ma'am. Excuse me." She doesn't reply.

What's happening? I have been walking for so long, yet can't reach her? She is getting further away. Do I know this girl? I can't see her face from this distance. But I know that dress, that hair…She looks exactly like…No! I have to go and check. Finally I reach her. She doesn't respond. She is not even aware of my presence.

I call to her, "Neera? Is it you?"

She looks at me. Oh God. What happened to her? I stumble and just save myself from falling at the last moment. Neera's face and hands are filled with cuts and bruises. What is on her hands? Is it blood?

"Morning sleepyhead! How much longer are you going to sleep? It's already 9. Time for work now." Rishi's voice blared in my ear like an alarm clock.

I felt disoriented with a bad hangover, a terrible feeling compounded by an unbearable headache. What a freaking nightmare! Why would I see her like that? Was I drunk last night?

I recalled going to the cultural association with Rishi, and then I remembered the rest as well. After what happened last night, I knew there would be questions I preferred not to answer. It's always difficult to confess your old sins in front of your best friend because it matters what he thinks about you.

I tried to get up from the bed in a hurry, "C'mon let's move. We'll be late for work."

Rishi hit the wooden corner of my bed with a fist, "No, sit down. Don't run away every time I want to talk about this. Enough!"

I looked at him. The lean boy has some attitude. "Rishi, we decided four years back we will not talk about that incident ever. Why are you pushing me now? These are hurtful memories for me. Why do you want to open my old wounds?"

"In the last four years things have changed Dev. When we decided this you were hardly in a condition to speak with anyone. Now you are successful, working in a good company. Why do you have to grieve over something that happened in the past? Just share it and forget it." Rishi stressed on the *share* word a bit too much.

"Then why don't we just forget it? You are right. I've moved on from the past. I am doing okay. You're doing fabulously. Let's just enjoy life. Why should we bring our past up to spoil the present? Don't do this man."

Rishi stood up, "You're not going to tell me? You did that in college as well. You chose them over me."

What next? Will he cry now? I tried to signal him to stop this act but Rishi shushed me, "Wait! I am not being a cry baby. Let me finish. It's not about me. It's about you. You didn't listen to me the last time and you got screwed up bad. I saw you yesterday. A look at Neera after all these years and you froze. Can't you see that? You need me; else you are going to end up where you did four years back. Let me help you."

I looked at him and gave up my reticence. "What do you want to know?" I asked in a tired voice.

"Everything! Every damn thing you hid from me during our college years. I knew your spark for Neera, so what happened? Suddenly one day Isha came into the picture. Ok, even if she did, what happened between you guys? And most importantly, why did you…do that thing which almost destroyed your life and career?"

I heard Rishi summing up my personal life in four sentences. As if I was Lord Krishna playing with Gopis throughout my college life. What looks pleasant from the outside is not charming when seen up close. If you make a mistake in your life, whether you are punished for it or not, a parasite of guilt grows inside you and eats at you every moment until you deal with what you have done. When you finally accept the truth, your only way to survive is to erase that memory or cut a portion of your soul and throw it away. Rishi can never understand what I went through.

While I was still thinking about answering, my phone rang. The screen showed 'Rajan.' So my team leader was already bothered about me being late. I didn't take the call, but entered the bathroom saying, "I have to go now. We'll talk about it later."

I slammed the door of the bathroom. "Damn," Rishi shouted. I chose to ignore it.

When I was leaving for work ten minutes later, Rishi was smoking at the main door. "See you!" I started down the stairs.

"Hey Dev." Not again! I didn't want to but looked up. "It's for your own good. Stay away from Neera." Rishi threw away the cigarette and went into the house.

⊕⊕⊕

Morning shows the day. Whoever said this got it bang on. My day started with an interrogatory session with Rishi, not exactly what you would call a perfect way to start a Monday. I had more miseries ahead that day.

My first actual contribution to the project ended up with a meeting with Rajan and Mr. Fish, aka Hiten. The agenda of the meeting was how I should improve my style of working in service projects for customers. And all this happened because I helped one customer a bit more than Rajan liked.

I worked in a service company before. There I worked with the customers. That company was small and we had only one big customer to rely on for our revenues. So, we used to go through heaven and hell to maintain a good relationship with them and that relationship was far more important than billing hours.

But today I realized things are done differently in giant IT service companies. If you speak to a customer, you bill them. You stay an extra hour at office for them, you bill them. Even if you open your office laptop at home to watch movies, and by mistake, you check your emails, you bill the clients.

I screwed up today because I responded to customer requests too soon. As per Rajan, if you get a request from the customer, don't respond quickly. Take some time and make it look more critical than it actually is. Respond to the customer after a couple of hours.

What the hell! Why should I drag a simple issue out for two hours and make myself look incapable of solving this sooner? Rajan didn't like my logic.

The second time he lost it when I created a software package for a customer when I should only be executing it. "What are you doing? I told you not to raise customer expectations. Now they will ask us to create custom packages every time." Rajan was visibly irritated.

"What's the problem in that? That makes them more dependent on us, right? That's a good thing." I really didn't get this 'expectation' stuff.

"No, we should not touch anything other than ready packages and jobs. We are not here to do development for them. Their development team takes care of that. Do only what you are told to do." He said the last quite loudly and all our team members, including the unsocial Gayathri, looked over.

Rajan was making me mad, though in all fairness to him, I wasn't in the best of moods from the morning. Why don't you accept that you can't write a package, that's why you are insecure with me? Don't try to control my life, dude. You are just the team leader. Though actually what was audible was, "Rajan, I don't agree with this attitude."

Rajan didn't say anything but I finally ended up being called in by my manager.

Hiten told Rajan to wait outside as he wanted to talk to me in private. Rajan's expression clearly said he didn't like it much but he left.

"So Devdas? What's wrong?"

I gave him a brief of my point of view and added, "Sir, I don't understand the problem in helping our customers more. Why do we have to think about billing every damn thing?"

Hiten smiled, he is cooler when he doesn't talk about food, "Look Dev, I understand you. I have been there, done that. But at the end of the day it's business. Do you realize why customers are coming to us to do this work, even though they could have guys in the USA to do the same? Why? That's because they have to pay 10 times more what they are actually paying for our whole team for someone in the USA to do the same work." Hiten stopped to munch on a chocolate bar, this looked like his energy booster.

He continued, "Now about helping extra? Of course we want to do that. But remember one thing; this is an IT service company. We don't have products from which we can make a profit. So how are we surviving? The billing. We are billing for each of our resources according to their skills and the complexity of the work. The number of human resources assigned to each project will depend on the amount of work and the nature of it. If our people are sitting idle, eventually we will have to reduce the number of resources."

I was finally getting it. I nodded at him.

"Same applies to skills. If you show you have extraordinary skills and manage the work alone, what will happen?" Hiten was acting as if he was hosting a quiz show.

"Ok, I got it." So the point is to save my team members' jobs and keep my company booming I have to act a bit less efficient and less skilful. It's pathetic but I can survive that.

"There you go! Now you got what Rajan was trying to say." Hiten smiled. I started thinking how Hiten's logic seemed totally money-minded. Somewhere down the line that results in averageness for our technical abilities but I can't really blame them. Ultimately it all comes down to bread and butter.

Hiten veered off-track and moved on to his favourite subject of fish. I waited till I finally found a pause and made an excuse to leave. I couldn't bear another 'Fishy' meeting with Hiten. I had to leave early today. I had to go somewhere.

⊕⊕⊕

"Eastwood Hall?" I double checked with the auto driver.

"This is the one," the driver confirmed.

"Oh, ok." I paid. Oh dear Lord! I would be bankrupt soon if I have to travel by autos in Bengaluru regularly.

I walked towards the hall. It looked so different than yesterday. Last night for the programme it was all decorated with flowers and lit all over. Today it looked a bit dull in the dark. Seeing a guard, I asked him about a manager.

"No booking! No Manager!" he declared. That sucked. Did I come all the way just to hear his brush off?

"Do you know anyone who can help me with some information?" I didn't want to waste my time and auto fare, "I need the phone number of the organizer of yesterday's party."

"Ok. Maybe Prasad knows." He scratched his head.

"Who is Prasad?" I saw a ray of hope.

"My cousin. He is the mini-manager," he declared proudly.

"Why are you waiting then? Call him." I was getting restless. He still looked at me with a bland expression. What? Does he want money? I tried that approach and it worked! Clutching a hundred-rupee note in his hand he went to call Prasad.

When he was gone for more than five minutes and I was thinking my 100 rupees had been invested to cover a guard's dinner tonight, I saw a short guy coming towards me.

"Prasad?" I asked hesitantly.

"Two hundred," he replied. What? Is that his name? "Two hundred rupees. Hand them over," he cleared up his requirement.

"I need my number first," I bargained. "I need the number of Bala Subhash Roy...maybe you have heard of him. He was the organizer of yesterday's event."

"Oh. Bala Sahib," Prasad smiled at me showing a row of black teeth, "Yes! He parties regular."

Did he mean Bala parties very hard or the cultural association holds its programs quite often? I guessed the second and forked the amount over. Upon payment, Prasad took out his mobile. I got Bala's number and checked my watch. 8:30, not too late to call anyone. I dialed.

"Hello. Bala Subhash speaking."

"Hi Bala! This is Dev. We met yesterday. Do you remember?"

"No, are you sure you are calling the right number?"

I didn't want to mention Rishi's name but unfortunately I had to, "...Rishi from your office introduced me last night."

"Oh! The part-time singer? So what is it?" Bala sounded eager to disconnect.

"I wanted to know about the group membership. How should I proceed?"

"Good. Come to our office tomorrow. It's on M G road. Close to where the event was organized. You will find a guy named Arup there. He can guide you. Do you know about the charges?" I had to admit I didn't.

"Why? Rishi didn't tell you? He gave you my number right?"

"Do you want to tell me the charges please?" I got a bit impatient. If I am paying, I should get the membership on my own terms.

"Yes. Joining is 2,500. And monthly it's 1,000. But if you pay 5,000 extra at the start you can get into our Pondicherry trip. We are planning the trip for the end of this month. But you'll have to decide quickly. You won't regret it." He sounded like a travel agent.

I wasn't sure though. I wanted to know about my main concern but it was difficult to ask, "Is it a family event?"

"Yes, of course. You can bring your family, at some additional charges. We always believe in family get-togethers."

I dug deeper, "Can I bring my girlfriend? More like a fiancée."

Bala thought a bit, "Yeah, sure. But no discounts. Don't worry. I am taking my fiancée too."

Bala had finally given me the information I was looking for. I was done with the conversation. "Okay Bala! I will come with the money tomorrow. Please count me in for the trip. I need the full address of the office." I noted down the address and disconnected the call. So my small fishing expedition was successful.

Something inside me said I was doing everything wrong. I was going back into the same pit that took me years to crawl out of. Why exactly do I want to meet her? Frankly I don't know. Do I want to ask her not to marry that loser? Or do I want to tell myself that she is doing well, she has recovered from the past, to give me a much needed break from the guilt which has been plaguing me nonstop.

I have my family and friends who love me. I've worked hard to achieve whatever I have. And here I am putting everything at risk for someone who doesn't even care whether I exist or not. But I still care. I realize that now seeing her again. It's too complex a feeling. It's like a drug, where you know you are going to harm yourself but still can't resist the urge.

Why do I keep visiting her Facebook page and fight with myself whether I should send a friend request or not? Can I truly say Neera's name never came to my mind when I accepted the offer from TTS? Didn't I remember her face when I decided I'd be moving to Bengaluru? These are tricky questions. Only I can answer, yet I can't at the same time. Call it anything—madness, passion, love or selfishness that makes me do crazy stuff for her. I had hoped everything would change with time. Thought I'd changed. But I was wrong.

I didn't realize while talking to myself that I had reached the back of the hall. It was the parking area. Damn! I came the wrong way. I turned back and started walking but had to stop because a strong light hit my face and body. I couldn't see anything for a few seconds. Then I understood it was a bike light.

To my surprise, the rider called out my name, "Dev! What are you doing here?"

I had forgotten. Last night Rishi left his bike here.

5
CHOOSING TO REMEMBER- A JOURNEY

Moral and immoral are overrated. It's all about the choices we make. But is there a right or a wrong choice? What seems to be right to me could be wrong for thousands of others. So what to do? Listen to your heart or follow a giant moral guide written by a society full of hypocrites?

I was supposed to convince myself that the decision of going to Pondicherry with the group and meeting Neera was the right thing to do. That was the best thing I could come up with to pass this sleepless night. But the problem was all that thinking and I still couldn't convince myself.

Should I really take this risk? Put my friendship with Rishi in jeopardy? What if she ignores me completely? Should I tell her not to marry that psycho? How is this even my business? Maybe deep inside I want to break her impending marriage up and see if I still have the slightest chance with her.

That last thought had my heart pounding. I felt sweat on my forehead. I sat up on the bed. Sometimes the devil inside you can shock you. You never fully realize the animal you actually are. Seriously, Dev? After all the misery you went through and the trouble you created for your family, you still want another chance to score with Neera? What a loser you are! My conscience slapped me hard on the face.

Wanting some fresh air, I got up. I looked at Rishi sleeping blissfully on the next bed. Poor guy! I don't know if he believed me or my poor excuse of checking out his bike at the Eastwood Hall that day. I wouldn't believe it had I been in his place. He knows very well how much I hate bike-riding. And after that morning he didn't bring up the topic about my past either.

But it seemed like the lull before the storm, which was something I was concerned about. I didn't want another *Clash of the Titans* before the Pondicherry trip. I carefully brought the topic up, mentioning I needed to be out for a weekend trip with the office team. He was unusually cool about it and just nodded.

I went out to the small terrace, picking up my phone on the way. It was already thirty minutes past midnight. Who should I call? Mom? Bad idea. What if Dad picked up? I couldn't survive another lecture on my irresponsible behaviour. But I had to talk to someone. Who else? Isha? She should be back already. It's a bit late. But who cares? Worst case scenario, she will not pick up. I dialled her number with a low expectation she would actually answer. To my surprise she picked up on the 2nd ring. "Hey Champ! How are you doing? Can't sleep?"

"Actually I can't. When did you return?" I was happy she picked up.

"Last week. I was thinking you would call me. Though I was having a damn busy schedule." She sounded sleepy, yawning away.

"Hey! If you want to go back to bed, please do. Why are you up anyway? I know you don't like to be awake after 9:30. Your body parts collapse after that." I laughed.

"Very funny! Don't lie, you monkey. Once I used to talk to you around this time almost every day." She showed mock anger.

"Yes. Among those conversations mostly you were dreaming and I used to sing *Lori* to you." I teased her.

"Then I used to give you a kiss…" she stopped realizing she had crossed a line. There was an awkward silence.

It's difficult to be friends with your ex. You have to be very careful about staying within the limits. She didn't speak for the next couple of minutes. I tried to control the situation, "So…you didn't tell me why you were up?"

"Thinking about you! What do you think, stupid?" Now what was that supposed to mean? Was it a joke?

"Today is the birthday of one of my roommates, so we just had cake." Isha was back to normal.

"I see. So how was your Hyderabad trip? Fruitful?" I wanted to change the topic.

"Not exactly. I am fed up with these technical interview panels. They keep rejecting a quality candidate profile in five minutes flat and their manager asks me to give them more. How am I supposed to get more applicants in these specialized technologies? Give birth to them?"

"Keep your cool! You'll find good people."

"And what if I don't?"

"Then it's a good time to update your LinkedIn profile," I joked.

"You rat! Are you making fun of me...you..." she was quiet for some time. "Hey I have to go. I have a call waiting."

"At this time?" I regretted saying that. It was none of my business.

"Uh...it could be work..." She was definitely thinking about the mysterious caller.

I didn't want to bother her anymore, "Okay. But I wanted to fix our dinner plans. You asked for that, right?"

"Yeah...dinner. I'll tell you later. Have to go now. Don't feel bad. Please? I'll talk to you tomorrow. Goodnight Divs." She hung up. But it was okay. After all these years and what we went through, she still cares whether I feel bad or not if she disconnects the phone in a hurry. That's more than you can ask for.

I stopped thinking as I heard footsteps behind the door. "Rishi?"

Rishi walked out with a cigarette in his hand. So he'd been up for a while already. What was he doing in the dark? Was he keeping an eye on me? The thought pissed me off.

"How long have you been up?" Rishi asked me calmly.

"I think you know." I tried to sound sarcastic.

He nodded and waited for me to say more. But I didn't reply. I just wanted to go back to bed.

Before I could walk inside Rishi said, "There is a trip organized by the Bala's club to Pondicherry. They are leaving this weekend."

I froze. Rishi knows. Scoundrel Bala! He had to open his big mouth. "So?" I acted as if I had no interest in any such activity.

"I thought you'd be interested to know." He was acting calm.

"I...I...Why would I?" I said in a shaky voice. I am normally proud of my lying skills but my guilt was on a roll here.

"Ok... good for you. Let's sleep." Rishi dropped both the topic and the cigarette.

I sighed. I want to tell you Rishi. I want to tell you everything. It's bothering me more than you. But I know you too well. You will start your moral lecture and leave no stone unturned to stop me from going there. I can't let that happen. For whatever reason, I need to go. I will tell you everything once I am back, I promise.

"Good night." I turned my back to my best friend.

⊕⊕⊕

Majestic. It is the biggest bus terminus in Bengaluru. I was here because Arup had informed me a couple of days back that we would leave for Pondicherry around 6:30am on Saturday. I was asked at least five times to arrive before 6 since Bala wanted everyone to reach there before time.

I, too, preferred arriving as early as possible. Rishi thought I was going to Ooty with my office team. Elaborate, detailed lies are not my forte. So he knew I was supposed to catch a bus from Majestic and offered me a lift which I definitely had to avoid. The early morning stint saved me. Rishi can't see himself in dreams dropping someone around this time.

My problem was I didn't know anyone else. I had met Arup when I'd visited their M G road office. All I knew was that our platform was 25, so I located it and waited there. Lots of people were already waiting there. Probably most of them were in our group but I didn't know any of them. I couldn't see Bala and, most importantly, Neera.

I saw an empty bench and settled down there. I am not an early riser at all. My morning normally starts after 7:30. Sitting idle gave me a chance to take a nap. I didn't realize how deep that nap was and jumped up to the loud sound of honking. I looked at my watch. It was 7:05!

Did I miss the bus? Spending 5,000 rupees even before getting my first pay-cheque and now missing the bus? I will kill Bala if he leaves me here.

The bus hadn't left yet. It was just taking a U-turn. I could see Arup with a list in his hand, taking attendance. Most people I'd seen at the platform earlier were already in the bus. I moved towards Arup before he could mark me absent, "Hi. I am Dev. I should be on the list."

"I was looking for you. Where have you been?"

"I was already here, just took a nap. Sorry."

"Okay...no excuses please. Get into the bus now," Oh! This little chap is also learning attitude from Bala.

I boarded the bus. It was full. I couldn't see a vacant seat anywhere. Arup came up the bus steps. "Do we have any seat numbers?" I enquired.

"Nothing fixed. Sit anywhere." Anywhere? I put down my backpack and stood there. The bus started to move.

"You can sit here," someone from the front row called. I could see him now, a big, thick-set man occupying almost one-and-half seats. No wonder no one had sat with him yet. But something was better than nothing. I sat there, trying to squeeze my body into the half-seat available.

He moved as if he were trying to adjust. But other than his facial muscles, not one of the other body parts moved. "Thanks, sir. I am Dev."

"Don't mention it son. I am Jiten Sarkar. I work in LIC. What do you do?"

While trying to figure out where Neera was sitting, I played along with this extraordinarily large gentleman. "I am a software engineer, sir. I work for TTS."

"TTS? It's a big company. Some of our IT projects are outsourced to them. Perfect. What's your surname?"

"Banerjee," I didn't understand what was perfect about me working in TTS.

"Meet my family. In the next seat here is Indu, my wife, and Diya, my daughter. She is graduating from HIT. BCA, final year." I could just make out there were ladies behind us so I waved at them.

LIC man didn't like the casualness. "No! No! Meet her properly! Hey Diya! This is Dev Banerjee. He works in TTS. Nice. Isn't it?"

I smelled what was cooking. This man was matchmaking! Some fathers can be a real pain. They start looking for a groom for their daughter even before they are out of their diapers. But at the insistence of LIC man, I stood up and said 'Hi' to Diya. She didn't reply, making a 'Get Lost' facial expression at me.

While standing up, I looked towards the back of the bus. In the 8th row, I could see Neera sitting next to Bala. I'd finally found her. A red scarf covered part of her face. Looked like she was taking a nap. I had an uncontrollable urge to remove her scarf and see her full face. But suddenly I saw Bala. He was looking straight at me. Damn...

I sat down immediately. LIC man was happy to get me back. "Where are your parents? What does your father do?"

Give me a break buddy. Why don't I give you my birth certificate too? I replied briefly and closed my eyes, acting as if I was taking a nap. This ride was going to be a long one.

⊕⊕⊕

We were on the verge of reaching Pondicherry. The roads were good, with my co-passenger and proposed father-in-law informing me it's one of the best highways in India. I had to act as if I was sleeping throughout the journey to slow him down on his matchmaking efforts. The bus stopped for a break somewhere near Krishnagiri. Most passengers decided to get down for some snacks in the roadside shops. I preferred to stay on the bus. Maybe I could get a chance to speak to Neera. LIC man invited me to join him for a snack but I acted as if I was sleeping. I need to stay away from this family, especially this man with desperate paternal instincts.

I looked at the back. Neera was still sleeping. Her fiancée also decided to stay on with her. We were the only ones who didn't get down. What a threesome left on the bus! I cursed my luck and looked out of the window.

Once the passengers were back after the break, LIC man asked his daughter to sit beside me and gave me a meaningful smile. Some fathers! The girl didn't seem to be bothered much and took the window seat. Initially I hated the idea but eventually I thanked her father. At least I could utilize my full seat.

We reached Pondicherry in five hours. I liked the small and neat look of the city. Arup walked towards the driver's seat to give some instructions. What I understood was that we would get down before the main bus stand as we'd be staying at the Pondicherry VIP Lodge. We stopped in a narrow lane. Arup shouted, "Guys! Get down quickly. We're blocking the traffic."

Before I could react to that, my proposed bride to be stepped on my shoes and got off the bus as if there was an earthquake. What is wrong with this family?

I had been sitting for more than five hours without much body movement. So it took me some time to stand properly. Arup shouted from outside, "Whoever is still inside! Get down."

I tried to move as fast as I could towards the gate. I reached the bus door and collided roughly with someone. "Can't you see?" I heard the voice. I had less blood circulation in my legs a few seconds back but suddenly I felt my blood pressure pumping. It was Neera. Of course I wanted to let her know about my presence, but not through this freaking collision.

I survived the shock pretty quickly as I already had an idea whom to expect. But for her, it was a shock of earthquake proportions, a 9.5 on the Richter scale. Arup was getting mad due to our lack of motivation to deboard the bus. Of course, he couldn't target his boss's fiancée. So I was the easy target, "You, Dev? Are you coming down or not?"

Bala was already down. I heard him, "C'mon Neeru, come down!"

Neeru? Seriously? His lazy brain couldn't think of anything better? I had to laugh. She raised her eyebrows. Those eyes. Why do they seem prettier each time I look at them? But it was time to be practical, not poetic. I said, "You go first."

She obeyed. I followed her. Arup was visibly mad at me. "Why do you have to be late in everything?"

I was in a cheerful mood after my small but effective encounter with Neera. I patted his back, "Let's go my friend. You are blocking the traffic." Arup stood there for some time to digest my reply.

Inside the hotel, Arup took charge and distributed the keys. Neera was sharing a room with Bala's sister. She looked like an exact feminine version of Bala.

I was hoping to get a single room, but Arup asked me to share with someone. "I don't know anyone here. Why don't you get me a single room?" I tried to bargain.

"No single rooms booked. Only double." Arup rejected my proposal outright.

"Come with me. We can share." I looked for the owner of the voice. Oh no! LIC man? No way!

"One minute sir…" I pushed Arup a bit away from him.

"C'mon, let's share a room. Please don't leave me with this man." I almost felt as if I was proposing to Arup.

Arup didn't seem that bad, maybe he acts tough just to be on Bala's good books. He laughed. "What happened? Does he want to fix you up with his daughter?" My jaw dropped. How did he know? "Don't flatter yourself. He tries that with most young Bengali boys in the group. That old man is nuts."

"Whatever! But don't leave me with him. I want to return to Bengaluru in my unmarried status."

Arup laughed again, "Ok. Let me manage this. Bala is getting a single room. Just for himself. I'll arrange another one for this guy. You can bunk with me."

I thanked him profusely. Arup smiled and went away. I looked back and noticed Neera was looking straight at me. As our eyes met she looked away. Did she not recognize me? I haven't changed that much. Yes, I have gained some weight, but Isha recognized me easily. My thought process was interrupted as she started to move away with Lady Bala aka Bala's sister!

Arup gave me a key and said he would join me later.

He shouted to the group, "We will meet in the dining room in the next 30 minutes for lunch. Please try to be on time."

I looked at the key: 310, 3rd floor. Is Neera staying on the same floor? I had my answer when I got off the lift on the 3rd floor. Bala was shouting at the hotel staff standing near the elevators. I could see Lady Bala and Neera watching him from a distance.

"What do you mean you don't have single rooms here on the 3rd floor? My family is staying here. I want to stay near their rooms."

"Sir, we don't have single rooms on this floor. If you want one you can move to the first floor with your family," the staff member explained.

"Pathetic! Neeru! Let's take the bags. We will all move to first floor."

I heard Neera's voice clearly for the first time in four years, "I am tired. It's just one day. I don't care. I want to stay here." She entered her room and slammed the door. I squinted to see the room number: 312.

Both the male and female versions of Bala remained shocked and silent. Bala was clearly having a hard time processing his authority was diminished by Miss Sinha. I felt great seeing Bala like this. I wished Rishi could see him; he would have enjoyed Bala's comeuppance.

Okay, now we are getting somewhere. Man, I love Pondicherry!

6
"DO YOU REMEMBER, MY LOVE?"

My happiness in Pondicherry was short lived.
I was really hoping to see Neera at lunch. When I reached the dining room, I saw people had already started tucking in. I could see everyone but Bala and Co. I sat down next to Arup. The food was pretty good but I couldn't concentrate on the taste. Arup might know something about his boss' absence. "So where is Bala? They already had lunch?"

"Maybe. They are dining in the room," Arup concentrated on a chicken leg.

"Why?" After asking, I realized my question was way out of line.

Arup looked at me strangely. "It's what he wants to do. Bala is the Boss." Then he thought a bit, "May be Neera, I mean Bala's wife-to-be, is not feeling well."

I knew exactly what had happened to her. She had seen a ghost from the past. I just nodded to Arup to show I was listening. Arup has a tendency to gossip, this man could help me with more information.

We were supposed to rest after lunch and go sightseeing in the evening. I didn't feel like going. I had a feeling Neera wouldn't either. I felt a burning sensation inside. Can't she tolerate me even for a day after four years? What do I have to do, Neera, to make things normal with you? Why can't you just forget the past? I started pacing inside the room.

Arup came to the room. "What are you doing? I thought you were sleepy. What happened to your eyes?" His concern was a bit of a surprise. Clearly he wasn't expecting me to be marching around the room all red-eyed. Arup, you won't understand. Sometimes your eyes depict the fire inside you.

"I wasn't feeling good. So I thought...never mind. When are you guys leaving?" I tried to change the subject.

"You guys? Aren't you coming?"

"I'd rather rest."

"Whatever. It's your money. But call reception if you need a doctor. We don't need any emergencies," Arup opened his suitcase while speaking.

"Where are we going?" I wanted to cheer him up.

"Mainly local sightseeing. It's a small city. The sea and the Ashram are the biggest attractions. We will visit The Promenade on Goubert Avenue first. It's a beautiful place, about 1.5 kilometres of beach road. Then we will go to the French Colony. People should get a taste of French food. There is a big market too. The best place to go for shopping. Then we will come back for dinner. Tomorrow we will visit Auroville. You'll miss out if you don't join us for that."

I was about to make another excuse, but someone knocked on our door. Bala!

"Is Arup there?" he asked me.

"Yes he is." Bala entered and stared hard at me.

"You look familiar. Have I met you before?" How many times do I have to introduce myself to this bugger? I am the one chasing your fiancée, you idiot.

"Yes, I am Dev. We met at the party you threw a few weeks back at Eastwood Hall. I was…" I didn't want to bring Rishi's name up but this fox remembers everything when he wants to.

"Oh, Dev? Rishi's friend? Right! Good to see that you're wiser than your friend. At least you didn't want to miss this trip. He's hopeless." Rishi could be a thousand bad things but no one can kick my friend's ass in front of me.

My reply came automatically, "I'd say he's smart. I don't see any aspect of this tour that is mesmerizing so far."

Bala seemed unused to getting replies that were like a slap on his face. Arup intervened, "Yes Sir, you wanted to ask me something?"

"Yes." Bala focused on him, "Let's start the sightseeing now. Neera is not well. I have to come back early. Ruby is insisting I go now. Let's make the tour short and quick," Bala commanded. Ruby must be Lady Bala. This man thinks the world revolves around him. He needs to come back early so all the other 30 tourists who have paid their fair share have to compromise for him?

Arup was hesitant, "But Sir, I had asked everyone to gather around 5 at the lobby. It's still almost an hour away." A look at Bala's thunderous face and he changed his mind, "No problem sir. I will go to each room and inform everyone about the change of plan. Give me 15 minutes please."

I felt bad for this guy. He was running around the whole day and just got an hour to relax and now this idiot wants him to start the tour right now. Why does Arup have to agree to every damn thing Bala says?

Bala said, "That's better!" He gave me another dirty look and went out.

"Why did you complain about my touring arrangements? I tried to do everything everyone asked for." Arup sounded offended. Unknowingly I had hurt his feelings. Bala may use this against him. I felt guilty.

"I am sorry Arup. It's not about you. You have done the best job possible. I just said those words in anger. Your boss was insulting my friend."

"He insults everyone, all the time. I am sure your friend doesn't mind anymore," Arup said in a tired voice.

"Then why do you guys keep saying yes to him for everything? He's just your boss at work. He hasn't made you his personal slaves. You should refuse sometimes." Arup's eyes rounded.

"Are you on drugs? I am going. Bala will be pissed off. Are you coming or not?"

I shook my head. He shrugged and left.

God save him. I'd totally wasted my time and energy trying to motivate this man to speak up against evil. But I thanked Ruby. She forced her wicked brother to go out. That gives me more of a chance to speak to Neera if she wants to speak to me at all. I have to take my final chance. The Pondi beaches can wait.

⊕⊕⊕

I regretted my decision of coming here over the course of the evening. My legs were hurting badly from walking down the 3rd floor lobby umpteen times with the hope room 312's door would open. I started with enthusiasm but as time passed, my moral and leg strength declined.

A couple of times I thought I should knock on her door but considering the equation we currently share, I didn't have the courage to do that. Though my sole purpose of coming here was to meet her, I had to make it appear accidental. Boys can be more manipulative to get a girl than politicians for their chairs.

It was almost 7:30 and I was sure Bala and gang would be back soon. I lied to my best friend for absolutely nothing. I doubt I would get to speak a single word with Neera on this trip, or maybe in this life.

Frustrated and devastated, I dragged myself out of the hotel's main gate. I needed some fresh air desperately. After crossing a couple of blocks I reached the promenade; the beach road. I could see scores of people strolling. The place was not exactly beach-y. There was very little sand. Then there were steps which lead to tons of rocks. These rocks acted as the perfect boundary between the sea and civilization. I remembered Arup mentioning this place. This indeed was awesome. The wind was mind blowing. My on-edge nerves got some badly needed relaxation. People were sitting on the rocks, snacking and chatting away. Occasional waves were coming in and leaving you all soaked. I continued walking and reached a café. My head was still churning trying to digest the disaster of Mission Neera. I decided to sip on a coffee and get back in shape mentally.

As I climbed the steps to the first floor of the café, I got a big shock. Story of my destiny! Whenever I hunted too hard for something, I didn't get it. But whenever I didn't expect the slightest bit of anything, there it was. Neera was visible at the very first table. Here she was and I was circling the 3rd floor praying her door would show mercy on me.

I froze for a second as our eyes met. It was awkward. I could see her situation was not exactly the most comfortable too.

"Sir? A table for one?" The attendant got me back to my senses.

"Yeah. Excuse me for a second," I actually needed some time to decide what to do. I tried to get over my nervousness. I should go and talk to her. Dev, whatever happened was in the past. Just have a normal chat with her. That's why you are here.

Slowly I walked towards her, "Hi Nee…Neera," my voice shook.

She didn't look at me. C'mon, at least you can say 'Hi.'

"May I…" I was about to ask if I could join her but she spoke first, "I…I have to go." Something inside me exploded. Why do you have to be so rude to me? Don't I deserve another chance at least to speak to you after all these years? Do you even realize how your action hurts me? No, you don't. You are a selfish girl, Neera.

The attendant was in my face, "Sir? Are you joining her?"

I looked back at him and shouted, "What's your problem dude? Can't you give a second to your customers? I don't want a table or a bed. I am done here."

"But Sir…" I didn't let him finish and ran down Goubert Avenue.

I wanted to move away as fast as I could but my already tired legs didn't co-operate. After a few tired steps I decided to clear my head by sitting on those boulders. I tried to sit as close as I could to the sea. But the rocks were slippery due to the sea water. I saved myself from falling more than once. But when I finally settled on a rock near the sea, I felt relieved. Nature does that to you. Lets you forget all the stresses and worries. It's us who keep screwing with nature all the time.

When I thought I had already been through the worst for the day, someone spoke very close to me, "It's so nice. Isn't it?"

I was literally shaken because I hadn't notice her walk up at all. I was so busy ensuring I wouldn't be the sea's unwitting prey that I didn't realise she was following me.

You are right Neera. It couldn't have been nicer unless I were sitting here with you. But the very next moment I remembered her behaviour from a few minutes back and my anger came back with a vengeance, I looked away.

"How are you, Dev? I didn't know you were in Bengaluru."

I didn't reply. How would you know that Neera? Actually the exact words should be, 'I didn't know you were alive.' You've abandoned me for years.

I couldn't see her face but she seemed to be smiling a bit, "Dev and his temper! You haven't changed a bit!"

"You are exactly the same too. You still like to hurt…"

She became silent. Then after what seemed like ages, said, "I was shocked, Dev. I didn't expect to see you here. Not after such a long time… four years?"

I sighed. It's ok Dev. Can you really blame this girl for not talking to you normally? Grow up!

I tried to act normal, "I have been in Bengaluru for a month now. By the way, congratulations on your engagement." She looked down. I craved Neera's vibrant eyes and smile. Today I couldn't see either.

"So when is the wedding?" I asked. Her expression made me curious. I would not have enjoyed it if she jumped around in joy talking about her wedding but one should show a bit more excitement. Something was definitely wrong here.

She replied, almost whispering, "Maybe early next year. Whatever the family decides." I kept quiet. If you are unhappy with this marriage, why are you doing it, Neera?

I wanted to cheer her up, "Where did you do your post-graduation? Did you do it in Electronics?" If anything could cheer up Neera it had to be learning. I have never seen anyone so passionate about their studies.

But I was proved wrong again. "I didn't. I am working somewhere. Can we go back to hotel now?" Clearly having had enough of me, she stood up and started walking back.

Well done Dev. You have managed to send Neera away again. I got up and followed her back, or tried to. I was wary of slipping and making a real fool of myself, but it wasn't me who slipped. She could have fallen badly but luckily I caught her. I hadn't seen her so close for years and looked at her full face.

No it can't be! I couldn't relate these tired eyes to the Neera I knew.

We walked back silently to the hotel. Before she could enter I asked her what I had wanted to for longer than I could remember, "Neera? Have you ever forgiven me?"

Did she even hear my question? She didn't look back and kept on moving.

But she stopped after taking a few steps, "Dev? Can I ask you something? Is everything good between you and Isha?"

Now that's a knockout punch! Why this question? Should I answer it? Should I tell her the truth? That we broke up long ago. But what if she asks about the reason? I can't share that with her!

I didn't want to but still I lied to her, "Yes. We're good."

She looked happy for the first time since we met. "That's nice! So when are you guys marrying?"

It was getting very uncomfortable for me, setting up an imaginary marriage date, "Let's see…I…we didn't plan…"

Her phone rang. Yes! The bloodsucker saved my day. She said, "Ok. I'll talk to you later," and left hurriedly.

I stood there. My whole interaction with Neera went in an entirely unexpected way. I had many imaginary encounters with her over the years. But this actual one was completely different. Where was the lively girl I knew who used to spread happiness with her vivacious smile? Why was she barely speaking?

If Neera had avoided me today, I could have tolerated that, but now, looking at her in this condition, something was killing me from inside. My thought process was interrupted. "Wait! Dev?"

The voice sounded familiar. I tried to find the caller in the dark. From the darkness the devil popped up. It was Bala.

7
LOVE IS BLIND; FRIENDSHIP CLOSES ITS EYES

Bala didn't make me nervous like he did Rishi and Arup, but they had their obvious reasons. But when he appeared out of the dark just after Neera went in, I felt for a moment like I was caught doing something wrong. Then I thought there should not be any hush-hush about my meeting Neera. We were college buddies. We talked and walked on the beach. It's a perfectly innocent friendship story.

"Hi…Bala."

"What are you doing here? Arup told me you were unwell." He looked at me in a peculiar way. As if he was trying to act as a lie detector.

"I…feel better now. Needed some fresh air." Small talk won't help you Bala. If you asked me directly, 'what were you doing with my fiancée?' I would have told you.

"Good for you. Will you be able to join us for the Auroville trip tomorrow?"

"I'll go. Anything else?"

"Nothing. Have a good night," Bala gave me a mechanical smile.

"You too," I walked away.

This man has a twisted mind. He must have seen me and Neera. There could be no other reason for him to come and chit-chat. He didn't care about my existence till just now. Do whatever, you clever guy; unless you have the bravery to ask the question I am not going to offer you any explanation.

I returned to my room. As I entered, I saw Arup holding a big, bulging paper bag.

"What is this?"

Arup tried to hide the packet and then saw me, "Oh! You! I thought you were Bala." He smiled. "Wait. I can show you," he took out a full Blender's Pride bottle out.

"Wow! Someone is going to celebrate tonight," I laughed. "But why do you need to hide?"

"No, I…" he hesitated for a moment. "I bought it from the tour budget. Bala will not like it if he finds out. I know it's not right but I didn't have enough money!"

What is this guy? An incarnation of Raja Harish Chandra?

"Gimme a break. How much does it cost? Rs. 550 or whereabouts? You arranged this entire trip and took care of everyone. You are working your ass off. You deserve this, man. Don't worry about Bala. He must have arranged some refreshment for himself too." I tried to cheer Arup up.

Arup thought about it, mulling it over and liking my perspective. The more I see of him, the more this guy strikes me as a kid in a grownup body. He smiled at me, "Yes! You are right.

Bala doesn't need to know. We can have our small party here. Bala will be busy. He has his fiancée to enjoy the night with…"

"Stop!" I almost shouted at him; not wanting to hear what he was trying to say. But I checked myself, I should not react. He just made a casual comment. How would he know about my association with the future Mrs. Bala?

Blissfully unaware of my suppressed reaction, Arup went on, "Let's have some food with our drinks, you like chilly chicken?" I discovered I was hungry. I hadn't eaten anything after lunch. But I was not sure about the drinking part. I can't be really awarded a 'gentleman drinker' title. I create enough scenes to involve a crowd when I am drunk, and other than Rishi, I doubt if anyone can handle me. Most importantly, after being drunk, I don't have any control over my actions. I don't want to be in such a situation in Pondicherry in the absence of Rishi and within 200 meters of Neera.

Arup got impatient as I took a long time to reply.

"Food is okay. I am starving. But I don't think drinking is a good idea for me. I…" while speaking I looked at Arup. He seemed disappointed, to say the least. I felt bad for him. I knew he didn't have any drinking partner here in the group. If I refuse, he may end up missing the fun himself.

"What the hell! Bring it on. But if I lose control, you have to take care of me and stop me from doing anything foolish. You ready for that?"

"Sure!" He looked excited about the prospect of baby-sitting me.

"Ok! Let's hit it then. Order whatever you want to. Order

soda for me, I don't drink whisky with water."

"Certainly." Arup almost ran out of the room in excitement.

I sighed. I just hope the drinking session ends in similar excitement.

⊕ ⊕ ⊕

I lost track of time a long while back. Neither could I remember the number of pegs. I could rate myself 7 on the scale of drunkenness of 10. I had to leave 3 points because I was still able to rate myself.

But the guy sitting in front of me, should be given a rating of 11. Arup was supposed to take care of *me* if I got drunk. What a joke! He looked drunk after the first sip and now, after God knows how many pegs, I was sure he was on a different planet. I thought I spoke more after drinking but Arup was in a class of his own.

So far I had found out about his orphanage in Kolkata, how he didn't have enough money to study after the 10th, how he worked in a restaurant and passed 12th privately, how his job is way too important to him since he sends money every month to his sister in Kolkata. I was slowly starting to wonder if anything good ever happened to him.

"Tell me about your love life." I was drinking slowly, almost at my limit.

"Nothing! Big zero!" Arup drew a zero in the air.

"Anything at all? Any crush?" I needed something cheerful.

"Yeah there she was!" Arup started another performance. "She used to come to the restaurant every day. She was so beautiful, so pure, so hot, so sexy…Her body…She was…She was…"

Arup's description started like a bhajan and ended with a cabaret. But as they say, 'don't blame the man, blame the whisky.' Before he could get too explicit about his dream girl's physical description, I stopped him.

"Okay…okay I get it. But what happened?"

"Nothing, she stopped coming." Arup said melodramatically.

Another failure! I was on an impossible mission to find something optimistic in this man's life.

"What about the club? I saw a lot of young girls come to the programme. You should try your luck there."

"No way. Bala will fuck me! You know F U…."

"I know the spelling. But why? What's his problem? As long as you do your work it's none of his business." I was amazed at the quality of my rational speech after so many pegs.

Wrong topic for a drunken man! Arup's eyes flashed, "That son of a bitch has a problem with everything. He doesn't wish well for anyone but himself. I work all day, all night for this association and still he finds fault with every single thing. If I had more education I would have left this job long back. I haven't got a raise for the last 3 years. 8,000 rupees! That's what I get. I have to send 3,000 to my sister. Can you survive in this city in just 5,000? Can you? Tell me…" He slammed his fist on the table.

"No…no you can't. But don't break the table." I needed to shut him up. "Hey Arup! The bottle is finished. Let's sleep now." I tried to end the party seeing Arup becoming violent. There seemed to be a full peg remaining but my instincts said we should wrap it up.

Maybe Arup was ashamed of his boxing act. He didn't say anything. I put the bottle and the empty plates away. I was trying to take the glass from his hand when he spoke up, "What about you guys?"

"What about whom?" I was confused.

"You and the fiancée? You know her right? We saw you guys coming from the beach road. There is something between you guys. I know it…"

My senses came back like a tight slap on the cheek by those words. So he'd seen us. But he'd mentioned, 'we.'

"We? You and…?"

"Who else? Bala! The asshole! You should have seen his face when he saw you guys together. Ha Ha Ha…" Arup laughed like a Shakespearean character.

So, I was right that Bala's special appearance in the dark was planned. I took the glass from his hand and tried to drag him off to bed. Arup co-operated as much as he could. Just before he conked out, he said, "Do you love her? I say elope with her. Let the menace suffer."

"We're just friends," I said and covered him with the blanket. That's enough yakking for one night!

Resting myself, I looked at my mobile. 5 missed calls. One from home and four from Rishi. What does he want? Is it a good idea to call him now? But I didn't have to decide. He called again.

Hesitantly, I said, "Hello."

"So you got time to receive my call?" He sounded pissed off.

Who is he? My mother? "I ...I was busy...What's the matter?"

"You tell me! Where are you?" Rishi sounded furious.

Why is he asking that? I tried to recall the place I had told him I was going to. Damn! I couldn't remember ...Mumbai... Hyderabad....oh! Yes ...Ooty...I remembered.

"Oo...Ooty...Why?" I felt something was wrong.

Rishi was silent. He spoke after a long pause, "I trusted you! And you are still lying to me? You don't deserve my friendship." He sounded a bit soft while mumbling those last words.

"Why? Wh...what happened?" I could not react as fast as I should have since my drunken nerves didn't co-operate.

"Bala called me up. I know where you are, Dev. Anything else you want to lie about?" Rishi was back to his rude self.

"I don't know...I..." Funny thing about being drunk is you can break a hundred glasses but fixing a broken heart belonging to your friend is out of the question.

Rishi disconnected. Did I just lose my best friend? Is it my head that is spinning? Or is it the room? Is it Arup who is throwing up on the floor? I couldn't think of anything anymore. I fell on the bed and immediately fell asleep.

⊕⊕⊕

"Good Morning!" Neera looked fresher this morning.

We had reached Paradise Beach. After our classy celebration last night, Arup and I were in no condition to wake up before noon. Finally, Bala banged on our door hard to get Arup moving. Thanks to Arup, our room was a large trash can after last night. It was impossible to spend the day there.

I can't say I was enjoying this beach tour much in broad daylight with a heavy migraine and hangover. If someone gave me a pillow and a blanket I would have gone for another round of sleep.

Arup may have been a terrible drinker and guilty of messing up our room, but he excelled at making arrangements. Even with a monumental hangover, he arranged for five SUVs from the hotel to take us to Paradise Beach. Then we were supposed to visit the Auroville and Aurobindo Ashram next. After lunch we would take the bus back to Bengaluru.

Since that beach meeting, this was the first time Neera had spoken to me. I tried to smile, "Good Morning." I was sitting on the sand. I tried to stand up but almost fell. I stood successfully at the second attempt. Damn alcohol!

"Are you ok?" Neera showed concern.

Definitely not! If two people with the capacity of two pegs complete a 750ml whisky bottle between themselves, they can't be okay the next morning.

"Yeah. Just a migraine. You look good today." She certainly did. Her eyes were still puffy but I saw a glow on her face which was signature Neera.

She felt shy, "Oh. By the way, I forgot to ask, how is Rishi? You guys were inseparable in college."

We still were till last night. That thought disturbed me. How am I going to face him tonight? What will I say in my defence? I lied to him and that's a fact.

"He's okay. We're sharing an apartment."

Neera seemed happy hearing that, "That's so nice. Just like old times." Then she was silent. What is it that she starts thinking about?

I asked casually, "So...how's your life? Are you in touch with Neel?" Her face changed. She looked like she would not answer. That's not fair, Neera. You can ask me about Isha and Rishi but I can't ask you about your friend?

"So you guys know each other?" I didn't notice Bala had joined the party, showing far too many teeth. I had never seen him smile until now.

Neera tried to act normal, "Yeah, we were in college together."

"That's so nice. College buddies! Let me tell you the truth, it's Dev, right? School and college is where you make friends. Work is work. People can be colleagues but never friends."

Forget about college, I doubt Bala made any friends in school. He's the type who liked to write other students' name on the blackboard to see them punished. I nodded. I could ignore my migraine to talk to Neera but not to this man. He's the one who called Rishi. What did you want to know? Ask me directly, you coward!

"Where are you working Dev?" Bala was taking quite an interest in me. Though I doubt how much of that was genuine and how much was under the 'let's screw this guy' category.

"TTS. Anyway guys, you have to excuse me. I have a migraine."

"Take care." Bala showed courtesy. I shrugged off his fake concern and left, not giving Neera a second glance.

When I reached the car I saw Arup standing next to it, holding a bottle of water. "You too?" he asked.

"What?" I didn't get it.

"You are here to throw up, right?"

"No. I am here to sit in the car," I corrected him, "but looks like you are about to clean up this place as much as you cleaned our hotel room."

Arup looked ashamed about his puking act. One should know their limit while drinking. But I excused him. The man has got nothing to enjoy in his daily life. Somewhere inside I didn't feel too good. May be Rishi is more important to me than I realized.

We visited the Auroville and the Ashram next. I didn't realize the beach road was a stone's throw distance from the Ashram. Arup and I walked up to the nearest rocks and sat down. Arup was nagging away at me about some more misery in his life, but I wasn't listening. I was watching the sea.

"There you are!" I looked back. It was Neera. Is she chasing me? How the hell did this role reversal happen?

"Hi Ma'am." Arup stood on the rocks to show Neera respect and stumbled precariously.

"What are you doing? It's very slippery," Neera shouted.

"I am ok Ma'am."

"You are Arup right? I met you at the association." Neera made some small talk, then concentrated on me, "Dev. Are you all right? You appear a bit sick." Concern! That's new. What happened to your concern for the last four years?

Arup understood we might need some privacy. "Ok Ma'am. I'll go now. Dev, I will wait for you in the car."

"So what's the deal?" Neera sat down on a rock near me.

I smiled, "Nothing! What about you? I think you want to talk about something and that's definitely not my wellbeing." As I finished, I realized it sounded too harsh.

Neera was a bit struck by my tone. She asked, "Why do you say that?"

I looked at her. It's difficult to stay mad at this face unless you are blind. "Sorry. I had a fight with Rishi. I am a bit disturbed."

She bit her lips. I missed that expression so badly. She smiled then, "Why do you have to fight with everyone?"

"I don't know. Maybe I like fighting." I shrugged.

She started laughing. That sounded like my old Neera. "What kind of excuse is that? You're mad."

That's a proven fact. "So what did you want to talk about?"

She hesitated a bit, "Dev. I want to confess something…I…"

"Neeru! Shall we go? We have the bus to catch in two hours. We have to finish lunch before that." What incredible timing, Bala. Knowingly or unknowingly you keep screwing with other people! Neera's expression said she too was disappointed. But she stood up.

"Come," she called me in a low voice while walking away.

I always thought I was the one with the guilt. What is that you want to confess Neera?

⊕⊕⊕

When I got down from the auto near Rishi's house, my heartbeat increased. I gained a lot from this trip. I got a friend in terms of Arup, and more importantly I was back on talking terms with Neera. But at what cost? I didn't have any idea how he would react when he faced me in just a few minutes. I climbed the stairs and found the door open.

I saw Rishi. He was standing by the window smoking. When I entered he looked at me with a blank face. I didn't want to bring any issues up right now, I wanted to freshen up first. When I was about to enter our bedroom I noticed that Rishi had pushed my bed out of the room and placed it in the hall. Is that my punishment? How childish, Rishi.

I shouted, "What is this Rishi? You want me to sleep in the hall? That's how you want to show your maturity? What are our ages? Five? This is so ridiculous." I couldn't believe he could do something that cheap.

"It's not ridiculous Dev. What you do is ridiculous." He uttered each word with enough stress to make his point.

Anger burnt inside me. "Why are you making a scene over a small thing? Do you want to know why I lied? Ok. Listen to me then. I lied to you because of *your* nature. You are a dominating freak. If I want to do something you won't let me, because it's not the correct thing as per *your* moral guide.

What if I think that's the correct thing to do? Why do I have to listen to you? If I feel like going to Pondicherry, I'll go. If I feel like contacting Neera, I will. You can't control my life, dude!"

Rishi laughed sarcastically, "I am dominating? Huh? You should thank me that I stood by you all these years. You are a selfish punk. You just think about yourself. You ditched your friend, your girlfriend, your parents, and even this girl for whom you are shouting at me right now. What a pathetic human being you are. Now you suddenly feel for her. That's the same girl whom you called a ...."

"Enough, Rishi! I don't have to listen to you. In fact, I don't even have to stay with you...I..."

"Exactly. Get out of my house...right now. I thought I would give you couple of days to find a place to go. But no... you don't deserve anything from me...Take your stuff and get the hell out of here...NOW!"

8
LOVE ONE, TRUST NONE, DO WRONG TO EVERYONE...

If you are being kicked out at 10p.m. you don't have many options available to you. I could have called Isha. I wouldn't have stayed at her shared apartment but I am sure she would have arranged something. But then I would have to confess that I had fought with Rishi.

The next option was to get a hotel. But my account balance after this ultra-expensive last month didn't permit me that. I needed something more within my budget. When I was wondering how to find such a hotel roaming around in the streets of this unknown city, I remembered something Arup had mentioned. He said he worked in a hotel/restaurant earlier. He might suggest something.

When he heard that I needed someplace to stay, he called me immediately to his place. Once I reached his place at Malleshpallya he was ready with a grand welcome. "Welcome. Please come in. This way."

"Will you stop it, Arup? Last night we drank together. What did I do in last 24 hours to get the formal treatment?"

"No...I didn't know..."

"What did you not know? That I am friends with Neera? How does that make me superior? And let me tell you a secret, your boss doesn't like me at all. So chill!"

He smiled then. "Ok Dev. This way, right up the steps."

To call these steps narrow would be quite an understatement. A guy with a 44 inches chest and 6 feet tall might not be able to squeeze through. We reached his room on the second floor. Arup called it an apartment but it was merely a room with a few divisions. I asked him the rent. He said it was 3,500.

Are you kidding me? 3,500 for this mousehole? What is wrong with the owners, and more importantly what is wrong with us, the tenants who are paying for these extremely overpriced jail extensions?

Arup said there was another cell similar to his on the 1st floor. It would be vacant in a couple of days. So I could go for that mouth-watering offer. That didn't excite me. But I needed to find a shelter for the night. I asked him about a hotel. He doubted if standard hotels would allow me to check in now. Another option was the 24 hour check-in hotels. But they were 1,600 Rupees per day or more.

"1,600? Nothing cheaper?" I started missing Kolkata.

"I don't think so."

"Impossible. I can't afford 1,600 Rupees a day."

Arup tried to offer some solutions. "Stay here tonight. You can find a hotel tomorrow. The other apartment will also be empty soon. And you will get paid by then. By the way, you have to give 10 months' rent in advance. You are going to need money."

"What? 10 months? What will they do with the advance? Open a new business? Send their child abroad?" I was really getting pissed off with the rental system in Bengaluru.

Arup smiled, "You can't blame them. Like the rest of urban India, rentals are an investment. People work hard to build one house and once you are done, you are the king. In Bengaluru there is no shortage of working professionals or students. So it's the safest business. Owners take advances and keep them in the bank to enjoy the interest. Mostly, they use it to invest in another house or business and the cycle continues."

"Enthralling! But ten months is too much for me. Even if I get a house with rent around ten thousand, I can bear it monthly. But depositing 1 Lakh rupees at a go is just out of the question." I was screwed.

I regretted my fight with Rishi the most at this particular moment. Arup understood my dilemma, "Look. Stay here for awhile. If you search hard you will get something. In Bengaluru the key is to stay near your office. Otherwise the auto fare and the excessive traffic will kill you."

Arup is a good man. If he were a bit more hygienic I would have surely kissed him to show my gratitude.

⊕⊕⊕

"What's the name of the newspaper for the rentals you were talking about?" I asked Rajan.

"It's Admag. You are looking for sharing right? Then you can check out craigslist or sulekha. Also, TTS has an internal portal. You may find an ad there," Rajan replied. We were discussing my house hunt over lunch.

For the last three days I had been staying with Arup. I would be thankful to that fool for the rest of my life. But his place could hardly accommodate one person, forget two. I felt like Gulliver. The first day I tried to share the bed with him, and three-fourths of my body was hanging out. The next day I decided to set a bed on the floor but regretted it the next morning. I could hardly move my neck and upper body and my butt hurt like hell. I need a new house badly.

I liked Rajan's idea of putting up an internal advertisement for TTS employees. Someone could be looking for an apartment mate or a tenant. There is also a good chance I could get a house nearer to office. I submitted the ad after lunch. I was not looking forward to another night of sleeping misery at Arup's house.

TTS internal network normally blocked social networking sites. But if there is a will there is a way. We used a proxy server to connect to the customer portals. With that proxy server there were no restrictions. We accessed Facebook and Gtalk through that. I was not that into social networking but for the last 48 hours I must have logged into Facebook more than I did the whole of last year. My reason was simple. After the trip I had sent a friend request to Neera.

There is a Dr. Optimist and Mr. Pessimist in everybody. Dr O says maybe she hasn't logged in at all. It's only been three days since the trip. Mr P crushes O's logic—but what if she has? O argues if she has to ignore you, why did she talk to you in the first place? She was quite friendly with you and even on the last day she was trying to talk to you, what about that? P counter-argues you can't predict girls. Maybe it's just out of sight, out of mind. She is engaged. Remember? Maybe she is just enjoying life with Bala. Who the hell are you to her?

But the problem is neither P nor O wins the debate. They sandwich me and I end up checking Facebook every 15 minutes, confirming my loser status.

I was doing the same right now when I saw Gayathri standing near my cubicle. Sometimes I forget Gayathri and I are on the same team. We hardly ever conversed. I tried to talk business with her but she only used 'yes' or 'no' to reply.

"I heard you were looking for a house near Bannerghata Road." Oh! She could speak in full sentences.

She continued, "I am looking to sublet my leased house. One of the rooms. It's in JP Nagar, but very close to our office and Bannerghata Road. If you want, you can have a look." Not used to speaking that much, she stopped to get her breath back.

I tried to refuse gently, "Thanks Gayathri! But I am looking for a male roommate you know." I tried to portray how backward my thinking was. Sometimes that can save your ass.

"Oh no, no...It's not exactly sharing. It will be more like rent. You will have your room on a different side. There is a passage in between. There is a separate entrance too. You won't have any trouble. You just have to share the kitchen with us. Please come and have a look, you will surely like it." She sounded quite desperate to rent it out. I wanted to refuse as politely as possible. The thought of having Gayathri as my landlady didn't excite me. But we would be working together so I couldn't be too straightforward.

"OK Gayathri. Let me think about it a bit." I delayed the decision.

"If you want to see the house, let me know," she left in a hurry.

I was discussing this 'Sensational Proposal' from Gayathri with Rajan during our coffee break. Rajan's viewpoint was the exact opposite. He encouraged me to have a look.

"Out of the office it's different. She will just be the owner and you are the tenant. What's the harm? She is just a team member." Rajan shrugged as if to confirm he was the team leader, not us.

But I liked his point. There's no harm in looking. I looked at my watch, it was 4. If it is nearby I could be back in an hour's time. I approached Gayathri and she seemed okay with the idea. Gayathri mostly had flexi-timing, so I knew she could get away to show me the apartment. Hiten made that exception for her for some reason. I asked Rajan once about that. He mentioned she had some family problems. I sought Hiten's permission before leaving. He didn't have a problem with me leaving early. But he had another issue, "Are you seriously thinking about staying at Gayathri's house?"

"I have not decided yet sir. I will just go and have a look now."

"But she is a Tamil-Iyer. She won't let you cook or eat non-veg." Hiten looked surprised at my ignorance.

Oh! That's true. I don't see myself cooking non-veg dishes often at Gayathri's house. Even if I did I sincerely doubt I could swallow my own creation. Cooking was out of question anyway. But at least I would like to have the option of bringing non-veg food from outside. Sorry Gayathri! I would have to support Mr. Big Fish on this.

Then Hiten thought of something else and changed his mind, "OK. At least go ahead and have a look. It may suit you."

We took an auto and reached Gayathri's place in exactly twelve minutes. Location was good, I thought. The house looked like a standard Bengaluru house, with small, spiral stairs across the floors and a demon mask attached on the outer wall. What's the deal with the mask? Is it to keep the demons away?

We reached the first floor and Gayathri started knocking, "Prabhu! Prabhu!"

We waited for some more time and then the door opened. A little boy, around 8 or 9 years old, stood in front of us.

"Sorry Amma! I slept in," he confessed with guilt. Prabhu was Gayathri's son!

Gayathri didn't seem mad at him. "It's ok. Meet Dev. He works with me in the office. Say Hi," she said softly.

He looked at me, not very pleasantly. I tried to act as a very child-friendly person and offered to shake hands, "How are you buddy?"

He refused and said, "Madaya!"

I didn't get the meaning but from Gayathri's reaction I understood he was not praising me. "Prabhu! Behave yourself!" She turned towards me, "He's not feeling well. Please don't mind."

To mind I need to first understand what he said. I nodded foolishly.

Surprisingly, I liked my room. The sorry stay with Arup seems to have lowered my expectations. It was spacious, airy, and the bed was at least twice as large as Arup's so-called double bed. Along with a cupboard, I even had a study table with a decorated lamp. I had a small but separate toilet and a back door that led to stairs that could be used only by me. Too good to be true! But now came the crucial part. I asked Gayathri about the rent.

She said, "3,000 per month. Plus 500 if you want breakfast and dinner. It's pretty cheap, better than what you will get at other places."

"Is the food part mandatory?"

"No...But where will you eat then?" She didn't look like much of a negotiator.

"If it is 3,000 with food, I'll take it," I declared. That's better. Even if I don't have the food here, I'll not be at a loss. Good thinking, Dev.

She was not sure. "But..." she was trying to think.

"Sorry Gayathri. I can only afford 3,000." I banked on her poor negotiation skills.

She sighed, "Okay. Deal!"

Now that was a total win. I couldn't stop praising myself for the remarkable deal I had made. I asked this last question, "You won't allow non-veg here, will you?"

Gayathri's Iyer instincts flared, "No…not at all," and then she thought maybe it was too harsh for the prospective tenant, "Look…Prabhu and I can't tolerate the non-veg smell. So please…I hope you understand."

I sighed. Sorry chickens and muttons, I will have to sacrifice you for my survival in Bengaluru. Anyways, I can always see you guys outside. I agreed. Gayathri seemed really happy. That was a rare expression on her face. A smile? She could do that? I had almost started to think those lines on her forehead were birthmarks!

I had a satisfactory deal. Gayathri didn't want rent in advance. The coconut oil whiff coming from her hair suddenly didn't smell too strong anymore and I almost got convinced she was an Avatar of Goddess Laxmi who had come to the earth to solve the problem of my Laxmi, I mean money.

I took the responsibility of getting the agreement formalities done as we didn't want to involve a broker. As I was going out the door, suddenly I felt someone pulling at my shirt. It was Prabhu.

"Are you coming to stay here?"

"Yeah! I am your new tenant." I could not hide my excitement. Even though this kid had cursed me in God knows what language a few minutes back, he looked like a child Buddha to me at this moment. He didn't look mad this time. From his expression it seemed he liked the idea of my staying there. I was about to leave, "Ok buddy. See you tomorrow."

He smiled, "Madaya means idiot."

I didn't get it at first. "What?" and then I remembered he called me exactly that when I had entered. Little rascal!

I laughed, ruffled his hair, and left.

⊕⊕⊕

I moved to Gayathri's yesterday. Arup got a bit emotional with his good bye and requested me to stay for a couple of days more. But I had to respect my sore ass and neck more.

The first night at the new place was good. Gayathri tried to show off her cooking skills and made rice noodles. The dish was not that fascinating, to be honest, and the chutney was too spicy but I acted like I was mesmerized by her cooking. My idea was to appreciate her efforts, but it didn't end very well. I had to eat another portion of the dish.

I noticed that her husband doesn't stay there. Maybe he is posted elsewhere or the couple is separated. But then I saw her Mangalsutra which affirmed her married status. Another strange thing is Prabhu doesn't go to school. He studies at home. I asked him yesterday about his school and he confirmed that. Gayathri returned and so I didn't bring it up again. Something is definitely out of place! However, the last thing I want to do is to piss off my new landlady by poking my nose in her personal affairs.

As the end of office hours approached, I didn't have much enthusiasm to start working on a new assignment so I logged onto Facebook. Neera hadn't accepted my friend request yet. I saw Rishi online. It was over seven days since I left his place, at least he could have the decency to ask if I got a place to stay.

But I decided to put my ego aside. I care for this guy and he does for me. I pinged him, "Hey!" No reply.

I wrote again, "U there?" He disconnected.

I felt a fire build inside me. Damn you Rishi! You don't want to speak to me. Don't. Get lost, you self-centred jerk. You…

I was busy thinking of more poisonous words when I got a notification that I had a new FB message. I opened the message and my mind went blank for a second. It was Neera.

"Hi Dev! How are you doing?"

Is this a joke? She didn't accept my friend request for a week, and there she was, suddenly messaging me. I wanted to ask why she did not accept my friend request. But I should act cool. "Hey! I am good. What about you?"

No reply for a long time. Did the girl ditch me again? After an era as per my impatience clock, finally she replied, "I am good. Mom is not doing so well. So was a bit busy."

I had forgotten about her mother's medical condition. Ok, so she really was busy. I scolded myself, why do I have to be so judgemental and impatient?

"So how is she now? Everything okay?"

"Yeah! She's better now."

"Look I have to go now."

I wasn't really done talking to her. Why did she have to ping me for these two sentences? I tried to keep her on, "Are you doing anything this weekend? May be two old friends can catch up." Yeah! The 'Friend' word hides my desperation a bit. I sent it.

Another five minutes of nothing. What is she doing? Testing my patience? Then I received a message, "I don't know. Maybe not. Normally I spend the weekends with my fiancé."

Now that was one rude awakening. Was she reminding me that she is engaged? Was she telling me to fuck off? I felt the same electric shock after so many years. Nothing has changed. I am still the one she loves to throw away in the dust. Why can't I forget this selfish girl?

My ego kicked me hard. What are you doing? Do you have any self-respect or not? You went miles to meet this girl personally. She did you a favour by talking to you. So what did you expect? That she would come running to you and perform a scene from a Bollywood ROMCOM? Did you think you have a chance? Did you think you will do her a favour by getting her away from Bala? Maybe she wants to marry Bala. Money and security, that's what a rich girl needs, right?

The last two hours at the office were torturous, I couldn't concentrate on anything. Gayathri offered to share her auto ride but I refused and decided to stay back. I needed some alone time. Around 7:30p.m. when most team members left, I got back to normal.

I logged in again as something inside me still said she might have left a message. No messages. I controlled my emotions this time and wrote a new message.

"Neera, why didn't you accept my friend request? Is everything okay?" I sent it.

Once sent, I tried to realize what I actually did. Any sane person would say what I did actually re-established my loser status. But I tried to convince myself otherwise. I refreshed the page but didn't see any of my messages on her 'timeline.' She was online. She had deleted them all!

For a moment I wanted to delete my Facebook account, break my computer, fire up Hiten's office, and explode TTS. I reached the emotional point where I was years back. Suffering, burning, and losing. Why has chasing her become an obsession for me when there is no destination to reach?

I was almost in a drunken state. I needed to go home and hit the bed. I didn't want to speak to anyone. But when had something happened as I wanted it to? I saw Isha standing at the entrance of Tower A.

I tried to look and act normal, "Hey Ish! What a pleasant surprise. You didn't say you were coming to Techno Plaza." She walked closer. Then I could see her properly. Her eyes were red. Had she been crying?

Isha spoke up, "Dev. I don't believe it. I can't believe you would do something like this again. Tell me it's a lie. Please."

Her words were dramatic and even funny but with that degree of intensity, it didn't sound funny at all. I got a bad feeling. Did she meet Rishi? Does she know about my trip to Pondicherry?

My guilt ate all my confidence, "Ish...Isha, I mean...I am not sure what you are talking about."

Isha came closer, "Dev Banerjee. I am talking about your journey to meet that slut! I know what you did. That bitch does some magic to you and you follow her like a puppy. That's what I am talking about."

"Stop it Isha. How can you use those words? What's your problem? Yes I went there. How does that affect you? We are not a couple any more. Who are you to dictate to me what to do or what not to? Stop being my mother." I raised my voice.

She was stunned. I could see tears flowing down her face. Shit, what have I done? Screw you Dev. You have hurt the girl who selflessly stood by you over the years.

She could hardly speak but she did, "Rishi is correct about you Dev. You are very selfish. You can't see anyone other than you. And you want to know who I am? I am the stupid bitch you used in college life to satisfy your physical needs and after all these years you have used me again to reach this place where you can meet your dream girl. That's exactly who I am."

She ran away before my shocked senses could react. For a second I thought I should go after her. But I didn't feel enough strength inside me. There were enough spectators already gathered to watch this spicy show.

I sat down on the ground in front of my office building. I had just lost the last friend in my life who truly cared for me.

DEV'S JOURNAL ARCHIVES-2
JULY 2006
Hearts are made to be broken

"Congrats Buddy. You made me proud," Rishi shouted in excitement. I had to hold the phone away from my ears.

"Really? I did well?" I was not exactly sure what the scale of pride for Rishi was.

"Massive, man. You got 8.8. Most probably you are in top 5 or at least 10. You cracked it dude!"

Really? I got 8.8? The last three semesters made me believe I could never touch an 8 or higher CGPA. I should have been there and witnessed the 4th semester results myself. Then I remembered Rishi.

"What about you?"

"Same buddy. I don't fluctuate like you." Rishi laughed at his own joke, "7.53. Can you freaking believe it? I got the same grades two semesters in a row." I felt a bit bad for him. You can't really enjoy your success without your best friend.

Rishi was unmoved though, "Forget about me. This calls

for a celebration. I'll come to your place. Ask your mom to make my favourite pakoras. By the way, still have fever?"

"Slightly better."

"Okay buddy, got to go. Have classes now. See you in the evening," Rishi was about to disconnect.

"Wait…Rishi?" I hesitated to ask, "…how did she perform?" I was defensive as I knew Rishi would not like this question.

"Who? The trustee's daughter?"

Rishi calls Neera that every time. I just said, "Hmm…"

Rishi took some time to reply, "I don't know. Does it matter? I thought you said you were over her?"

Sometimes Rishi behaves like a kid. We've had hours of discussion on this topic. I don't think discussion is the right word because it was completely one-sided, the main agenda being Rishi convincing me to stay away from Neera. Frankly when you fall for someone hard, unless you are drugged or electrocuted, you won't listen to anybody. And I mean nobody! Not family, not friends, not even your own rational mind. But I couldn't confess that to Rishi as I didn't want to lose his friendship. So I lied to him. I had to justify my interest level, "Oh, c'mon Rishi. This has nothing to do with feelings. I just want to know how she fared. If you don't want to tell me it's fine."

Rishi laughed, "Ok. Ok. The truth is I am not sure man. I couldn't check everybody's marks. The place was crowded. But your friend was weeping and her puppy Neel was consoling her."

I got mixed feelings. So Neera didn't do well? I thought she still managed better than I did. Top students have a different way of looking at life. The fact that didn't comfort me was Neel consoling her. This bugger has been the bane of my existence for the last two years.

I informed Mom that she had something to feel proud of me after more than two years; and she was ecstatic. She called up Dad, two of her siblings, and some neighbours too. Things were getting too embarrassing for me so I decided to go up to the terrace. I was thinking about Neera.

I need to tell her about my feelings. It has been almost one and half years now. The urge to be with her is becoming intolerable. We speak a lot over the phone, but we had this mutual unspoken agreement where we didn't interact much in public. I sincerely doubt if most students in our class even know we are friends.

Should I call her? I almost dialled but resisted. What if she is with Neel right now? This guy had been a slow poison for me every day for more than a year. Neel has everything—looks, talent, good dancer, and confident as hell. Frankly, if he wasn't after Neera like a leech, I might have liked the guy. But his association with Neera makes him my biggest enemy. He attracts a lot of girls. Just leave Neera alone!

New message alert. I opened it in a hurry. Is it hers? Nope. It was the crazy girl, Isha.

"Champion! Champion! You did it buddy. Where's the party tonight?" This girl can make you smile with her sense of humour on any day. She is my good friend. I even got help from her on a couple of computer subjects.

"Thanks girl. But you share the honours too. How did you do?"

She replied promptly, "Not good. 7.7. I sucked." Isha did very well in the first couple of semesters but then somehow she lost her way.

I consoled her, "It's ok. You will hit big next semester." It was not as if she needed it. She is cheerful by default 24x7/365 days a year. Her brain is wired like that.

"Thanks! Call you later." She ended the message swapping. So Isha already knew about my results. In that case Neera must also know. Is she too busy mourning for her 0.02 grade degradation to congratulate me? Or is she enjoying Neel's consolation too much?

Why do people say being in love is the most wonderful thing? What crap! From the day I realized I was in love with someone, I have just been screwing around my brain with insecurity, jealousy, possessiveness, and God knows what other evil traits I never knew existed within me. Sometimes I feel I was a better person before I met her.

It started raining. I could hear Mom's "Dev! Dev! You'll catch a cold!" from two floors down. I got going.

⊕⊕⊕

Rishi and I were having fun today. The drama king brought pastries to celebrate my results. We enjoyed Mom's homemade pakoras and decided to revive our 'Lord of the Rings Project'. We had decided to watch the 3 parts of *The Lord of the Rings* together on my computer last year. But what a mammoth and painful project it was. The length of the movies was 3 hours plus each and we couldn't even remember all the characters when we got to the next movie. After four evening sessions we were able to complete only two parts.

I tried to find the DVD and told him, "The third part should be good. It received lots of Oscars."

Rishi's trust was already broken, "To hell with Oscars. None of the parts have any end or make any sense. Trees are fighting, horses are flying, and that old man doesn't bother to die. It's crap. All for that silly ring. That Gollum zombie thing keeps on saying precious…precious…Tell me, does that ring even look precious? Huh?"

Rishi didn't like Hollywood movies. I was the one who kept pressing him as I needed a partner to watch movies. He was mainly interested in action movies because his soccer buddies recommended those. I tricked him into watching this one as I promised him it would have lots of action. He just didn't expect the action would be performed by flying animals, zombies, and tall trees.

However, I wanted to encourage him today, "At least we have an end this time. It won't be bad."

We started and things were getting real exciting with those black demons when my cell buzzed. Rishi picked up the handset and announced the caller's name, "It's your cousin, Narad."

Rishi had this tendency to check on my mobile, so as a precaution I saved Neera's number as Narad. I looked at my watch. Almost 8:30! So Neera finally found time for me at the end of the day? Maybe I shouldn't pick up at all but there could be disturbing consequences of that. She could send a message. Rishi could easily guess that my conversation with Narad is unusual.

"What? You don't want to take this call?" Rishi didn't give me enough time to think, "Shall I answer and say you aren't here?" He moved to pick up.

I jumped and snatched the phone away, "No, no! I have to take this call. Give me five minutes. You continue watching the movie," I went out of the room to the balcony.

"Hey!" I was breathing fast when I picked up.

"Where were you? Were you running?" She laughed. Not sad at all. Neel's consolation worked well.

"So what's up?" I asked.

"You did brilliant. 7.6 to 8.8. That's a big jump, dear. Well done." She said that in a way as if she was proud of me. I was overwhelmed and touched. Maybe you are my inspiration Neera.

"What about you?"

"Not good." She sounded depressed. "I dropped to the 5th position. 8.97." She said this as if she'd failed in all subjects.

I tried to be a good friend, "Don't worry! It's only one semester Neera. I am sure you'll bounce back." She got a grade better than me; still I was the one consoling her. Hilarious!

She came back to a jolly mood, "Yeah! I hope so. Neel was telling me that. He…"

"What's his score?" I needed to know. Neel was not on the list of the toppers but he used to score over 8.5.

"He did well. Got 8.6," Neera said. Yes! I beat that cheapo. Now tell me who's the boss, Neel?

"Forget about him. Today it's Dev Banerjee who is making the news. Everyone is talking about you and you only."

"And what about Neera Sinha? Does she speak about me?" I joked.

"She does ...as always," she laughed.

"Then why didn't you call me earlier? I was expecting your call."

Neera remained silent for some time. "I am sorry. I should have. But I was upset with my grades. So Neel took me to a café to cheer me up. There I lost my purse again. I called you just as I reached home."

Losing her purse has to be Neera's favourite pastime. I have already lost count of how many purses she misplaced in college. But right now I ignored that. She was with Neel all day and now she wanted to call me. Can someone please switch off these electric shocks inside? They are getting too much to tolerate.

I said in a low voice, "Neera? Are you guys engaged? Please tell me the truth."

She hesitated for a moment, "Why do you ask that? Not yet. I would have told you if something like that happened."

We both stayed quiet for some time. She spoke again after the pause, "So how is your fever now?" Ok. So now she cares about that?

"Whatever!" I said in anger.

"You are very short-tempered, Dev. Don't let it take over your good qualities. You will harm yourself and others too."

The last thing I needed was a moral lecture. "I have to go Neera, bye."

"Bye. But Dev, I don't want to see you hurt. Don't do anything stupid." She disconnected.

What was that supposed to mean? When you have a one-track mind you just listen to what you want to. She said two sentences but I chose to hear the first one only, "I don't want to see you hurt."

I came back to the room. Rishi was watching the movie with too much concentration.

"What did I miss?" I asked him.

He didn't give an exact reply, "Your five minutes are much longer than normal people's," he smiled sarcastically.

"Yeah. I talked a bit longer. He was asking me…"

"About your grades right? And how did he perform? Or shall I say *she*?"

So Rishi overheard me. If he could read my phone messages, overhearing is child's play for him. "Look Rishi. It's complex. I am sorry I hid this from you…but she is…I mean we are just good friends."

"Whatever man. It's your life. You want to fuck up bad, it's your decision. Enough of this movie shit. I have to get going now."

Rishi was clearly mad but I didn't care. I believed he was wrong. He was always wrong about Neera! One day I would show him.

⊕⊕⊕

"Wow! The view is beautiful from here," Neera said.

We were on the terrace of our college main building, along with some other students. Normally this was closed. But there was some building maintenance work going on so we had a rare chance to take in a view from such a height.

Six boys and two girls, all from the electronics stream, decided to explore the opportunity. We even took a wooden step-stool used by the workers to climb up to the high water tank. It was a bit risky but the view was truly mind-blowing. Luckily I couldn't see Neel accompanying Neera.

After 10 minutes, everyone had more or less lost interest, including me. We all decided to come down except Neera. When everyone started to move she expressed her desire to stay a bit longer. Though I didn't speak much to her in public, I did say, "Let's move Neera. It's not safe up here."

Neera casually touched my hand, "Wait Dev. Look it's so beautiful from up here." I don't think she even realized she was holding my hand. But I noticed it and sparks were running all over my body. Even the other students accompanying us looked at each other. I bet they didn't know Ms. Topper was friends with this regular guy. I moved my hand away but stayed back. This was my moment of the year. Sitting alone with Neera with no one to disturb us!

Neera got excited seeing an aeroplane. "Wow. Look Dev. It appears so close from this height. You like flying?"

So far in my life I was on a flight only once, when I was very little and my father was getting posted to a different city. So my experience of plane travel was almost the same as my expertise in dancing the Salsa. I thought Neera knew that already. I tried to come up with something, "Yeah. Sort of."

She looked glad at hearing that, "Me too. I just have to force Dad to fly long distances during all the holidays. Last time we travelled to the US, my cousin was disgusted with 18 hours of flying, but I want to fly more."

This conversation was giving me an inferiority complex. She was talking about foreign travels and I don't even have a passport.

"My dad says I should marry an NRI. I am seriously thinking about it. Then I can travel between India and foreign countries. Wouldn't that be great?"

I felt like turning to dust. We had been interacting for almost two years, but she never seemed obsessed about status and money. I was hoping she would burst into laughter and say I was kidding with you, Dev. But she didn't.

"It's too hot. Isn't it? July is hotter this year. I don't know how people can survive without air-conditioning nowadays...I just can't...at my house I have one in each room..."

Now that was it. If she was here to show off I didn't want to be here. I said, "I have to go Neera."

She looked at me. Then she said, "Okay. I should get going too. Neel will be looking for me." What is wrong with her today?

We started to take the stairs carefully. She stopped, "Dev, you go ahead. I will stay a bit longer." I was surprised at her sudden change of mind.

I double checked, "Are you sure?" She nodded. I didn't want to, but came down.

Why was she behaving like a different girl altogether? What about that NRI marriage shit? My head filled with disturbing thoughts.

I took some time to control myself. Then I told myself she must be faking it. She's just pulling my leg. She couldn't really mean that Daddy's Rich Girl stuff. She was different. I should go and check on her.

I started back. When I took the wooden stairs and reached the top I couldn't see anyone. Had she already left? But I would have noticed. Maybe I missed her. I turned to go down.

Then I heard a giggle from behind the water tank.

I went closer, now I could see them. Neel was holding her hand and she was holding a red rose. My heart started pounding harder than my body could bear. They started kissing next. I turned around and tried to run as if the demons of hell were behind me. Bad idea for such steep steps! I missed the last four of those steps and fell straight onto broken brick pieces. One hit my left leg badly. I didn't feel much or maybe I didn't care. I could see blood coming down my trouser leg. Shit! But I couldn't stop. Not now...

August 2006
Curing Evil with Evil

"Who told you to go onto that terrace? Everyone knows it's risky," Isha said that with full-on drama. She even looked at

Rishi who was sitting next to her for moral support. He nodded silently. They'd both visited my house to check on me.

After the accident initially I felt only the flow of blood. When I got it cleaned up at a local doctor's, we found a small piece of brick was still sticking in my leg and pressing on nerves, so things turned complex. I spent a couple of days in the hospital. The doctor said I was lucky that it was done without surgery, just some stitches. I was put on strict bed rest for 20 days. I'd started walking a bit though. I needed to go back to college soon, having missed lots of lectures already.

Surprisingly, Rishi didn't show too much of his parental instincts after the incident and didn't scold me about how I could do such a foolish thing. He just said, "If you decide to do something like this again let me know." Would he stop me? Would he come with me or book a hospital bed in advance?

My cell phone buzzed. I picked it up before Rishi could sneak a look. It was a message from Narad. "Why aren't you picking up my calls? Not replying to my messages? How are you Dev?" I deleted it just like I did the last 26 messages sent by the same person over 20 days.

I deleted the contact as well. I don't need you anymore, Narad. I don't trust myself. I may weaken and wish to call you as time passes.

Isha couldn't sit silent for long, "So this is your house. NICE!" I don't know how much she meant it and how much was sarcastic. She belonged to a well-to-do family and I have seen their 4 BHK in Lake Town.

"So when are you..." my message notification beeped again.

"One busy guy! Lots of well-wishers," Isha commented.

I read the message, "I feel so guilty for taking you there." This time I switched off the phone.

Rishi said, "I should get going now. So are you sure you can come to college on Monday?"

I smiled, "Yeah Rishi. I am sure."

Isha got up, "I should go too."

They left. I wanted them to stay. As long as someone is there to talk to me about something else, I feel comfortable. Once I am alone I start thinking about the same episode with all the permutations and combinations. I have to admit I saw this coming but ignored the facts. Why? Is it because I felt those emotions for someone the first time in my life? And I thought I would have a picture perfect ending! Who was I kidding?

I always believed first loves are overrated. Trust me they're not. Here I was acting a perfect Devdas and lying on the bed. But instead of alcohol I had a glass of glucose in my hand.

Is my male ego hurt because I lost to my arch enemy, Neel? Or is it about that girl who showed me feelings I never knew existed within a shy and loser boy like me? Maybe both! But what matters most is to get rid of this weeping wound inside me.

I am thinking about doing something unthinkable. I have questions! My morality, my senses, my conscience; all of those are continuously questioning me about my decision every damn second. But I can't look back now. Before loving Neera I didn't set a limit. Why should I do that while forgetting her?

⊕⊕⊕

"What?" Rishi looked at me with round eyes. "Yes! You heard right," I assured him.

"Look Dev. I don't think you are talking sane. Let's talk about it after a few days. You just had the accident. I think you are still in shock." Rishi tried to distract me.

"What's wrong Rishi? Why can't I have feelings for Isha?" I wanted to make my point.

"Think man. Yesterday you had no feelings for her. We used to joke about her. Suddenly you say you are going to propose to her? It's crazy!"

Who better than me knew how crazy it was. But I stood my ground, "Nothing is crazy. Love can happen suddenly. I fell for her. I am going to propose to her."

Rishi shook his head, "No something is wrong. If you had said that about someone else I might have believed you. But not Isha! You had nothing for her before the accident. What's going on Dev? Is it about *her*? The trustee's daughter?"

It was always about her. But I couldn't admit that to myself, forget about you, Rishi.

"Rishi! This is my final decision." I don't know if I wanted to force Rishi or my conscience to accept what I was saying.

Rishi stayed quiet for a second, "I am not going to stop you Dev. But you are playing with an innocent girl's emotions. I don't want to be part of that."

I felt anger, "Don't act like my parents Rishi. Why do you have to discourage me on everything I decide to do? I feel you don't want me to be in a relationship for your own sake. Maybe you fear you will be left alone if I hook up with someone." I sounded harsh even to my own ears.

Rishi was silent in shock for a moment and then said, "I am pushing you away from girls for my sake? You actually believe that? Keep thinking that. And do it alone."

Rishi stormed off. I felt a pinch of guilt. I couldn't be truthful to my best friend. How could I? Some things are difficult to share. If Rishi was not as judgemental as he was maybe I could have told him.

As usual, like with my all other screwed up decisions, Moral Dev, who was a minority inside me said, Who am I kidding? I am doing all this to get rid of my agony of defeat. I loved a girl and she didn't love me back. I want to show her I can be happy without her. For that selfish reason I am dragging an innocent girl into all this.

Shut the fuck up! The devil inside me slapped the moral fool. Don't think too much about this Dev, just do it.

⊕⊕⊕

"I need to talk to you Isha."

"Dev... I have heard this thrice already. I have a class in five minutes." Isha looked irritated.

We were walking in the garden behind college. Mainly couples used to walk there and it was infamous for lovers' naughty activities. So when I called Isha to this place she hesitated. But she knew me so she played along. Now for last 10 minutes I was boring the hell out of her and not getting to the point.

"Ok. I wanted to tell you …shit!" I kicked at the dust in disgust. Why am I such a fool? I have known this girl for two plus years now and still I can't say I like her.

"What are you doing Dev?" Isha was laughing.

I had to finish this, "Isha. I like you very much. I mean too much. I…think…we should get…" I needed a break after such a beautiful proposal.

Isha looked serious this time. "Dev. It's not about you. Maybe I know you very well in this college. But I have other priorities in life. I don't want to get into this stuff. I am not open for any relationship right now."

Another slap. I had taken her for granted. What a fool. What's next? Go ahead and propose to the girl from the next bench?

Isha was not done yet, "I just hope our friendship is not affected by this. But trust me, I have my eyes set on my career only."

She left me alone in the garden. Moral Dev got out of the chains. That's what you get when you try to do irrational things. You got it back straight in your face. Now will you finally wake up and behave like a responsible adult?

I did. I didn't bother Isha for a week.

⊕⊕⊕

Rishi hadn't spoken with me since we fought. And I had not seen Neera since my accident. I was sitting alone on the stairs after lab. I should have gone directly to the bus. But maybe

I was hoping my only friend would miss me too and come looking for me.

I was about to get up and get going when I saw Neera standing near the bottom stair. I didn't have any idea if she just got there or had been standing there for a while.

"Hey Dev," she greeted me in a tired voice.

"Hi." I couldn't act rude standing right in front of her.

"What's going on? What did I do?" She looked into my eyes. Those eyes showed me an impossible dream Neera. Take it away.

"I am busy nowadays…so…nothing personal…" I mumbled.

"That's why you don't pick up my calls? That's why you don't answer my messages?" Did she have tears in her eyes?

Our mind is a monster. When you are extremely angry with someone, their tears look fake to you, their concern seems drama to you, and their sorrow causes annoyance to you.

"I miss talking to my friend, Dev."

"It's about what you miss Neera? It was always about you. What about me?" I got a bit excited.

"What about you Dev? Tell me what did I do wrong? You can't imagine how I felt when I heard you were injured." Her voice cracked.

You have no idea about my wounds, lady. But her emotions were moving me a bit. Maybe I would have gotten softer if she was there alone with me for some more time. But that didn't happen. Neel came running, "Oh Shona. Here you are! I was looking for you."

Shona? I felt as if someone put some burning charcoal inside my ears. Why don't both of you get the hell out of here? I don't know what Neera was thinking. She didn't say a word. Then Neel saw me and noticed Neera had tears in her eyes. He shouted at me, "What did you say to her?"

Fucker! Why don't you ask your 'Shona' about this? Neera spoke, "C'mon Neel. He didn't say anything. Something got into my eye. Let's go!" Neel turned to me, "Stay away from her." they walked away. I could see Neel putting his arm around her while they were walking.

Why Neera? Why? I was dying on my own terms. Why did you have to pay this little visit and rip open my wounds again? If you can't come close enough, just stay away from me.

I boarded the bus. I chose the second seat from the front. I didn't want to go to the back as I knew Rishi would be sitting there. I didn't want Rishi to look at my defeated face. I hadn't seen Isha on this bus or the auto stand for the last few days after my rejected proposal. I saw her today getting onto the bus. I had an empty seat beside me. But she chose the first seat instead of sitting with me. Story of my life.

"What happened to you?" Isha called out at me before I could move away when we got off the bus.

"What? Nothing."

"Your eyes! So red. Your hair, your shirt—all messed up. Are you ok?"

I am not ok. I need relief. I need to forget about the last one and half years of my life. Can you give me a single clue on how can I get rid of this constant pain inside?

I replied, "Nothing. Maybe I am a bit stressed out."

"Let's take the auto."

I refused, "No Isha. I need to walk a bit. Clear my head." I didn't look at her and started walking.

I reached my house late and went to bed immediately. I woke up when Mom almost broke down my bedroom door. "How many times do I have to tell you not to sleep before dinner?"

"Ok Mom. I am coming. Chill!" I had a look at my mobile. One Message. Could it be Neera again? To my surprise, it was Isha.

"Hey Champ. Don't be so sad. You look like a baboon."

Since I got good grades, Isha started calling me champ. I liked her sense of humour normally. But today I was not in the mood. I didn't reply. I went to bed again after dinner. Two more messages. What is wrong with this girl today?

"Are you thinking about that day? Don't feel bad."

"Just one reply? Am I lucky enough to get that?"

What day is she talking about? Oh! I understood. The day she rejected my proposal!

I decided to reply, "I am ok. Just had a headache! I was not thinking about that day. I respect your decision." No reply. Good for me. I needed more sleep.

Normally I sleep soundly and don't bother about doorbell or telephone rings. But that night I woke up with a single message beep.

It's 3:30a.m. Who is messaging me now?

I opened it, Isha again. Has this girl lost it? "Dev will you hurt me if I trust you?"

Oh God. Is she falling for me? What did I do to deserve this? Actually, if I think about it, I should be happy. She will be my first official girlfriend. But then why am I having this feeling that she deserves better than me? Will I forget about Neera? Can I be true to Isha?

I didn't know what to reply. My mind was messed up just like my situation. I wrote, "I don't know Isha. May be you deserve better. I am not that good a person."

After sending that I decided to write another message, "Isha, please forget about my proposal. I was not in a correct state of mind that day. I love you as a friend." I received another message before I finished. It was a long one.

"Dev! For the last seven days I have been thinking about your proposal. None of us is perfect. I have been in relationships before. So I can judge people. If I want to be with someone right now it has to be you. Will you accept me the way I am? If yes, then I want to take this chance."

I closed my eyes. She wants to take a leap of faith with me. Why don't I? Clearly she is the only friend I have who still cares for me. What about Neera then? She chose Neel over me. I should forget this girl who didn't understand or value my emotions. Isha had been in other relationships. Why not me? Screw Neera.

I replied, "Will you go out with me for a dinner date tomorrow? PS: Budget is limited. So cheap Chinese is preferable."

I got a reply. "Yes. PS: Anywhere, Anyplace, Any budget."

I smiled for the first time in days.

⊕⊕⊕

FEBRUARY 2007
A cheat code for Love

"So when are you coming? We don't have much time. Mom and Dad will be back soon."

"I am coming Ish. It's raining, I don't have an umbrella." I tried to justify my slow response.

"Oh! Who wants an umbrella in the rain? I am drenching myself on the balcony. C'mon Divs. I am waiting."

Normal people prefer an umbrella while walking in the rain. Isha doesn't. She has her own rules and own terms to live her life. That actually makes her more attractive. But sometimes it becomes a pain in the ass for her boyfriend—me. If Valentine's Day was a normal college day I could have met Isha at classes. But no! It had to be on a rainy holiday. St. Valentine might have understood this was not exactly the weather to celebrate love, but Isha didn't. She had this crazy idea to meet me at any cost. So when her parents left for a doctor's appointment she made this quick plan to meet at her place.

It was six months since we started our official relationship and I was starting to understand Isha's expectations. I blundered last December when I went to meet her at the back of her house on her birthday empty handed. I thought my going to meet her within the semester exam was a big gift for her. But I realized that day I am not exactly the best boyfriend material. Isha first wanted to see her surprise gift, then the flowers, and then the chocolates. I disappointed her with the fact that I was her sole gift. Finally I saved the day with a five-minute-long kiss.

Today the God of rain didn't shower mercy on me. It had been raining heavily for the last 8 hours and even on Valentine's Day most cake and chocolate shops were closed. They didn't expect people to celebrate love with colds, coughs, and sneezes. But I noticed a flower shop was open. I had to get something.

"A bunch of red roses please."

He looked at me from head to toe and said, "What? Are you nuts? Out in this weather?"

I am not nuts, buddy. My girlfriend is. Now do me a favour and give me the flowers before I drown.

I said, "Can you make it quick please?"

"Roses are sold out. If you want I can give you a few tuberose sticks."

Where is the comparison between Rose and Tuberose? I had a bad feeling this was one of those screw-up situations.

I didn't have time to think. My shoes were feeling like elephant legs and I needed to get moving quickly. "Whatever." I tried to make up the lack of gift accessories with a romantic attitude. I rang the doorbell. She opened it. She was trying to say something but I pulled her closer and kissed her lips. She trembled a bit initially but started kissing me back within the next few seconds. Breaking away, she said in a very low voice, "Mom and Dad are back."

What? I pushed her away immediately. She started laughing, "Got you." This girl has her own version of fun. I almost had a heart attack. Still I didn't believe her. I walked through all the rooms to confirm no one was there.

"Believe me now? We are alone baby," she laughed again.

"Whatever. These are for you."

She looked at the sorry sodden bunch. "Who died? You brought tuberoses? No roses?" As expected my gift was substandard.

I really got a bit offended, "I walked in this damn rain to get you these and you don't even bother to appreciate it."

"Oh, my poor Divs! I didn't mean that. I meant roses express love much better than these. I love them. Look how beautiful they are. How do I look, tell me?" She posed like a model with a few of the sticks in her hand. Her theatrical performance got me laughing. It's difficult to stay angry with this joker.

Her dress was already drenched. Was she doing a rain dance?

She stood near me. "So, do you want to get rid of the shirt? You're all wet." She came close enough to get my heart pounding.

Where was this going? Bollywood hero and heroine standing close in the rain with flowers colliding and birds kissing each other? The reality is so different. In movies you get a place to get laid very easily. A room, a hotel, a hut, a jungle, or even paddy fields! It's not that easy in real life. Your home is too insecure, hotels are costly and scandalous, and other options are just not viable. In reality your girlfriend's parents can arrive at any damn second.

So I wasn't exactly sure what to do next. Isha was always the driver in our relationship and I was firmly in the passenger seat. Even when we kissed for the first time in a cab, it was her idea and my execution. But today I had the feeling it was going further. Her parents were supposed to come back any minute.

She hugged me tight and my animal instincts were slowly getting involved. I pushed her away, "Ish. Your parents will be here any minute."

"Don't worry Divs. They'll be late. Dad called."

Something told me I should not move on to the next level with Isha yet. We should stop here.

"What? Why are you resisting? You don't like me in this dress?"

"It's not that Ish. You always look good. I just…We will do it eventually. Today is not the best time."

She looked at my face for some time. "So you don't like me in this dress? Wait. Let me change." She was about to go.

This girl is mad. She wouldn't listen to me. I tried to stop her. She giggled and kissed me again. Her phone rang suddenly. "It's my cousin," she said in a low voice. Don't tell me they are visiting?

She gestured me to stay quiet and went to the other room. She seemed to be taking quite some time, so I took her laptop and decided to check on my emails to pass time. Her Facebook account was already open. I first saw her relationship status: 'in a relationship.' Thanks to her talkative nature, most of the college already knew about us. Initially it bothered me because

I am not really comfortable making my affections a public affair. But now I have learned to be cool with it. I checked her friends list. 1239? I hardly have 70. Is it her friendly nature or hot looks? May be both! Well, enjoy the heat from a distance guys. She has a boyfriend.

While going through her friends list I saw Neel's name. Is she friends with *Neel*?

Possible! They're both in computer science. Also, Neel is a mini celebrity in college. I don't know what prompted me to open Neel's profile.

I got into his pictures. There they were. Neel and his girlfriend. Nalban? Shikara, the boat house? Victoria Memorial? Where is this one? Has to be outside Kolkata! So are you guys spending holidays together? You guys must be sleeping together too!

I got a shiver in my whole body. The pain Isha helped me forget over the last six months was back with a vengeance. She was having all the fun and here I was, thinking twice about getting physical with my girlfriend. I can do it too Neera.

When your anger blinds you, you start believing the world is blind too. I wanted Isha badly. She calmed my wound earlier. She could do it again.

I went to the other room. Isha was done talking and was standing in front of her wardrobe looking for a dress to change into. For me, of course! I don't need that girl. I want you now as you are.

I picked her up in my arms and took her to the bed. She was shocked at my sudden savageness, but didn't resist. I wanted

Isha to push my pain away. Only she could do that. As I went on to kiss her, she said in a firm voice, "Dev, wait!"

Isha's voice snapped me back to my senses. Feeling ashamed, I stood up but Isha held onto my hand. "I am not asking you to stop," she smiled, "…just be gentle, you fool!"

Standing up, she helped me take off my shirt. I started to say something but Isha stopped me with an open-mouthed kiss. Then, she whispered, "Do I have to tell you everything?"

Soon all our clothes found their way to the floor. She drew me closer towards her. We tumbled onto the bed, breathing harder now, panting in anticipation.

Brushing my hands from her breasts to her belly, my lips followed my hand, working their way down. She moaned softly and held me stronger. As our bodies came closer, Isha's head dropped back, her body shivering with the intensity of the sudden adrenaline rush. She closed her eyes but drew me towards her. Her lips silently asked, "Kiss me." I obeyed her unspoken wish. Primal instincts took over us until all that separated our bodies was her thrilled breathing on my chest. That moment both of us lost our control and surrendered to passion.

After our passions were sated, I lay next to her. Isha put her head gently on my chest and I could feel hot tears.

"What's wrong?"

"Nothing. I feel so special now." She looked at me and smiled with tearful eyes, "I love you, Divs!"

A guilt was killing me from inside. I mumbled, "Yeah."

She was visibly disappointed. "What?"

I sighed, "Ok. Yeah Neera, I love you too."

I didn't know if she heard it correctly or not. But she looked at me curiously, "What did you call me?"

I realized I had blundered. Recovering fast, I said, "Now, Isha I love you. What else? My Ish!"

Before she could say anything, I moved towards her again to make her forget my *faux pas*. Soon she was too busy to remember any conversation.

⊕⊕⊕

"Don't you remember it?" Isha looked surprised.

Oh dear Lord! Now what have I forgotten? I agree I am not good with dates but most boys aren't. I may be an extra notch higher in that I don't remember even my own birthday. But now I am trying to improve my date skills. I remember the 19th of December is Isha's birthday. But we just celebrated it two months back.

We had Valentine's Day a few days back. So what is so special about today? What the hell, I couldn't even remember today's date. I looked at Isha for more clues.

"You are hopeless. How can you forget so quickly? You men are all alike. You change after the girl says yes!"

I have been bad with dates since my birth. Also, I have heard, 'you have changed' at least 12 times in last 6 months. My hair style and clothing were changed as per Isha's wishlist. Even after all this if you complain about my frequent changes, I guess it's a good time to accept that I was defective from the start.

But these dialogues don't really help you make up with an annoyed girlfriend. So I had to use my CAG or 'Convince the Angry Girlfriend' Algorithm.

Step 1: Downgrade yourself immediately with words like fool, idiot, Dumbo or similar. Make sure you start the sentence with *sorry*.

Step 2: Make her remember that she loves you. This is very important.

Step 3: Give her the authority to forgive you. Don't give yourself any importance right now. Use words like, "Give me one last chance." Don't worry, it's never the last chance.

Step 4: Show your eagerness to fix things later. Promise something that she'd like to hear. Avoid being too specific while promising things like dinner or gifts. And remember the same principle; don't take the exact words too seriously.

I've used this algorithm a few times already and I was getting good at it, "Sorry Ish. You know I am a fool. But that's why you love me right? Give me another chance. I will make it up to you, I promise. Please?"

See? Told you. Works every time.

When she was back to normal I asked, "You didn't tell me what's so special today?"

She looked at me for some time, "When did we get engaged Dev?"

That should be easy. It was August, right? Or July? Oh God. It's too much pressure. If I mess this one up Isha will get mad again. CAG doesn't work well when used too frequently.

I took my chance, "August right?"

She wasn't excited with my achievement, "Whatever. What about the day?"

Now that's being too specific. I tried to brush my brain cells to remove dust, but no. No matching records found. She understood the question was way out of my league so she asked the next one.

"Dev, do you even know what today's date is?" Now that was embarrassing but truly I couldn't remember. Maybe the extra pressure caused a few of my brain cells to collapse.

Luckily for me her reaction was the exact opposite of what I thought it would be. She started laughing and hugging me, "You are too cute. Today is the 23rd of February, our 6 month relationship anniversary, you Dumbo!"

I tried to stop her from showing any further signs of PDA. We were standing at the bus terminus. I was confused because as far as I knew the dictionary meaning of anniversary was 'the annually recurring date of a past event'. So how could there be a six month anniversary?

"What are we going to do today?" Isha muttered. Oh no! Another celebration? There is a Bengali proverb; we celebrate 13 festivals in 12 months. But with Isha's active contributions it may turn into 26 or 39.

But I had to play along. What was bothering me more was the date. Somehow today's date was important to me. But I couldn't place it.

"What about dinner?" she asked me.

Today's included, it would be our fourth dinner this month. No wonder my t-shirts were getting shorter and tighter. Also I was out of pocket money.

"But…" I searched frantically for a reason to cancel.

Isha understood, "It's on me Divs. You don't have to worry."

Isha spent far too much on me. She already gave me more shirts than I usually bought in a year. She normally carried a healthy amount of pocket money. What she didn't understand was it was not easy to justify that to your parents; why this good friend of yours was giving you expensive gifts. Also I didn't feel good myself about with the whole process. Frankly, I hardly had enough pocket money to give her a single expensive dress. Though I had bought her something during Durga Puja, it was way cheaper than what she generally wore. So I wanted to stop her mostly to relieve my ego.

"You already spent a lot Isha, I don't like …" I didn't want to hurt her.

"What difference does it make? It's us who are celebrating. Not me or you alone."

"It's not that. I feel small. I can't give you expensive gifts even if I want to nor can I take you to dinners. I feel helpless."

She looked at me for some time, "It's ok Divs. From now on we only celebrate what we can afford. Alright?"

Do I really deserve her? I proposed to her with a manipulative intention. But as the days are passing I can't dream of hurting her. But the care or affection I feel for her, can it be called love? If yes, then why do I still spend sleepless nights thinking about that heartless girl who crushed my emotions over and over for the last two years? Maybe with time I will forget about her. I have to.

Neera, you only gave me pain so far. You... I remembered at that exact moment while cursing her...23rd February was Neera's birthday.

⊕⊕⊕

I should be sleeping or watching TV. It was almost 11:30 at night.

I don't know what I was doing out on the terrace. I normally had a phone session with Isha between 10:30 and 11 every night. She couldn't stay awake after 11. I teased her that she had the 'After Dinner' syndrome. She couldn't keep her eyes open for long after dinner. I should have gone down and slept after we hung up. But I was still there.

Fuck! Who am I kidding? I still couldn't decide if I should wish Neera on her birthday or not. When you have already decided to do something, checking about the rationality of it is a mere formality. Finally I sent a message to Neera: "Happy Birthday."

Her birthday was almost over. She might be partying or sleeping. Also my number was changed in last 6 months. Now this wish from an anonymous sender shouldn't even bother her.

But Dr. Optimistic doesn't die easily. I walked around the terrace for another 15 minutes hoping for a reply. It was almost 12. I should go inside. While going back to the apartment my phone beeped. New message! I couldn't even wait to open it properly. "Thanks. But sorry I can't recognize your number. Please let me know your name. Apologies."

Should I let her know it's me or should I hide it? No, I can't tell her it's me. You wanted to wish her on her birthday, you did. Don't fall into this trap again. You have a loving girlfriend now. Just move on, Dev. Don't think about the good memories. Remember how she rejected you and chose someone else. How you spent those days in pain and agony. Think about that you moron!

The phone buzzed.

"Dev, is that you?" I read that message at least 10 times. How could she guess that? Do we still have a connection? Is she missing me?

This time I couldn't resist, I replied, "Yes. How are you?"

I expected a message. But instead got a call!

"H...hello," my voice shivered.

"Dev? It's me." I didn't need that information. I remembered those 10 digits too well.

"How are you?" I tried to sound normal, formal actually.

She sighed, "Good...good..." Is she unhappy? Uncomfortable? She continued, "I heard about you and Isha. I am very happy for you."

You were not supposed to be happy Neera. I wanted you to feel bad about it. Why don't you ever feel a single thing the way I want you to?

I sighed, "Yeah. She is a great girl."

She sounded a bit more excited this time. "I am so glad you're happy with her. I was so disturbed when you were angry with me." It didn't really give me much comfort that she was enjoying my hooking up with another girl.

I asked her, "If you were so concerned why didn't you call or speak earlier? Why wait for me to message you?"

"How could I Dev? I tried to wish you on your birthday. You changed your number. I could speak to you in college. But I wasn't sure how you would react. Last time we spoke you made me cry." Her voice was getting soft and moist.

I felt bad about our last encounter. She just wanted to see if I was okay. But I behaved so badly. I can be a menace at times.

"I am sorry Neera. I was angry with you, with me, with the world at that time. I am sorry."

"I told you, you have a temper problem. How is Isha coping with it?"

I tried to think about that. I don't remember a single day I had shouted at Isha or scolded her. On the other hand I shouted at Neera may be a 100 times during our telephone conversations and we made up later. Is it that Neera is so close to me that I feel more comfortable showing my tantrums? I don't know.

I almost whispered to myself, "Maybe I've changed."

She seemed to be smiling, "Not the angry young man anymore? Good!"

I asked, "So how are things going with Neel?"

She was silent. What is the problem with girls? They extract every bit of information from you and when you ask something about their personal life they avoid the question.

She spoke finally, "We are good. Though …" I got impatient.

"What?" This silence was killing me.

"He doesn't want me to talk to you. He has this crazy idea that you are after me. That you want us to break up." Crazy?

That bugger has some grey matter after all. I want you for myself Neera and no one else.

"I tell him that we are just friends. But that doesn't reassure him. If he finds out we are talking he will...forget it. You are not that supportive either. I know you don't like him. No one wants to know what I want."

I do. Tell me Neera, "What's that?"

"I want both of you. I need my friend back. I could speak with you about everything. I miss talking to you. You abandoned me. My boyfriend doesn't trust me..." I could feel she was on the verge of an emotional outburst. That bastard might have treated Neera badly. But can I say that I treated Neera right?

"No need to tell him you called me. He doesn't need to know if we speak again." My proposal sounded evil to my own ears. But I didn't care. When you are chasing your obsession you don't want righteousness to come knocking.

Maybe she liked the idea, maybe she didn't. She stayed quiet. I was about to say something...but I saw a call waiting. What the hell? Why is everybody on a calling spree after midnight today?

I looked at the caller's name, Isha? Does she know? I started to freak out as if I was caught red-handed. I had to take the call. I couldn't tell her I was talking to another girl. I told Neera, "Neera...give me a second," and put her call on hold.

"Hi Isha. Up so late?" I tried to sound perfectly normal.

"Forget that. Who are you talking to at this time?"

"I...uh...It's my uncle from the US. You know right? My mother's brother? He wanted to discuss post-graduation options..." I kept on lying. Poor girl, she believed me.

"Oh...I was missing you. I can't sleep tonight. Since the day we...I mean Valentine's Day... I miss you so much, Dev!"

Any boy would die to hear something like this from a smart, good looking, and caring girl like Isha! And here I was waiting to disconnect her call and get to the other line. What am I doing? I read somewhere you should always select a person who loves you rather than one whom you love. Easier said than done. I surrendered to my obsession.

"Isha, I have to go. You sleep now. My uncle is waiting on an ISD call."

"Umm... no, you have to say 'I love you' first."

"Ok. I love you. Bye now."

I disconnected Isha's call and reconnected the waiting one.

9
THE INVISIBLE SCARS

"Don't you have any friends? Why don't you go out with them?"

It was a valid question. I looked at the questioner.

Prabhu was standing just in front of my door. I closed the journal. It's been a couple of months now since I moved in at Gayathri's. My routine was restricted to home, office, and back to home. My outdoor activities were little to none. Frankly, I didn't have any one to spend time with.

The truth is it kills me sitting alone on the weekends and reading my own bullshit journals over and over again. Arup calls me and asks to hang out with him. I went there a couple of times but all those sessions ended with Arup's drinking and throwing up. So I decided to skip those.

But I got a small friend in last two months. Prabhu. He seemed the happiest at my decision to stay at their house. I could understand. Gayathri was out most of the holidays and even some weekday evenings. I guess she has some other job.

Prabhu and I gelled well so far. He had told me that he fell ill last year. That's why he'd stopped going to school. The poor boy didn't have much of a clue about what happened to him.

I noticed Gayathri didn't want him to move around much. One day I took him to a nearby park. Gayathri made a big issue out of it and requested me not to take him anywhere else.

I took a long time to reply, so Prabhu entered the room. "What do you keep on writing?"

"Nothing important. Just stuff," I shrugged.

"Can I read it?"

"Not now. Maybe in a few years." Trust me, kid. My life is the last thing you want to take lessons from.

He went to the window. "Hey Dev! That car again," he shouted in excitement.

"Are you sure?" I jumped to stand beside him.

Gayathri's house was in a narrow lane. From the standard of living of the other houses it was clear the area was mostly occupied by middle class people. But I noticed an Audi Q5 which used to park in that lane for hours. It had a specific routine. Weekdays: in the evening. Holidays: both morning and evening. You had no choice but to notice it as it blocked most of the lane.

But the funny thing was the car didn't stay for long. And I didn't see anyone getting out of the car. So the whole suspicious behaviour got Prabhu's detective instincts ticking and we tried our best to solve the mystery.

Prabhu ran and came back with his binoculars.

"See anything?" I asked.

"Nothing! But I am telling you. It's my grandpa."

Yeah! Right Kid! And Ratan Tata is your father-in-law. Do you have any idea how much an Audi costs? If your grandpa could afford an Audi what the hell are you guys doing here in this cheapo 2 BHK?

"You don't believe me?" he sounded desperate.

No, I don't. But you can't say that to a 10-year-old. I shrugged, "How are you so sure?"

"I know. Will you ask Amma?" Sure. That's the best option I have.

The doorbell rang. Prabhu ran to open the door. I was still admiring the Audi. I heard some male voices inside the house. Relatives? Did Prabhu just shout my name? I rushed out from my room.

A couple of tall, dark, and not-so-handsome moustached men were standing in the drawing room. Prabhu was standing apart. I slowly walked into the scene, alert.

"Who are you?" SM (Shorter Moustache) asked me.

"I…I, the tenant. Are you looking for Gayathri?" I tried to measure the situation.

They started talking to each other, in Tamil I guess. I tried to look at Prabhu and gestured what was it about? He slowly walked towards me.

He told me in a very low voice, "Chittappa." What does that mean? Was he giving them a slang name like he did earlier with me?

"So do you guys want to meet Gayathri? Then please have a seat. She will be back soon." I tried to play the host.

They didn't listen to me. LM (Longer Moustache) came near me, "How much are you paying for rent?"

Hello? That's far too personal. "Why? Who are you guys anyway?" I expressed my irritation.

SM sat down on one of the chairs and asked me to sit too. I did. I needed to know what this was about.

"Look. I don't think you should stay here. Your landlady is not innocent. She is a devil. She ruined my brother's life."

My mouth hung open. Gayathri could be bad at social skills but how could she ruin someone's life?

SM spoke again, "You must be wondering what I am talking about. Listen, she's my elder brother's wife. But she has never given any happiness to him. Nothing at all! Not even a healthy son," he looked at Prabhu with disgust. "Of course you can understand how my brother cannot bear to live with such a witch? He wants a separation. But this bitch is asking for alimony. We wanted a peaceful divorce but she is not compromising on the money. She and her so-called rich father didn't even fulfil all my brother's demands during the marriage. Now she is asking for money every day and for what? This imperfect son? This boy is not going to live much longer …Why should my brother waste more money on the treatment of this defective piece of shit…"

"Madaya," I shouted in anger. Idiot was not the correct word to describe that rascal sitting in front of me. But I knew just a few Tamil words.

"What? What did you call me?" SM didn't like my abuse. I could see LM coming towards me. Did Prabhu lie to me about the meaning of the word?

Prabhu shouted, "Fight Dev. Hit them. Give them an upper cut." What the hell, boy? You want me to get killed here?

Gayathri saved the day. I didn't notice when she had entered the house. I was too busy saving myself from those two rhinos. "What are you hooligans doing here in my house?" Gayathri shouted with a frequency that could break glass.

That worked. SM and LM backed up a little. But they were not done yet.

"You are asking for more money from my brother and here you are keeping tenants in this house? You are living with a young guy! I can see what you are doing. I always doubted your character."

I tried to stay quiet considering the last threat, but I couldn't. How can you say something so ugly to your brother's wife? I shouted, "Chittappa."

For some unknown reason everyone got silent and started looking at me curiously.

Prabhu whispered, "What are you saying? 'Chittappa' means father's brother."

I gave a dirty look to him. I trusted you to provide me with good Tamil abuses when I needed them.

Gayathri asked me to calm down, "Let me handle this Dev. And you two? This house is under my name. My worthless husband signed the document long ago. I will show it in court if needed. And about money? You rascals have to give me alimony. If you don't give it straight away your brother won't get a divorce.

And then he can't marry that slut. Can he? So don't even think about making these little visits to me in the future and get out of my house right now before I call the police."

SM and LM were terrified at Gayathri's screaming, frankly I was too. Luckily I was on the right side this time. They said some stuff in Tamil and went out. Gayathri crashed down on a chair as if she were boneless.

Prabhu told me, "You should learn more Tamil slang."

I looked at him blankly. Looks like the kid was the first one to get out of this trauma!

⊕⊕⊕

"Amma is calling you," Prabhu said to me.

I didn't feel like facing Gayathri after what happened today. I came to know a lot about their personal life in the last hour. But if she wants to talk about it, I should go. I knocked at the door, "You want to talk?"

Gayathri looked devastated. But she tried to act normal, "I am so sorry Dev. I know what happened shouldn't have. I really apologise. I promise as long you are here, you won't be dragged into my personal…"

I had to stop Gayathri. She was missing the point. "Gayathri, you don't understand. No one dragged me into this. I couldn't leave Prabhu alone with those ill-mannered guys. I don't have any issues at all staying at your house because of this. On the contrary, if I can help you with anything, I will be more than happy. Consider me your friend."

Gayathri's expressions are so peculiar I don't understand whether she likes what I am saying or not. I couldn't understand if she liked the idea of being friends with her tenant, so I changed my offer a bit, making it more traditional.

"I mean, I look at you as my sister. You can share any problems with me."

She clearly preferred sister over friend. She got quite emotional. "You are a good boy Dev. You have taken care of Prabhu. I can't thank you enough. I can't give him enough time …I feel so bad about it…"

I asked, "Are you working somewhere else too? You are out most of the holidays."

She stayed quiet for some time. "Mostly I need to meet the lawyers for the case, you must have understood why. Also, I talk to the doctors. I need a lot of money for Prabhu's treatment."

I just remembered what the guy had said about Prabhu. I felt anger again towards that heartless guy. I asked, "What is wrong with Prabhu?"

She cried, "He has CHD. Can you believe it? My Prabhu…."

I would have believed it if I understood the term. Can you say it in English please?

Gayathri understood from my expression. "It's Congenital Heart Defect. His heart shape is deformed. It obstructs the blood flow from the normal pattern."

"So how bad is it? There must be some treatment right?" I had no idea about it whatsoever.

"It's not easy Dev. No guarantee. With some children it automatically cures as they grow up. My son is not that lucky. He is under diuretics medication, but still last year he had a stroke." Tears welled up in Gayathri's eyes.

I was sitting like a statue. It can't be true. Not Prabhu? I can't relate death to that little smiling face.

Gayathri continued, "Doctors says we can try surgery. It's complex and expensive. If that doesn't work as expected, the last option is to try a heart transplant. But there is no guarantee that too will work out well. But I have to try." Her eyes flashed with anger as she continued, "His father doesn't take any responsibility. I don't need him, not his family or money. But I have to fight for my son. I will."

I tried to find a solution, "Does his father know about his condition? I can understand things didn't work out well between you, but Prabhu is his son."

Gayathri covered her face with her hands, "From the day I entered their house I only heard complaints I didn't bring enough money and jewellery from my parents. He brought me to Bengaluru deliberately and left me in this house five years back with his ill son. He told me he was going to the USA for a couple of months. He hasn't returned. He lives with a girl there. He doesn't care whether we live or rot. He just wants a divorce from me and doesn't want to give me or my son any support."

Sometimes the cruelty of people leaves me stunned. An ultra-educated asshole who works for a multinational company and gets paid mega dollars still doesn't have any sympathy for his dying son or his struggling wife. What a shame.

I remembered hearing something else from those goons. "Those guys...they mentioned your father! Does he know about all this?"

Gayathri fumed, "He is the one responsible for all this. I was such a bright student. I never wanted to marry early. He forced me into this arranged marriage. Now look what that has gotten me. I and my son will rot in hell, but we will not take help from him. He destroyed my life..."

I got the point. I needed to calm her down. "Gayathri, please cool down. I'll be back in a minute."

I went to my room and took out my wallet. Luckily, it wasn't empty like most days. I returned to her. "Gayathri, you didn't ask me for my rent. I know it's not the right time. But if you don't mind, it's already the 3rd. So..." I handed over the money to her.

She took it and looked at me, "This is 4,000. We fixed on 3,000."

When I spoke, true emotions came out through my voice, "If my friend is in trouble, what am I going to do with this extra saving of 1,000? Tell me? By the way, by friend I mean Prabhu."

Gayathri stood up and hugged me, "I can't take it Dev. But you are my true Thambi!"

I was totally unprepared for the hugging part and now another alien word? I asked, "Gayathri, I hope this is not a gaali."

She smiled which happens may be once in a decade, "No silly. It means younger brother."

I felt proud. This lady is a true spirited woman fighting for her dignity and son. I know 1,000 rupees doesn't really help the cause. But she had been fighting it all alone for years now. I just wanted to say, *you are not alone.*

I ignored the strong coconut oil smell and hugged her back.

10
FORGIVE, BUT DON'T FORGET

"Your meeting is over?" Prabhu asked.

When I came back to my room, Prabhu was standing beside my window. I felt a pinch inside me when I looked at his cute face. I said, "Yes. You should go to your mother. She needs you."

Prabhu was about to go. Then he looked back. "Dev, you are my friend right?"

"Yes I am buddy."

"Am I going to die? You know. I heard Mom saying…" he was so casual speaking about his own death.

I couldn't bear to listen to it fully. "Come here." I hugged him. Those little hands around my broad shoulders gave me the best feeling ever. The best hug of my life!

"Dev, are you crying?"

"Yeah buddy. I am sorry. I am bit upset right now," I admitted.

"Have you ever done anything wrong?" Good question my friend. Alas, the list is too long.

"Yes. I have offended all my friends. I let them down," I informed my only friend left.

"Amma says if you make such a mistake never leave it like that. You should try and fix it."

Sometimes a child's innocence gives us knowledge one can never get in all the pages of all the books combined. I suddenly knew what I had to do.

I sent Prabhu to his mother's room and went out.

What was the address? I remember Indiranagar. I remember 80 Feet Road. But that's all I remember. Oh God. I hate my memory. I entered a cyber café. It was already 9:30. The owner declared, "We close at 10."

"It's ok. I'll just take 10 minutes," I announced. I started checking my old emails. Here we go. I had the full address now. But I needed to find the exact location.

"Indiranagar, 80 Feet Road, 3rd main near the Defence Colony," I gave all the information in a single breath to the auto driver.

"300," he said.

"What? Are you mad? How many kilometres is it?"

"It's after 10. It's 1.5 times the meter."

"Then switch on the meter. I will give 1.5 times that," I tried to bargain.

"I will return vacant from there. Go or no go?"

I cursed him in my mother tongue and got in, "Go."

When I reached Indiranagar, I tried to locate the house number. What about the street lights? I couldn't read the house numbers properly. I asked someone. He informed me, "Power off. Six hours."

My luck! Anyway I concentrated on the house number. Finally! This must be the one: 212. But it looked like a house. I expected an apartment. I went up to the first floor and rang the bell.

"Yes. Who do you want?"

I thought she was sharing the house with her colleagues. But this lady was much older than I expected any of her roommates would be. I said, "Hi. I am looking for Isha."

"No Isha here. Bye." She was about to close the door.

"One minute please. She should be here. You are a roommate right? Do you mind if I come in for a second?"

"What? Shall I call my husband? I know you guys too well."

What the hell? This woman believes I am here to molest her? Lady, please don't flatter yourself! Things worsened fast as she started yelling for her husband. I needed to disappear. I got down the steps quickly. I could hear the lady still cursing me and a male voice joined her.

What terrible luck! I tried to run as quickly as possible. But before I could cross to the next house someone called out to me, "Dev? Is that you?"

Thank God! Isha found me.

⊕⊕⊕

Isha walked towards me with an 80's horror movie getup. I mean with a candle in her hand and wearing white clothes. I was still trying to catch my breath.

Isha was accompanied by another girl. "What are you doing here?" Isha was more shocked than surprised.

"I...I came to see you. But that old lady thought I was teasing her...forget it. I wanted to speak to you. Your house number is 212, right?"

"No, 211. Why are you here so late? You could have called."

Oh damn! So I messed up with the house number. And calling? As if Isha would have picked up.

Isha's bodyguard spoke for the first time, "Isha? Do you know this...guy?" She said it as if she was not sure I was a guy or a werewolf. I couldn't blame her. In the pitch black darkness no one could see properly. She could easily turn out to be cat-woman.

Isha said, "What do you want Dev? I have work tomorrow."

"Isha, I need to speak to you for five minutes in private. Five minutes only."

Her bodyguard friend intervened, "Why private? Talk here."

Look girl! I knew this friend of yours before you were born. I don't mean that literally, but in Isha's life you came later. So just back off.

I was about to say something. Isha spoke first, "It's ok Naina! I know him. You go ahead. I'll be back in five minutes." Clearly Naina didn't like the proposal but she left.

I was trying to form an apology but Isha surprised me, "Dev! I have had enough of you in the last 8 years. What more do you want me to do for you?"

I didn't have any answer for that.

Isha paused and said, "I had relationships before you Dev. But I don't know why, with you, I thought this was it! I wanted to live my life and my dreams with you…But then…" Isha's voice was lowering with each word.

I tried to put my hand on her shoulder, "It's ok Isha. Please don't hurt yourself like this…"

She pushed my hand away, "Why do you care now? You never cared for me. Let me finish…"

She continued, "After we broke up I was so mad at you. When you sent me that email a month later, I couldn't read it that time. I was so not over you. I spent sleepless nights trying to forget about you." She fought tears.

"…then after six months when I had enough strength to read your email I felt guilty. I wasn't there when you needed me. I contacted you myself, remember? I wanted you to become successful in life with or without me. I thought you valued me, or at least my friendship. But you didn't. You asked me the other day who am I? I don't know really. Who am I, Dev? I feel so embarrassed for all my actions. I made a joke of myself."

I sat on my knees in front of her.

"Isha, do you want to know your position in my life? That's where you are. I am on my knees and you are standing tall. That's where I see you. I always did. Can you believe the idiot who used to pass computer subjects just because you guided him, is now working as a database administrator in a big company? I owe an important part of my life completely to you. If I dare to forget you, if I don't value you, I don't value my own existence, Ish."

I stood up. My knees were aching badly. Isha hugged me and burst into tears.

I tried to calm her down. "I am truly sorry Ish! I am sorry for every damn time I made you cry. You can give me any punishment, but please don't fade away from my life. My life would be incomplete if you are not a part of it."

Isha was coming back to normal, "It's ok. I am not angry with you anymore. You can stop flattering me."

I looked at her face. This girl deserved every bit of happiness she didn't have. I wanted to put something right which I couldn't years back. I moved in to kiss her. Maybe I lost all rationality being too emotional or maybe I thought for that particular moment she wanted that from me. Maybe I was just living old memories where we used to kiss and make up.

Isha pushed me away, "Hey! What are you doing?"

Oh God! How embarrassing. Trying to kiss your ex and she kicks you away. My face turned red. Luckily it was so dark. Even 'sorry' didn't come out right. We both stayed quiet.

Isha spoke first, "It's ok Dev. You don't have to feel ashamed in front of me. It's just me. Don't sweat about what I think." What the hell? How can this girl read my mind?

"I know you. I can feel why you did this. I was mad at you. You wanted to make me feel special. I get that. And believe me I cherish your care. But it doesn't work like that. Stop living in moments, will you? You can't fix everything with a momentary brainless display of affection. What will happen if I kiss you back right now? How long will it take for you to regret this? One night? One month, or one year?"

I couldn't look her in the eye.

"Over the years I have made peace with this fact Dev. We share something very special. But not this! Don't unnecessarily complicate things again. We will regret it."

Then she hesitated, "Also…actually there is someone now. I am not exactly sure yet, but I like him."

Oh! Girl, you fell for someone else. If I would have heard Isha was seeing someone during a casual conversation, I would have congratulated her outright. But the whole situation with me running madly at night to see her and going ahead to kiss her and now her telling me she was hooking up with someone else made me feel like a perfect fool with a capital F. Bad timing!

"What? Aren't you going to say anything?"

I recovered in the next few seconds, "Oh! Sure. I mean it's so great. I am so happy for you. Is it that night caller?"

Isha smiled, "Yeah! We met in a recruitment drive. We…"

Yeah-Yeah. I know we are the 21st century young generation. I am not exactly a firm believer of live-together & die-together Romeo-Juliet stuff myself. Still we are not really ready to enjoy our ex's latest love story in Technicolor. I had to stop her from providing vivid descriptions.

But I really meant it when I said, "What matters to me is your happiness, Ish! Make sure this lover-boy of yours takes good care of you. Else he has someone to answer to."

Isha giggled. "I know. I told him about you. How important this friend is to me. He wants to meet you."

I hugged her. "And you are important to this stupid friend of yours. I wish you all the happiness in life, Ish."

What timing. The power came back. Along with the streetlights something inside me lit up as well. After our breakup, whenever I closed my eyes and thought about Isha, I could see her pale face as if she were in agony. Not anymore. From today I will see her face glowing with happiness as it is right now.

11
BACK TO WHERE IT ALL STARTED

Freaking unbelievable! How did I reach this place again? I
must be dreaming. The same garden, birdcages, and yes,
the girl in the swing. The question is how should I get out of
this dream? I didn't want to face the scary Neera this time.
How the hell am I ending up in front of this swing each time?

Ok, Dev. That's the riddle. To get out of it, you need to
see Neera. It will be painful but that's the way out. I walked up
there with a pounding heart. How will she look?

I stood by the swing. The last time I had called out to her.
So I did the same this time. "N…Neera?" She looked back
with her wounded face. Damn! Can you have a heart attack
within a dream?

"Dev? Are you scared to see me like this?"

I was. But her voice was so agonized, it touched my heart.
"How are you Neera? What happened?"

"This is how I actually look."

"But who hurt you like this? You are bleeding! Who did
this to you? Neel? That Bastard…"

"No Dev. It's not him."

"Then Bala right? I knew…"

"It's you, Dev. You did this to me. Don't you remember?"

I searched for words, "But how can I harm you like this Neera? I love you more than anything."

"You just want to win me Dev. I have become an object of obsession to you. Your love was always conditional. You were nice to me when you thought you had a chance to get me. How did you treat me when you learnt I loved someone else? Look at me. This is how I look from the inside! Are you sure you're still in love with this hurt and broken me?"

This feeling of guilt is killing me. Can dreams be so painful? "I realize that now Neera! I have been too selfish. How can I make things better?"

"Get up, Babu! It's 9 already!" I jumped out of bed. My forehead was all sweaty.

Same dream? Why do I see Neera like this? Is she alright? Alas, I can't know. I am miles away from Bengaluru.

Mom was already drawing the curtains. Daylight hit my sleepy face. "Get up. Don't sleep late on a festival day. We have guests."

It had been couple of days since I reached Kolkata for vacation. The main idea was to attend the Durga Puja. Rajan was initially doubtful about approving seven days of leave as he believed the festival was a single day, Dussehra. I had to convince him it's a five days extravaganza for us. Hiten was quite excited about my visiting Kolkata. Duration was not a problem for him. He specially requested me to carry some home-cooked fish back to him.

"Babu, get up now." Mom knew I was planning another round of sleep.

"Oh Mom. Don't call me Babu. Which guests? Do I know them?" I slowly sat up.

"It's Gupta uncle and family." Mom went away.

Gupta uncle has to be my favourite uncle from childhood. He is a colleague of my dad and we used to share a great rapport when I was a kid. He was a real cool guy when he was single. Later he got married and frankly I didn't like his wife much. They had a girl. She was around 7 or 8 years younger than me and annoying. I tried but couldn't remember her name anymore. It felt nice about meeting Gupta uncle again after such a long time.

"Hello Uncle. How are you? So nice to see you after such a long time," I went forward to hug him.

Gupta uncle was busy helping himself to Mom's home-cooked Kachori. He looked at me and tried to clear his throat with a loud sound, "Uhh…"

"Hello Aunty!" I continued my greetings and suddenly remembered their daughter's name too, "Hey there Minty. You have grown up."

"You have grown up too," she smiled snidely, as if with a double meaning. Why is she looking at me like I was an Amazonian savage?

"Dev, go change right now!" Dad commanded.

Oh, now I got it! In my excitement to meet them I forgot to wear proper clothes. I was still in my night dress, the Ganji, and my shorts. Shit! But the damage was done. I tried to act cool and returned to my room. When I came out suitably attired, our guests had recovered from my semi-strip show.

Gupta uncle spoke to me, "Dev? How is life in Bengaluru? Enjoying the new job?"

I smiled, "Yes Uncle. It's a very professional city. Everyone is serious about their work. I like it. About the job? I am enjoying TTS so far."

"That's nice. TTS is a big company. It has to be good." That's how most of us still rate our jobs. We go for brands other than the quality of work.

I kept quiet. Mom asked me a couple of times to sit near the Guptas. I ignored her initially. But Aunty made her intentions clear, "Dev? Would you mind joining us here?"

I felt strange but went ahead. Aunty started, "Dev, how do you see yourself in next 10 years?"

That's a perfect HR interview question. Is Gupta uncle opening a new company? What's the deal here? I took it more like a joke. "Aunty, with this trend I will definitely gain more weight. Liver conditions one just can't predict. With junk food and oily stuff…"

"Dev! Enough!" Mom shouted.

"Ha Ha. Dev has a very good sense of humour, I like it." Uncle seemed to be the only one who enjoyed my funny side.

"Thank you Uncle," I smiled at him. Aunty's expression was not cheerful though. However, she continued her Q & A session.

"Dev, don't mind me asking, how many levels down are you right now compared to a manager?"

I don't know why, but my funny bone was tickling too much and all I could come up with is, "Two floors. You can take a lift though to reach my manager's office." Aunty's expression was epic, as if she was listening to a lunatic, but Minty enjoyed it. I saw her giggling.

Uncle tried to take my side again, "As I said Dev has a very good sense of humour…"

Aunty asked him to stop. She glared at me, "Dev. I don't know how comfortable you are with making fun of your elders but I think you should know something first. We, I mean us and your parents, are planning Minty's marriage to you sometime next year. I guess your parents needed to have a talk with you separately before calling us."

I looked at my backstabber mom who gave me a dirty look in return. After 10 minutes of non-stop begging by Mom, Dad, and Gupta uncle, Aunty finally calmed down.

She requested Mom to send my astronomy profile to a guru for match matching. I was sure she meant astrology. I don't know what happened to me but I couldn't afford to lose this last chance to have some more fun, "Mom, send her my NASA resume." I burst into laughter.

Things were getting out of hand so Gupta uncle left in hurry with his wife and daughter.

⊕⊕⊕

"Mom! How could you do this to me?" I couldn't believe Mom had betrayed me like that. Seriously? Marrying an 18 year old kid? Freaking unbelievable!

"What's the problem? You don't like Minty?" Mom tried to make a point.

"Yes, I do like her, but not as a marriage partner. How old is she? It will be like adopting a child. I don't get the hurry. It's not like I am hitting 40 next year."

"Don't talk rubbish. You are 27. The best time to get married. I don't think you should stay alone in Bengaluru. I am concerned about your health and food!"

That's not my mom, that's the typical Indian mother speaking. I disagreed, "How will marriage help my health Mom? Is she a doctor? No. She hasn't even completed her bachelor degree."

I continued, "Which era are you living in? Do you expect a wife to get rid of her wedding jewelry and immediately enter the kitchen and start cooking for me? It doesn't work like that anymore. Why would I like that anyway? I don't want a doormat for a wife. I want someone independent and working with whom I can discuss my career options and she can discuss hers."

"What makes you think Minty is not smart enough to do that?" Mom argued.

"I am not saying Minty is dumb. She might be the brightest teenager ever. But the point is there will be a big difference in our thinking. Ultimately it's her decision. But how can our mental wavelengths match? She is still a teenager for God's sake."

Dad came into my room and gave his expert opinion. "When I was about your age, you had been already born. Your mom is 9 years younger than I am. How did our wavelengths match?"

I am not really comfortable discussing about how my parents maintained their chemistry or biology levels, but this is a classic dialogue of all parents. 'When I was your age, I did this, I did that.' Dad, not all the things you did turned out well. Take me as a prime example.

"Dad, being a father so early was nothing but bad family planning. I don't think you should take pride in that." I regretted after saying it. But the shot was already fired.

Dad took a second to react, "See what this boy has become? That's the education you gave him!"

Actually all my educational expenses were taken care of by Dad, so logically he should be the one responsible for any disasters. Mom tried to calm Dad down, "I am talking to him. You go."

Dad was still furious, "I don't know how he turned out like this. Tell him to behave when he goes out with Minty. He has already shamed me enough in front of everybody."

"What was he talking about? I am not going anywhere with Minty. Forget about it Mom." I declared.

Mom was tired of being sandwiched between me and Dad for years, "I don't have enough strength Dev. I can't take these tensions any more. That girl expressed interest to go out with you even after your morning drama. If you don't want your dad to be humiliated in front of his friend, you should go." Mom left the room too.

I sighed heavily. Dev, you have already survived enough calamities. You can survive one evening with Minty.

⊕⊕⊕

Kolkata has her own charms during Puja. Calling her overcrowded is an understatement. This city is always crowded. During Puja, it just becomes insane. Even with all the lights, all the decorations, all the roadside snacks, all the hot girls, the excessive traffic and the sound pollution; it is really attractive as a whole. If you haven't experienced it yet, you are missing something.

This festival is fun, especially with friends and families. No one accompanied me this year. Dad dislikes crowded places. When I was a kid, we mostly used to hang out only in local surroundings. The last few years it became a ritual for me to spend the most of these days either with Rishi or Isha.

Unfortunately Isha didn't come this time, thanks to her new boyfriend. I didn't have any clue where Rishi was. It's been months since I last heard from him. He should be in Kolkata. He always is during this time.

"Sorry! I am late." Minty arrived. She was wearing a green sari. I must say she was looking more mature in this get up.

"It's ok. Where do you want to go?" I was looking for a peaceful snacking experience and getting back home.

"Let's see. Let's start with New Alipore. There are a couple of good places to visit there." What is this girl up to? Is she planning to run around all night? I sighed and called a cab.

"Dev? What's your favourite movie?"

"None. They're all crap." I know this game, girl. Your favourite movie, colour, actor, and then 'Wow! We have so much in common.' We can skip that.

She looked disappointed but didn't give up, "Why are you so underdressed?"

I looked at myself. She was not actually wrong. My boring blue shirt and regular cut jeans really didn't gel with the festive mood.

"Dev, how about your personal life?" Minty asked.

"What about my personal life, Minty?"

"Call me Sunaina! I prefer that. No, I am asking if you have any girlfriend."

"I am single. What about you? Are you seeing someone?" I asked casually. If she is, maybe I can save my ass from this marriage shit.

"Hmm...nah. I have to think about us first. How was your college life?"

"What about it?"

"I mean did you have any girlfriends in college? How was it? Wild?" She made a face to make me understand the degree of wildness.

She asked for it, "Ok. So here you go, I liked a girl. She liked another boy. So I couldn't score. Then I proposed to this second girl who was just my friend and we hooked up for a while. After a few days, I chased the first girl again who liked this other boy and they were already engaged. But I didn't leave the second girl who was earlier just a friend of mine but now we were together…"

Minty's mouth remained open for quite some time hearing such a cute relationship saga of mine.

"Here comes New Alipore." I smiled. I had given Sunaina enough food for thought for one night.

After one hour of walking we entered some overcrowded Puja pandals. I was sweating, boiling, and melting in human heat all around and just wanting to go back home and chill out. On the other hand, my date for the evening was bursting with more and more energy.

"Let's go to that beach," Minty announced.

"Beach?"

"That beach. Can't you see?" She started moving. I followed and we reached an artificial beach just across the road.

What the hell is this organizer's theme? Goddess Durga relaxing on a beach?

I saw a lemonade stall. Perfect. I was desperate to drink something cold.

"Where are you going? Let's sit on the sand," This is sand? It looked less like a beach and more like a trash dump from a construction site.

I gestured I would be back. Two glasses of lemonade saved my life. When I felt a bit better I started looking around for Minty. Where did the girl go? It's so crowded. If you are lost, you are screwed.

"Dev? What are you doing here?"

I thought for a second it was Minty. "Yes. Where were you? I was looking…" I turned around and couldn't speak anymore. She was standing just in front of me in a maroon dress.

"Sorry, stupid question. Obviously you guys must be here to enjoy the festival. Where's Isha? Anyway, have you seen a purse around here? I dropped mine…" she bit her lips to express embarrassment.

Unbelievable! How many times will this girl lose her purse? "What? You lost it again, Neera?" it came out automatically.

12
LOVE AND OTHER IRREVERSIBLE MISTAKE(S)

I looked around. I couldn't even see my own hands and legs sometimes, it was so crowded. Searching for this needle in a haystack didn't seem like a practical idea.

"It's black. It's a clutch and I need it, I have something important in there," she said hesitantly.

"OK. Let's see. Where did you put it? May be where you sat last?"

She tried to think, "Yes. I sat by that soft drinks stall. Dev? What is it?"

I was too busy looking at her 'thinking' expression. These signature Neera moments kept me awake for countless nights. Seeing it again I couldn't take my eyes off her, not after so many years. "Oh! Nothing! Let's check there," I moved. Before I could find the purse, Minty found us.

"Hey Dev, I was looking for you all over. Where were you?" She came running towards me.

"Never mind! I was looking for you too." I was speaking to her with my eyes still searching around for the purse.

"Who is she?" Minty noticed Neera behind me.

"Oh! She's my college friend...Neera."

"Hi, I am Neera," Neera introduced herself, "and you are?"

"I am his fiancée, Sunaina," Oh no! Don't you have any idea that you need to be formally engaged to be called a fiancée?

I had to stop her, "No...no...She means our family is just thinking about this relationship. But it is doubtful...I mean.... we are just friends." I tried to save all the passengers on this sinking boat.

Not appreciating my efforts much, Minty almost shouted, "Nothing is doubtful Dev. I will marry you."

I should have been overwhelmed that a college student was dying to marry me but I realized it was more her feminine rivalry speaking rather than actual desire. "Minty, just cool down."

Neera's big eyes got even bigger. "But Dev...What about Isha?"

"Who is Isha?" Minty had a valid question.

I stopped both of them together, "Ladies, please. I think you are missing the point here. I was looking for a lost purse. Neera, should I remind you it is yours? And Minty, I need to help her out on this so can you please wait somewhere nearby? We will leave in the next ten minutes."

I didn't know how convincing my speech was but both of them were silent for a minute. Minty walked away, her high heels clicking hard enough to convey her being pissed off.

Neera spoke up, "I think we should ask the guards. Maybe they have a lost and found section."

Yeah, but what are the odds that a purse will be taken there? I was right. No luck there.

"Where is your future husband?" I asked.

Neera hesitated, "Subhash is waiting for me in the next parking lot. I can't go without the purse."

Subhash? Oh, I had forgotten Bala's full name. The eternal love story of Subhash and Neeru! And loser Dev only gets the chance to search for the purse. A small bomb exploded inside me. The Angry Dev was back! "Neera, I have to go. Why don't you call your Subhash to help you?" I started to walk away.

Then I don't know why, but I looked back. Neera looked devastated. She had no clue what to do next. I felt bad. I suppressed my anger and walked back, "What's the problem? Why can't you call Bala without this purse?"

"I...I kept the engagement ring inside," tears fell from Neera's eyes.

"Why?" I was more shocked than surprised.

"I thought someone may snatch it."

We tried to locate it separately. Just behind the soft drinks corner I saw a small sand castle structure. I had a hunch and looked there. There it was. Neera's purse and someone's goggles had made the perfect base of this brilliant architectural model. Unfortunately I had to break it down and get the stuff out. Yes! I found it. It felt like I found Red Rackham's treasure. Now I looked around for Neera. No trace.

"What are you doing here?"

Bala is making a habit of showing up suddenly in the dark to scare the hell out of me.

⊕⊕⊕

"You want to tell me what are you doing here?" Bala asked me with a tough face.

It's a free country. I didn't want a showdown during a festival day but this person needed to be taught it was not always him who could ask the questions.

"I have my reasons. What about you?"

Bala was about to say something, but Neera appeared. "There you are. Wow! You found …" She stopped as she noticed Bala. Her face changed. Why are you so afraid of this man, Neera?

"Where were you?" Bala's next question was for Neera.

"I…I was…" This girl sucks at lying. I knew she couldn't come up with a quick story.

I intervened, "Hey Bala! Sorry to interfere but actually it's not her fault. She collided with someone and her purse dropped. She was looking…"

Bala ignored me completely. "Where is your ring? Now you don't want to wear it in public? You want to pretend you are single?"

Neera mumbled, "I am sorry. I kept it inside the bag for safety."

"You lost it?" Bala shouted.

I couldn't take it anymore, "Look man, that's what I was saying. It dropped. But I have found it now. Neera, here, take this." I gave the purse back to her, "It's all good. So just enjoy the festival."

I thought I managed the situation well. But Bala was not mollified. "Why did you ask him to find it? Why didn't you call me?" That was actually a valid question. But Neera was already filled with shame and fear. Neel never misbehaved with Neera in front of me. I didn't know this new feeling.

"Bala, she is a bit afraid right now. She will…"

Neera spoke up, "Dev, I think you are done here. Thanks for the purse. It's our personal matter. Please excuse us."

What? I am trying to save you here, girl.

"But Neera…" I still tried to make a point.

"Leave us alone, Dev."

I had no one but myself to blame. Again and again and yet again! I slowly walked away with my head down. Where the hell is Minty? I found her, she was angry.

So now I am a punching bag. Dump all your angers and frustrations on me. I just said, "Let's go."

"No. I wanted to spend some time with you on the beach."

This was not even close to a real beach. But I was too disturbed to argue. I crashed down on the fake beach. Minty enjoyed it. "There you go. I have a perfect solution to cheer you up. You will forget about Isha."

I said in a low voice, "Isha and I broke up long ago."

She glowed in happiness, "That's even better. Dev, I will show you a great time."

Normally when a girl says these words, boys of a certain age get a single meaning from them. I got terrified thinking what

Minty, my childhood friend, was actually planning to do. But Minty proved she was just a kid.

She wanted to show me a good time by playing sand ball with me. She threw one straight at my face. I wasn't prepared for it so when I realized what she was about to do, it was too late. The sand entered my eyes, mouth, and nose.

I had a burning Hell inside my eyes.

⊕⊕⊕

"FIRE…" I might have just broken the Guinness World Record for screaming in the highest decibels.

"Sorry Dev…I am so sorry…what should I do?" Minty cried. I couldn't see a damn thing and was flopping about in pain and sand-induced blindness.

Minty's panic and hysteria were no good to me. "Minty… calm down…You need to take me to water…wa…ter…" the more I spoke, the more sand I was swallowing.

"No…I can't do that…what if you go blind now?" she cried harder.

Oh God. Do I need to find water on my own in this condition? Seriously Mom? Is this the girl who is supposed to take care of me?

I tried to stand up and open my eyes. Bad idea! It burnt more. Shit. I had to keep them closed. I tried to run with my eyes closed. I fell on the first step. Someone held my hand. Someone with very soft hands!

"What did you do to him?"

It's Neera! What's she doing here?

"He's my fiancé. I can take care of him. Dev, let's go!" Suddenly Minty took charge of me. Feminine jealousy was in full swing. But 'let's go'? Am I really in a condition to run a marathon right now? Stupid kid!

"Minty, hold my hand," I said somehow. Neera for whatever reasons was still holding my hand. I pulled my hand away. Take care of your business, lady. Let me die in peace with my destructive self-proclaimed wife-to-be.

But Minty seemed stunningly stupid. In the next couple of steps I fell down again. "I ...I am sorry Dev." Minty cried and slowly her sound faded away. Did she leave me here? Like this? I swallowed the sand in my mouth to speak more freely, "Water...please....My eyes..."

Someone helped me up. I seemed to be getting good at touch recognition. I could tell it was Neera's hands. My anger smoked again, "Mind your own business. Leave me alone."

I pushed her hand away. This time she came very close to me. I could have enjoyed the feeling a bit more without sand in my vital organs. She whispered in my ear, "You need to wash your eyes out immediately. Let me take care of you please."

At the first touch of water in my eye I shouted like hell.

"Don't touch or scratch it. You need to wash it first," Neera played the perfect nurse.

After five minutes of continuous washing, I started to feel my body was back to being sandless. My eyes were still hurting though. I couldn't open and close them properly. I complained to my voluntary nurse.

"There is nothing there. Let me see."

That proximity got my heart pounding madly. Is this really happening? This is the girl I have always worshipped from a distance. Today she was eye to eye.

What she did next got my heart beating faster. She blew air into my eyes to give me comfort. She asked, "Better now?" Better? Are you kidding? I am on cloud nine.

Then I could suddenly see it. The ring. It was back on her finger. This encounter with my dream girl ended in a nightmare.

I turned away. Surprised, Neera asked, "What happened? You feel better now?"

"Yeah! Let's get going."

"Ok. I should go then." She hesitated but stood up.

"Where is Bala? Does he know you are nursing me?"

"He left long ago. I will take a cab."

Typical Neera! She will come into my life, take care of me, and when I start to think of her as an inseparable part of my life, she will vanish into thin air. I can't take this anymore!

"Wait," my voice was strong and she stopped.

"Let me walk you to a cab. You owe me some answers too."

⊕⊕⊕

"Are you marrying that girl?" she asked first.

"Yes. But I will skip the beaches for a honeymoon." We both looked at each other and burst into laughter.

"Oh! That girl is crazy. Where is Isha? Did you guys fight or what? Make up with her."

What's your fascination about matchmaking me and Isha? "Why do you keep asking me about Isha?"

"Is it one of your questions?" Neera smiled.

"Yes. Tell me." I needed to know. Why couldn't Neera associate me with her even once?

"You looked happy with her. You guys were perfect with each other."

"Yeah, I was so perfectly happy I had to call you every night..." I regretted saying it. I never expressed my emotions to Neera directly. She didn't have any clue how much I loved her. It didn't make any sense to convey it now.

She looked at me for some time, "Did you guys fight because of me? You said everything is okay between you, right? Tell me Dev." Why is she so concerned?

"Yeah, we are good! But I have more questions."

Neera sighed. "Ok..."

"Are you happy with this marriage?" I looked at her straight for the reaction. Did she look pissed off? Strangely she didn't.

"Does it matter Dev? I loved someone. We broke up. I don't have any romantic feelings left in me. If my family thinks Subhash is perfect for me, he is."

So, it's about Neel. Is Neera still in love with him? I felt the same pain from years ago. I am still losing to that guy. He is not even in the picture but Neera is thinking only about him.

Neera composed herself, "What's the next question?"

I didn't reply. She never took me for more than a friend. It's not her fault. She always had feelings for Neel. I don't know what I was thinking meeting her after all these years. Did some part of my heart believe since Neera didn't like Bala, I had a chance? How do I manage to see these impossible dreams every time I am around her? Why can't I accept the reality and just move on?

I didn't reply for a long time, and Neera spoke up, "Dev, you are too driven by momentary emotions. One second you are the dearest friend, and the next you are ..."

My phone rang. Home. I disconnected. Both of us stayed silent for the rest of our walk. She signalled for a cab.

Before going she looked at me, "Dev. I know you wanted to help me earlier. I am sorry I pushed you away. But from now please stay away from me and my problems. Subhash and his family are conservative. It's not good for anyone."

The cab was already moving away. I slapped its door so hard the driver stopped the car, "One minute." I looked at Neera, "Neera! You can ask me anything. But don't ask me to stay away from you. I never could do it nor can I do so in the future. I care for you and if you are hurt I have to be there."

Neera fought tears, "Did you say you care for me Dev? Is that why you called me a slut? Driver, please go."

I stood there. My brain cells didn't work. What had just happened? My phone rang again. Surprise, it was Dad. He never called me. Something was wrong.

"When are you coming back?"

"Soon Dad! What's the hurry?"

"Your mom's health is not good. Her blood pressure is high. I need to go out and buy some medicine."

What? Mom is ill? "I am coming right home!"

⊕⊕⊕

The door was cracked open. No locks! I entered our house.

"Dad?" Where is he? Has he already left before I could reach home?

I went into their bedroom. Mom was sleeping there. I slowly walked towards her and touched her forehead. She opened her eyes.

"What happened, Mom? You okay?" I whispered.

She smiled, "Yeah Babu! How was your evening with Minty?"

Not a good topic to bring up right now. I avoided an answer, "Yeah, good Mom. You rest."

I got up and turned to go and let her rest peacefully. I was surprised to see Dad standing just outside the bedroom door. He had a packet in his hand. So he had gone to buy Mom's medicine. "Oh Dad! You freaked me out. Why didn't you lock the front door? You could have waited for me...."

Dad didn't let me finish, "Why don't you tell your mom what you actually did today?"

I got a bad feeling inside. "Dad, let's go to my room and talk. Mom needs to rest."

"No. Your mom should know. She is so proud of you. She

needs to hear it." Dad raised his voice, "Deepa, your son left Minty on the road for another girl."

So that was Minty's version? That stupid girl didn't even mention the sand episode. "Dad. Please don't overreact. Minty is exaggerating. She left *me*. She threw sand…"

"Lies, lies, and more lies. I am ashamed of the fact I have a son like you. Why don't you poison me and your mom now so that we don't have to experience humiliation every day?"

"Dad, you are being melodramatic. I am not interested in this. I am going to my room."

Dad was really mad. He followed me, "Don't you dare walk away from me. I have given you everything you wanted. Clothes, books, education. What did you give us in return? You couldn't even complete your B-tech in 4 years. Your irresponsible behaviour caused you to lose one year in college. And you are giving me a lecture about melodrama?"

A volcano erupted inside my head, "Who told you to give me those things? Did I ask you to give me an education in a private engineering college? No. It was your decision. Because *you* couldn't make it in engineering! So it was your selfish intention. Don't blame me for that. And about giving me books and stuff, you didn't do any favours. All the parents do the same. You are no Superman. Yes! I lost a year in college. But I took care of my career. I will take care of it in the future too."

"That's the way you talk to your father?" Both of us looked at Mom .

"Mom? Now you are also taking Dad's side! You guys are teaming up now!" I shouted.

"Shut up Dev! You ungrateful boy! Do you have any idea how your dad arranged your tuition fees? You wasted one year of your life doing something so filthy I feel ashamed to even mention it and here you are arguing in our face that you took care of it. I thought you had changed after that incident. But no. You have no love or respect for your family or your own life. I sometimes regret I have a son like you…"

When did Mom call me Dev the last time? When did she shout at me like this? Never! I always thought Mom was the only one in the world who was proud of me. I stood stunned when I heard a loud bang as if something had fallen.

"Deepa …?" Dad reacted first.

Mom was lying on the ground. Is that blood coming out from her nose? What have I done? Have I lost my mother?

"Dev…is your mother …?" I saw tears in Dad's eyes.

"No Mom…Please wake up…Not like this…Mom!"

Dad got hold of himself first. "She's had a stroke. I am calling the ambulance. Just make sure she is breathing."

I put Mom's head in my lap. "I am sorry Mom. One last chance! Please…"

Dad came back, "The ambulance is coming soon. Be strong."

I got up and hugged Dad. "Dad, please tell Mom. I am sorry. Please ask her to give me one last chance…please… Dad….do it for me…"

Dad put his hand on my head.

The two men who had been fighting for years driven by their egos, generation gaps and individual viewpoints somehow collaborated. The reason was simple. The most important woman of their lives was lying in front of them, fighting for her life.

⊕⊕⊕

DEV's JOURNAL ARCHIVES -3
MARCH 2008
The final lie

"It's ok Divs. There is always next time," Isha touched my hand. She looked more disappointed than me.

We were sitting on the grass outside the main building. The ICM Campus interview results were just out. I was not in the final selection list. I could clear the written aptitude round but had screwed the technical interviews again. Being an electronics student I sucked at all computer science subjects so far and frankly I didn't have any interest in programming either. That was the rock standing between me and a software engineer position for the last five companies which visited our campus.

Isha already had an offer from Cognixant long ago. She tried to prepare me with my C and Java programming skills and I was slowly starting to develop interest in it. But you can't digest three plus years of ignored knowledge in one month and spew it up in front of the interview panel.

A couple of guys from computers and one each from IT

and electronics were selected. They were currently performing the 'Look Mom! I got the job' act in front of us.

I felt bad for Isha more. She had this crazy idea that she wanted to declare our relationship to her parents once I got a job. I disagreed. We are barely 22. Also, Isha wants to go for an MBA next. If she has another two to three years dedicated to studying, what's the hurry then?

She also tried to convince me I should apply for Masters. I am unsure. Dad has been talking about our financial conditions every day. I need a job first. Isha needs to understand this.

I saw Rishi coming towards me. We got back to talking terms early this year. But the closeness we used to share was still missing. Maybe he couldn't take Isha's presence in my life very well.

"Bad luck buddy." He sat next to us. Rishi couldn't clear the first round of any of the companies yet. He messed up in the aptitude round for all of them.

I tried to make plans and hang out with both of them mainly to cheer Rishi up, but things didn't work out well. Isha, around me, behaves like there's no one else in the world other than us. That pisses off most of my other friends, including Rishi. I always liked the caring part of Isha but sometimes I feel it is alienating me from everyone else.

As usual, Isha ignored Rishi's presence completely, "Dev, you have to improve in data structure programming. We must get that fixed before Sattyam comes next month."

"We'll talk about it tomorrow." I tried to change the topic. C'mon girl, gimme a break.

Isha didn't listen, "You have to act more seriously, Dev. Only two months left of the last semester. You have to get a job before that. Walk-ins are much more competitive with hordes of students trying to break in if you don't make it in campus interviews." Now that's pressure. You have to get a job in the next two months. You have to meet the girl's parents and declare your 'hooking up with their daughter' status to them. It's getting too much for me.

My thoughts were interrupted as Rishi stood up, "Ok guys, I have to go. Dev! I'll call you."

I wanted to stop him. I missed those mindless boy hours we used to spend together. "Hey Rishi, wait. Let's return together. I need to chill out a bit. My body is craving computer games."

"Dev, you are going with me right? You will need that networking book."

Was she always this bossy? Or is it that I have changed so much that I find loopholes in each of her statements?

I couldn't say anything more. Rishi laughed sarcastically, "It's ok buddy. I'll see you later. You study hard."

I felt anger towards Isha. It's my career, my job and my life. You don't own me. After a few minutes we took a bus. When we reached at Isha's place it was already dark.

"Hello Aunty!" I greeted Isha's mother. Isha had inherited her good looks from her.

"Hi Dev. How was the interview?" Oh! Isha has already told her I had an interview? More embarrassment!

"Not good. It didn't work out."

She tried to console me, "It's ok. Isha talks very highly about your capabilities. You will eventually crack it. It's all a bit of luck too." Oh, Isha! Don't make me a Superman in front of your parents. Too much expectation can kill one.

Isha didn't want to waste any time. "Let's go Dev. Get your book."

Sometimes I feel I have a nanny inside my girlfriend. I took the book from her. "I'll go now Ish."

"Stay here for half an hour at least."

I didn't feel like staying. Somehow I am losing interest in spending time with her. Is it her excessive clingy nature? Or is it that I don't feel any excitement being with her anymore?

She came closer and leaned in for a kiss. I don't know why but I turned away. She was shocked at my response. "What? Now you don't want to kiss me anymore?"

Oh! Another array of complains? It's true that boys have a gland which secretes the same hormone all the time spelling S E X but we are not machines either. Isha sat silently away from me. Is she crying that I refused to kiss her? Now I have to perform a consolation act.

"Hey Ish. Why are you crying? You know I can't stand to see you like this. I am not in a good mood today. Please stop crying."

She sniffled, "Are you angry with me Divs?"

I was but she was looking too upset to hit her with that, "You have to understand. You can't make me a Zuckerberg or Bill Gates in a couple of months. You have to accept I am weak in computer subjects. Just don't push me too much. I feel suffocated."

"You don't get it Dev. What if I get posted in a different city in next few months? If I get into a decent MBA college next year, I will be away for another couple of years. I know you will lose focus if I go. I want you to get a job and meet Dad soon. I also want to be introduced to your family formally. Please Honey! Just get a job quickly. For me! Please..."

Round and round we go. I am trying. Can't you see that? Don't force me 24x7. I wanted to stop her from talking about this anymore. So I scooped in and covered her lips with mine, effectively ending further conversation.

⊕⊕⊕

It was past 11:30. What is she still doing? My phone rang.

"Where were you? I was waiting for your call for so long," I complained.

"Sorry Dev. I was not feeling good today. How was your interview?" Neera asked.

"I screwed up again. I got selected in aptitude and GD. But rejected in technical interviews." I sighed.

She stayed silent for some time. "Ok. Don't worry Dev. It's all luck."

Yeah! When we get what we want, it's our doing. When we fuck up, it's all luck.

Neera didn't have any interviews yet. She was going to do M-tech next. She didn't have much interest in the big fat engineering rat race of software jobs. Her family background had ensured that her priorities were different from ours. Education was more like a passion to her as opposed to most of us who wanted to get our bread and butter out of these four years of mugging up.

"What happened to you? Don't tell me you guys fought again?" I changed the topic.

"Yeah. Unfortunately. I don't know why Neel is behaving like this. As the college days are coming to an end he is going insane…" she sounded really disturbed.

My first love speaks to me every night and discusses her personal life. Initially I used to get irritated hearing so much about Neel and I still do, but somehow I've learned to live with it. I am just the extra pillow you ask for from the hotel attendant to get that added comfort while sleeping. But you can survive the night even if you don't get it.

Neera's problem was always Neel. He had a problem with Neera speaking to any boy. I felt that after getting a job offer a couple of months back Neel's male ego was on a roll. Why was she tolerating this? It was beyond my scope of understanding.

"Why don't you leave him…" I stopped.

"Forget it Dev. Tell me something else. How are things between you and Isha?" Now that's Neera. If you don't need my advice and I don't understand the complexity of your problems, why bother to open up to me? Why bother to even call me? What do you want from me Neera?

I don't know if I love Neera with the same intensity anymore. Most of our conversations end with me getting frustrated, but still I have to speak to her. I have to make sure she is fine.

I didn't reply to that question. I was trying to say something to change the topic but I got call waiting. It was Isha again. She just called me. Is she checking up on me?

I stopped Neera, "Neera. Sorry I have another call. Please wait for a sec."

I switched. "Hi Ish! What's up?"

"You're on call waiting. This is the third time this week. Dev? Are you hiding something from me?" Her voice sounded moist.

A shiver went up my spine. So she was checking on me. What should I say to her?

"Dev, do you remember what I told you when I accepted your proposal?"

Now this is typical Dev. My memory doesn't co-operate in pressure situations.

Isha continued, "I guess you don't remember. But I do. I asked if you would hurt me if I trusted you. I am asking you the same question right now. Will you hurt me Dev?"

I felt like she hit me with a bullet. I felt so small in front of her. Did I keep my promise? No, on the contrary, I have hidden something from her every single day.

Enough of your selfish act Dev! You have only taken from Isha! Time to return something.

"I...I was talking to..." I wanted to tell her the truth this time. But I didn't know how to put it.

"No Dev. I don't want to know who you are talking to. Just answer me. Will you hurt me? Will you leave me? Tell me right now before it's too late." She couldn't control her tears anymore, I could hear her crying.

I knew what I had to do. "Ish! One sec." I connected the other call.

"Hey Neera. Isha is calling me. I need to talk to her. I have to go now." I disconnected.

"Ish. Don't worry. I will not break your trust!"

But I did. And so very soon after I promised I would not!

⊕ ⊕ ⊕

APRIL 2008
Those 72 hours, an unforgivable sin

"Don't forget the networking part. You suck at that." Isha smiled.

I sighed. I crossed the aptitude and Group Discussions round successfully for Sattyam. They took some time to get the results out. It was already late so they called us, the selected candidates, for technical interviews the next morning at different slots.

My interview was around 1 p.m. Isha wanted me to brush up on my computer skills. I trust this girl more about my technical knowledge than myself. I disconnected the call but listened to her.

I couldn't concentrate though. Something had happened that morning which was disturbing me. I was just informed that I was selected after the aptitude tests and I should wait for the group discussions. I was sitting just outside the meeting hall waiting for my turn. My phone beeped. It was Neera. When I accept she is out of my life, there she is back again. I last heard from her around a month back when I disconnected her call rather rudely. Since then no calls, no messages from either side!

Here she was messaging me just seconds before I was entering the GD round for the most important venture of my life at this moment, *A Job*.

A guy started calling out the names; what timing! I started to move with the phone in my hand. The guy asked me to switch off the phone. "Yeah! Sure." I wanted to read the message before I switched it off.

"Dev, we broke up. I am so down right now. We…"

I didn't read the last part. It was enough for me that she had broken up. I read the line at least 10 times. Has this finally happened? Neera has broken up with Neel? I wanted to hear these words for so long.

The organizer guy yelled, "Hey You? Get rid of the mobile and come now."

"Yes sir," suddenly I felt the day was wonderful.

When I got out of the GD room, I was more or less sure I was going to make it to the next round. I switched on the mobile. 4 messages! 3 from Isha and 1 from Neera. I read Neera's first.

"Sorry. I just remembered you have interviews today. I am sorry for bothering you."

I tried to come up with an answer. I was happy that she broke up. But should I tell her that? I messaged Isha to meet me after her classes. Then I replied to Neera, "Please don't feel bad. You tried your best to make this work. I think what happened is the best for both of you. If you need to talk, call me."

She sent a reply, "Thanks." Just Thanks? I wanted to hear more.

What was I thinking? Did her breaking up with Neel open a door for me? What about my promise to Isha? Was it really worth to sabotage my own last job opportunity in college? Maybe I was not thinking at all, I was driven by madness, insanity.

Six hours later and here I was, supposed to be preparing for the next day's interview but actually waiting for a call or message from Neera!

I eventually messaged her, "Hey. I haven't heard from you. Are you okay? I hope Neel is not bothering you. Call me if you want."

No reply. I got a message. Is it her? Shit, No! It was Isha. Girl, why can't you give me some space? I couldn't concentrate on anything right now. I dialled Neera. She disconnected the call. Why did she disconnect? Maybe she was with her parents.

I waited till 8:30. Then sent another message, "Why don't you reply? Are you okay?"

As soon as I received the delivery message, I got a call. Neera. "Hey. Where were you?" I said with a lot of intensity.

"Dev? I need to tell you something," Neera's voice sounded formal.

I had a feeling something bad had happened. "What happened? Are you fine?" I asked again.

"Don't bother, Dev! Please do me a favour. Don't try to contact me by any means after today."

I took some time to digest what she was actually saying. For a second I thought she was kidding. "Wh…what?" My voice shivered. Did she patch things up with Neel? Is he making her say these things?

Neera continued, "Dev, I mean it. Don't call me or message me ever. Ok?"

I lost my words. But I was still finding it difficult to believe she could say something like this to me. We had talked every day for years. Now you are telling me not to call you ever? You said you needed to talk to me, remember?

"…Is anyone forcing you to say these things?" Please say yes, Neera. Please!

"No! It's my own decision. And I don't see a reason to justify myself to you. Have I made myself clear Dev?"

I didn't realize my face muscles were still able to move, "O…Ok…" She disconnected.

What exactly had happened? She crushed my emotions, my friendship and my love which I kept inside and nurtured over the years. This was the same girl for whom I risked all the other close relations I had.

I sat down on the ground. I didn't realize for how long. My phone alerted me to another message. Unknown number!

"That's what you get when you chase my girl you loser. Do us a favour; don't ever show your loser face to us. Fuck off!"

I didn't need an encyclopaedia to guess the sender. I kept reading the message over and over. Each word struck me as a shock, converted to grief and fuelled an uncontrollable anger. There was an eruption inside my head. I had nothing but revenge on my mind. I needed to show this rich girl and her rotten boyfriend their place. She toyed with me for four years now. Enough humiliation and insult!

Those next five minutes decided the course of my life. If I had kept my promise to Isha and ignored Neera's morning message, maybe my life would have been different. Even after this humiliation, if I would have called Isha or Rishi and confessed everything, I could have lived another life altogether. Maybe I would have got a job the next day, I would have graduated in one month and lived a simple 9 to 6 working life. But just like the last four years, when it mattered the most, I took the wrong turn.

I sent a message to Neera, "You selfish bitch. You think you can use me all these years and kick me out like that. Now you don't want to talk to me? You had a boyfriend, still you called me every damn night. Do you understand what that makes you? A slut! I damn you right now, you characterless rich brat. Stay away from me. Go keep your multiple boyfriends happy. Spare me."

One should think I did enough to hurt my enemy's ego. But Dev's mindless anger was not done yet.

I sent another message to her boyfriend, "Hey Son of a Bitch! Call me a loser? Think again. Your girlfriend called me every night for the last 3 years. She had to talk to me. Are you sure we haven't done anything more? Yes, we have slept together. Now what are you going to do about it? You can have the rest of the fun. I am done with her."

I don't know if sending those messages gave me any relief or not. I skipped dinner. I didn't return any of Isha's calls. I couldn't sleep. Finally, I don't remember when exactly, I slept. I thought my day of misery had ended.

But this was just the beginning.

⊕⊕⊕

My eyes opened to my phone ringing. It stopped and started ringing again. I was forced to wake up. It was broad daylight. I saw the caller's name. It was Rishi. What did he want so early in the morning?

"Hey Rishi! What's up?"

Rishi sounded agitated, "You tell me. What's going on? You should be in college by now. It's almost 11."

It was 11? How long did I sleep? Why didn't Mom call me? My interview was scheduled at 1p.m. I still had time to make it. "It's ok Rishi. I overslept. My interview is at 1p.m."

"Screw your interview. Do you have any idea what's going on? What did you do?" Rishi shouted at me.

What was he talking about? "I don't get it. Tell me clearly."

"You moron! There's a notice from the regulation committee. They want you to meet them at 4p.m. Nothing much was written there. But there is a lot of buzz around. Some students were saying…" Rishi stopped.

"What are they saying Rishi?" I was feeling as if the ground beneath my feet was shifting and I was entering a deep, dark hole.

"You…you…" Rishi hesitated, "You have harassed a girl. Either you will be charged with the sexual harassment or the text harassment policy. Did you by chance send any obscene content to any girl? Maybe by mistake?"

Poor Rishi. He couldn't believe his friend could do anything like this. But I did, my friend. I let you all down. Did Neera complain? Or Neel? What are the consequences? We have final exams in less than a month. What about today's interview? What about Isha? How would she react when she found out about this? What about my family? Oh God. What have I done?

I covered my face with both hands. The phone fell to the ground. I was there for 20 minutes or so till Mom came into my room with breakfast and started small talk. I didn't react much. As long as she didn't know it was better.

I told Mom I had a day off. I didn't have enough courage to go to the college. How can I justify my actions to Isha? What about Rishi? My teachers? What will I say in front of the regulation committee? Will Neera be there? Oh No! I waited for years to see a drop of love for me in those eyes. I won't be able to bear it if those eyes only portray hatred towards me. Can't we rewind a few hours and change what I did? Please God.

My phone rang. Rishi? I checked. Damn it! It was Isha. I took the call. "H…hello," my voice broke in fear of the unexpected.

"Did you do it Dev?" Flat and straight. Isha's voice told me she already passed the tears phase.

"I…Ish. Please understand. I…" I didn't know what to say. Should I make up a story? It was all somebody else's fault. Or should I tell her the truth? I wanted to stop her from hating me at any cost.

"I don't care Dev. I have enough evidence you were lying to me day after day. I just want to know about this one. Did you send that message to Neera?"

Clearly Isha knew more than Rishi.

"Isha…I…I made a mistake. Please forgive me," That's the best I could come up with. I believed I had control over my emotions. Then what were these? Tears?

"Dev, you played with my emotions for years. I loved you. But you kept on lying to me and cheating behind my back. Did you ever love me? Why did you ruin my life like this? You… you…don't show your face to me again," she exploded into tears.

I couldn't say anything. I wept. I couldn't hold it any longer. Why Dev? You had everything. Good friends, caring family, loving girlfriend, decent grades, nice career prospect! Why did you have to give in to this moment of madness that ripped everything apart? What did you get out of it? Nothing! But here you are. You've lost everything.

I didn't know when Isha disconnected. I couldn't speak to her anyway.

I tried to control myself and looked at the door. Oh no! Mom was standing there with a lightning struck expression.

She walked slowly towards me and put her hand on my head, "Babu, what did you do? Why are you crying?"

I hugged Mom tight and shouted out in uncontrollable pain, "I made a terrible mistake Mom. It's all over. My life, my career, my education, my relationship, everything is over."

⊕⊕⊕

"Where is Dev?" I heard Rishi's voice.

Mom said something in a low voice.

I had been in my room for the last 24 hours. Rishi called me at least 100 times.

"Why didn't he go to college? He missed the regulation committee hearing. If he doesn't show up today they will punish him."

I thought I heard Mom crying. I still didn't feel any urge to get out of the room. Rishi banged on my door. "Dev? Dev? You have to go to the college right now. You could be suspended. You need to defend yourself. Tell them you didn't do it."

Defend? How am I going to defend myself? I know I am guilty. And in the process I have to face 300 plus students. Including Isha, and yes, Neera too. No Rishi! My life is over.

I was in that dark room for more than two days. I didn't eat anything, I didn't drink anything other than tap water. Mom banged on the door every now and then and tried to talk to me through it. I didn't reply. Dad tried multiple times. He even had a plan to break open the door. Mom stopped him. She was fearful I might do something worse if I was forced too much. After 48 hours I couldn't ignore their pale faces any more.

I stood up and tried to move, almost fell. My body muscles could hardly cope with two days of hunger and lack of movement. I opened the door, surprised to see Rishi there. Did he stay the whole night?

I dragged my body straight to Dad, "Dad! You can go to the office. I will be okay. I promise."

Dad didn't know what to say, "But…" Mom gestured to him to listen to me so he moved away.

I was about to fall down. Rishi helped me to sit on a chair. "Let's get him to eat something first."

Mom tried to feed me with a spoon. I didn't know why tears continued to fall through my eyes. Rishi held my shoulder, "Hold yourself together buddy. We're with you."

With food, bath and sleep, I was better by evening.

Dad was back. He didn't look at me. Mom was trying her best to make me feel normal. She came up with my favourite snacks. I told her, "Mom, Dad is not talking to me."

She looked at me, "He's a bit disturbed. I'll speak to him…"

I stopped her. "Don't. Let him speak to me when he wants. I deserve this, Mom." She tried to fight the tears.

Rishi came quite late. I could read from his body language he didn't have much good news to convey. "Here buddy. Looking much better now!" Rishi patted my shoulder.

"Rishi? What's my verdict?"

Rishi took some time and finally spoke, "You made it easy for them, Dev. They decided to suspend you for four months and you can't appear for any more interviews. Normally, if you skip a regulation committee hearing, you are given 7 days to report. But in your case everything was decided within 48 hours. I don't understand."

But I understand Rishi. It was about a trustee's daughter. They didn't need to hear any self-defence from the convicted. They wanted to finish it quickly and neatly. "4 months? But that means…"

"Yes…You can't appear for the final exam next month."

"But this is my last year…how am I going to…"

"I am sorry Dev. If you miss the last year's last semester, you have no choice but to wait for the next year to appear for the exam and get the degree."

"Oh Rishi! I have lost one year…" It came out automatically.

Rishi said yes with his silence. "I don't care what happened Dev! But you should have fought. You should have defended yourself. Maybe we could have saved the year loss. Was it about *her*?"

I looked away.

Rishi took my silence as affirmative. He sighed. His expression told me, 'I told you so buddy.'

I asked, "Isha?"

He looked away, "I tried to bring her to your house. That girl…she refused. She said you guys broke up."

That's what I deserve Rishi. Before Rishi could leave I needed to confess something, "Rishi? What will you say if you know I am guilty?"

Rishi stopped me, "We will not talk about this. Not now. But remember whatever happens I am here for you."

I was about to have another emotional breakdown. I had ignored this guy for half of my college life when he tried to stop me from going in the wrong direction. Here I was today having done something worse; and he was still standing beside me.

My voice almost broke in emotion, "Rishi I am sorry! I fought with you, I didn't listen to you. I messed up! Forgive me buddy!"

Rishi's face was showing similar levels of emotions. I don't know if his tough soccer buddies approved of this or not. But he hugged me tight.

13
FIRST STEP TO NEXT THOUSAND MILES

"Dev Banerjee?" The nurse called out my name.

I stood up. "The patient is asking for you. Don't raise your voice and avoid any excitement. She needs to sleep as much as possible. Visiting hour ends in 45 minutes."

I looked at Dad. "Dad, why don't you go?"

Dad and I were doing our rotational day and night shifts at this hospital for the last 48 hours. Luckily for my mother she didn't have an actual stroke. According to the doctor what she had is called a transient ischemic attack, or a mini-stroke. It's more like a warning for the actual stroke. Her blood pressure was dangerously high. We were not out of danger yet, not even close. Mom was shifted from the ICU to a room today. But I didn't go and meet her. I was happy stealing glances at her while she was sleeping. It's because of me she was in there. I believed seeing me would only harm her.

"Dev, she's asking for you. Go and see her."

Why doesn't Dad understand? "Dad! Please. What if her condition worsens? I can't take that risk."

Dad stood up, "Go ahead, son. Nothing is more important to a mother than her child. She needs you."

Dad walked away, maybe intentionally.

With shaky legs, I entered the room. I couldn't look at her. With all these tubes and needles and white sheets I couldn't place my lively mother who wouldn't stop talking. Mom, please speak up. It kills me to see you silent like this.

"Dev...What took you so long?" Mom said as if she was having difficulty in speaking.

"I wanted you to rest. The doctor said you have not recovered yet. You need more sleep." Why were my eyes getting moist? No. I couldn't break down in front of Mom.

"I'll be okay. I have seen you now." She stopped for a while. "I've hurt you, Dev. I know how emotional you are."

I felt some of my muscles were paralyzed. I tried to speak, but couldn't. Only tears came from my eyes. Mom was still concerned about my feelings only.

"If ...something happens to me, I need to tell you something. Listen to me. Please understand your dad. He loves you more than anything. You always misunderstood each other. You are both emotional, you expect too much from the other, and both have a temper problem. He is your dad, Dev. You wouldn't lose anything if you go ahead and hug him yourself. Why wait for him to come to you? He won't say it but he needs you. Promise me you will take care of him."

I covered my face. Mom, don't say these things. I need you to do it for me like you did for years. I can't do it without you.

"Dev, I didn't say it earlier. But I was very disappointed when you did something so horrible years back. You were too weak at that time for further criticism. I feared you would break down completely. But I didn't console you because you made a terrible mistake and had to repent. You had to get out of the pit on your own that you dug for yourself. You did. You managed good grades and a respectable job. I am proud of you, son..."

I held her hand. My tears just ran.

"But when I look at you today committing another mistake, I fear. You deserve better. Don't do this to yourself. Don't lose everything again." She paused to catch her breath.

"I always knew it's about a girl. Don't force it, Dev. If she is not for you, learn to accept it. It's not always about winning or losing. And never push Rishi away. He stood by you in the most difficult time of your life. True friends are difficult to..."

"I think she should sleep now." The nurse was back.

Mom was trying to disagree. I stopped her. "Mom, listen to her. I will never let you down again. But I need you. Come home soon." I got up from the visitor's chair.

Before I could get out of the door, I looked back, "Mom?" She looked at me.

"Never call me Dev again. It doesn't sound good from you." I tried to smile.

She smiled back.

⊕⊕⊕

I was searching for Dad all over. Finally I saw him in the park outside the hospital sitting on a bench.

"Dad? You want to go home? It's already late. I can take care of things here."

"How is she?" Dad's voice almost broke. I felt a pinch inside. I was habituated of seeing my dry, emotionless dad.

"She's okay. I am here. You can go home now."

"Why do you care? Tomorrow you will just go. Go away." He almost pushed me.

48 hours earlier I don't know how I would have reacted. Today, I hugged him forcefully, "It's ok Dad. I am not going anywhere. Don't push me away. Calm down please."

Dad stayed silent for a few minutes and then hugged me back, "Dev, everything is falling apart. I can't take care of it all anymore."

I fought tears, "You've done enough Dad. I will take care of it all from now on. Trust me. Now you go and get some rest."

I saw Dad off in a cab and came back to the hospital's park. I had something else to do.

"Hello?"

"Rishi? How are you?" I tried to sound normal.

He was silent for a minute, "Dev? Is everything okay?" How does he know? Nothing is okay, Rishi. I need my friend back badly.

"Yeah. Why didn't you call me during Puja? I expected we would hang out like always." I tried to make a casual conversation.

"You called me for that? What happened Dev? Tell me the truth."

I couldn't hide it any more. I told him about the Minty episode, my showdown with Dad, and Mom's condition.

"Which hospital?"

"Are you in Kolkata?" I couldn't believe my ears.

"Message me the address. Be there in half an hour." He disconnected.

Mom you were bang on. I dare not lose this idiot friend of mine. Never!

⊕⊕⊕

"How will your moving back to Kolkata help your parents? Do you realize you can't even get close to half your salary? How childish!" Rishi looked pissed off.

"It's a cheaper city. I can save more." I'd already decided, it was more like informing him.

I'd already informed Hiten and Rajan about my mom's health and spent most of my allotted leave. Mom had recovered a bit. She should be okay with good care at home.

Over the last few days, I have decided to look for a job in Kolkata. I'd already started appearing for interviews in some companies.

"Rishi, calm down. I have time. I have only started the interviews. It won't happen overnight. Even if I get an offer, I have to serve the notice period."

"What about taking your parents to Bengaluru? After your dad retires?"

Poor guy! May be he didn't want me to move away. I patted his shoulder. "We'll see Rishi. But I can hardly afford a room there. How will I manage a full house? And my parents will never leave this place. They have a sentimental connection here."

Rishi was looking for some other way out, I stopped him. "Rishi! It's not only about my parents. I need to get away from Bengaluru."

"What?" He looked surprised, "Are you nuts?"

I couldn't make myself clearer to Rishi in this conversation. I needed to confess to him. But I was not comfortable listening to his taunting words which would follow. I had to think of another way. I got my backpack.

"Here you go. Read them."

"Your journals? Are you kidding me? You know I suck at reading."

"It's up to you! You had questions for me. I am not comfortable answering them face to face. Read them or throw away, I don't need them anymore. Just do me a favour, don't start reading right now in a loud voice." I made a face at him.

From Rishi's expression, it seemed he was actually planning to do that. Thank God I stopped him in time.

"I should get going…" Maybe he couldn't wait to dive into my traumatic past.

"Remember we have to book the tickets to Bengaluru for Sunday! I'll call you tomorrow to confirm." Rishi left.

I connected to the internet to check prices. Damn. After paying these credit card bills, how will I survive next month? I opened Facebook out of habit. 1 message! I might have expected it a few days back but not now. I didn't want to hear from her any more. Not after what happened in the last few days.

It was sent the day after our little 'sandy' encounter. I should have deleted it. But Dev is not a saint, he never was. He is driven by weak emotions.

"How is your eye now? I am sorry that day I brought that incident up. I should've not mentioned it. Take care."

I closed my eyes. A mad lover's mind is a devil's den. It sees a flame and imagines a wildfire. One message from Neera and I start wondering if she is missing me. Why doesn't Neera understand?

You stupid girl, this boy is crazy about you! Whenever you come even an inch closer to show just friendly affection he starts hoping again that you can be his someday. Caring for him will only bring harm to you. Stay away from him.

I opened my eyes to focus on reality. Neera and I both had enough of each other. I need to leave Bengaluru permanently.

14
FRIENDS, THE FAMILY WE EARN

"Why do you have to leave?" Prabhu cried hard. Gayathri didn't like the news herself.

I just got the confirmation call from ITCON Software. After almost a month of negotiation, they offered me something acceptable. I would still be going back at a lesser salary. But salary was the last thing on my mind when I decided to leave. I shared the news with my landlady and her son. Hence this nuclear shock wave filled the house.

"Come here. Give me a hug." I asked Prabhu. He ran away.

In my short but effective interaction with this family I'd started feeling like one of them. It was natural that they wouldn't want me to go away. But I had my own reasons.

I walked to the kitchen to talk to Gayathri, "Hey! I am sorry. But you know all about my family. I have to go back."

Gayathri composed herself, "I understand. In this short time you have become a family to us. So it's difficult to think you won't be staying here."

Sometimes I feel the spreading happiness and making

friends wherever you go philosophy is just bullshit. Why can't we make everyone happy?

I didn't know what to say. I tried to cheer her up, "Please don't think that I won't be contacting you. I will visit. You guys can come to Kolkata. It will be fun."

"Don't give me that story Dev. People say that. They never look back." Is Gayathri angry with me? I couldn't blame her. She had lost enough close relations in her short lifetime.

My thought process was interrupted as something clicked in my mind. I couldn't leave this family alone again. I promised myself I would do something for Prabhu. The time had come.

I wanted Prabhu to come with me. But he didn't reply. Alright buddy, I'll do it alone. I went down to the road and waited near the tea stall. Soon the infamous Audi was back. It stopped exactly where it stopped every other day.

I felt apprehensive. What if it all turned out to be a big confusion? I controlled my fear of the unexpected and knocked on the black glass.

The window eased down. A uniformed chauffeur spoke, "What do you want?"

"Can I speak to the owner?" God, please save me from any embarrassment.

"Why?" the belligerent driver started closing the window. Someone spoke from behind, "Wait."

The back window of Audi opened halfway. I couldn't see the speaker's face. "Do you stay in B-21?"

I could see a ray of hope. I nodded.

"What do you want from me?" the deep voice asked.

"Sir, I am Dev. I have a message from your grandson."

I waited breathlessly. Was Prabhu right about his grandfather? Am I doing a sane thing believing a 10-year-old?

"Get in the car," he opened the back door.

⊕⊕⊕

"Hey Buddy?" I gently called Prabhu. "I have a guest to meet you."

Prabhu looked interested this time. "Who? Is it one of those bad guys?"

"No. He's a good guy. Go and have a look in the drawing room. Don't tell Amma yet. I'll talk to her."

Prabhu couldn't hide his excitement and ran to the room. He looked at our guest and shouted, "Tatha," and hugged his grandfather.

Bad idea! Gayathri came out from the kitchen. She took a minute to judge the situation, and then came the screaming which is Gayathri's forte. "How dare you come to my house? You want to spoil my son's life too? Get out of my house."

The old man hung his head. I could tell he regretted his mistakes. I had to interfere, "Gayathri, listen to me. I invited him. He is my guest. Please don't speak to him like that."

"What? You invited him? After I told you everything about my life? I trusted you, Dev. Now get him out of here." She walked away.

Prabhu cried out, "Amma? Why don't you let Tatha come in? He's my grandpa."

I shushed him and chased Gayathri to the kitchen. She was clearly trying to avoid any conversation.

I shouted like hell, "Gayathri? Will you please listen to me?" I did it for her sake. She was shocked into silence, maybe she couldn't believe someone could give her competition in screaming.

"I am not taking anyone's side. Hear me out. This man has been waiting at your doorstep every day. For years now? He could have left a long time ago and lived his own life. Why is he coming to see you? Your father made a mistake forcing you marry a crook. He is repenting, Gayathri, every single day, every single moment. Doesn't he deserve one more chance? Hasn't he waited long enough to hug his grandson? He has tears in his eyes when he mentions you. Don't do this to yourself. You deserve all the love he has for you. Forgive him for Prabhu and for yourself! Please talk to him once."

Gaythri silently walked into her room.

I walked to her father and asked him to go and talk with her. Your daughter has lots of bloody wounds hidden inside her, mister. It's up to you now to heal them all. He touched my shoulder and went inside.

Prabhu stood close to me, "Will Amma forgive Tatha?"

"She will." I smiled at him.

⊕⊕⊕

I came down to say bye to Gayathri's father. Gayathri rejected her father's offer of financial help. But at least they bonded. She invited him to come to her house whenever he wanted. I am sure the rest will be sorted out with time.

"Thanks, son. I don't know how I should thank you. You have given me the gift of a lifetime. Take my card. Call me for anything. I mean anything."

"Thank you, sir." I looked at the card. Venkat Iyer. Why does this name sound so familiar? Oh Damn. Can't be!

I asked, "Sir? Are you related to any Bengali cultural association located on M G Road?"

"Yes! How do you know?" He looked surprised.

"Sir, I am a member there," I smiled.

He looked happy. "That's great. I forgot you were from West Bengal. I have a very close collaboration with Bengal. I worked there for more than 15 years. I wanted to create this organization so that people like you visiting here don't miss their home too much."

This man looked genuine and his intentions sounded honest. Should I tell him about how Bala was forcing employees to be a member of it? I shouldn't. Why would he believe me?

May be he understood I was hesitating about something. "Dev? Do you want to tell me anything? Don't worry! Speak up."

Hesitatingly I mentioned how Bala was forcing his team members to pay for the functions and to be a part of those. I skipped over ugly details but from his expression I understood Venkat didn't like it.

"That's disturbing. I gave this responsibility to Bala because I thought he was passionate about this organization. It's not about making money, Dev. I have worked all over India. What I have felt is that due to diversity it gets very difficult for a South Indian person to settle in North India, and vice versa. I wanted to give them a platform where they can learn to accept this new city as their new home. It disturbs me that Bala could do this." He looked upset.

I felt respect for this man. Very few of us could think beyond our regions. Regional discrimination in society and the workplace is an ugly truth.

Venkat got hold of himself, "Dev, if I request you to take care of this organization, will you do it?"

What? I would be the worst choice. You need someone who can keep things organized. I take 15 minutes in the morning to locate my toothbrush, forget about running an association.

"Sorry, Sir. I will be leaving for Kolkata shortly. I have family issues. But if you don't mind I can suggest someone's name."

"Who?" Venkat looked curious.

"Arup is working in your organization. Believe me sir, he works day in day out for it. I think if given an opportunity he can excel in a responsible position."

Venkat nodded. "Thank you Dev. You don't want anything for yourself?"

I just smiled. He smiled back, "You are a good lad, Dev. Don't lose this helping nature of yours. Remember if you need anything, you can call me anytime."

"Thank you, sir." Venkat left. I felt good. I could help out a couple of my new friends who took care of me during my short tenure in this business city.

I wanted to give a hint of the good news to Arup. I called him.

"Hey Dev! You forgot me. You haven't called me for so long."

"Yeah I was busy. How are things going for you? Got a promotion?" I teased.

"Are you joking? I feel like I am working as a personal butler for Bala."

I smiled. "You will have everything very soon Arup. I have a feeling. But what are you doing? Shopping for Bala?" I took my last dig at Arup. This man would be a manager soon.

"No man. I went to collect the medical report and medicine and deliver them to the hostel. That's what I have been doing for the last two weeks. I need to leave this job soon."

"Wait! First of all, don't even think about leaving your job at this moment. I am telling you, you will get a raise very soon. Is anyone sick in Bala's family? Who is staying in a hostel?"

"What? You didn't know? Your friend…" he stopped.

"What happened to her?" I almost yelled.

"She is severely ill. Her fever is not coming down…" Arup was not done but I disconnected. Neera has been sick for more than two weeks? How serious is she? Wait! What can I do here? Other than just wish her health from a distance? She has her family, her fiancée, and to-be-in-laws to take care of her. She will be okay. I walked back.

✦✦✦

"Dev? Is everything alright?" Rishi yawned.

"Hi. Sorry buddy. I need a favour from you."

It was 1:30 at night. It was well beyond the permissible time of calling, even your closest friend. The last four hours I had been practising insomnia. I was deeply mourning my decision to call Arup. Since then I couldn't think about anything but Neera. I needed someone to slap me hard with a few taunting and hurtful words to make me realize how dumb I was. Oh Neera! You are down with a fever somewhere and your secret admirer is awake and troubling his friend.

"Couldn't it wait till tomorrow?"

I wanted to start with something that would interest Rishi. "Actually I got this offer from ITCON."

Rishi almost shouted, "Are you mad? You want to leave TTS for ITCON? Why do you want to play with your career?"

I sighed. "I've already decided. The pay is less but I need to be in Kolkata."

"You and your foolish decisions! I know very well why you want to leave. I have read your bullshit journal. You want to run away like a goat."

So Rishi already read them. "I am not as strong willed as you. Why don't you accept the fact and let me leave Bengaluru in peace?"

"Whatever. Axe your own career, my friend. How many employees are even there? 30? 50? You want to leave a billion dollar CMM Level 5 Company for that?" He disconnected.

I expected my best friend to understand my mental condition and give me comforting words. Huh! Me and my wise decisions. My phone rang. Rishi. What does the scoundrel want now? Did he miss some other adjectives to describe me?

"What happened? You missed adding some more spice to your name calling?" I smoked fire with my words.

Rishi sounded milder this time, "Sorry man. I was out of line. Ultimately it's your decision. But I…"

"You are right. It's my decision. It's like only you have the authority to run my life." I realized it was a bit harsh just as I finished.

Rishi didn't fight back. "Dev. Believe me. I want well for you. Ok. If you want to leave this job, do it. But I want you to read something first. Just don't make any decision in a hurry."

"What's it?"

Rishi sighed, "Dev, I read your journal. Frankly I don't support you on any of the things you did. Maybe you lost your sense of morality and wisdom. But I do believe that you love this girl."

I remained silent.

Rishi continued, "The question bothering me was what about the girl's psyche? I always imagined Neera as a rich spoilt girl who used you to pass time. But after reading all the details, I had a feeling she had something more to her character. Why did she care about your wellness? Why didn't she stop calling you even though she had a boyfriend? Finally, why did she call you and ask you to get lost? There was a missing thread. I got it now."

"What's that?"

"I'll let you see that yourself. Check Gmail. I forwarded you something. Think about it." Rishi disconnected.

I rushed to the laptop and logged on to Gmail.

I took a few seconds to understand the whereabouts of the email. It was an old email which Neera had sent to Sapna four years ago. She'd forwarded it to Rishi recently. That means Rishi and Sapna are still in touch. Hmm....

The first few lines gave me an idea Neera and Sapna were much closer than I realized. It was personal and Sapna shouldn't have forwarded it to Rishi. But it's good in a way that this was first time I could see myself with Neera's eyes. How did you like me Neera? Was I just a toy for you? Why did you always care for me?

I started my journey through Neera's mind for the very first time.

⊕⊕⊕

Neera's letter

Dear Sapna,

I know you'll be angry with me for many reasons. I accept all my mistakes. But I had my own reasons. You are one of the best friends I have, so I am sure you will forgive me. I have ignored your calls since that incident for months now. Believe me I didn't want to do that. But I was very disturbed. I knew you had questions for me. I wasn't in a condition to answer them. I am going to tell you everything today. In the last six months I have lost my passion for knowledge. I don't feel that I want to get my Masters anymore. Something changed, Sapna! Something died inside me. It's all because of this boy, one of the best friends of my college life.

I know, you'll say you never liked him. I don't blame you. He's not the friendliest person to be around. But he was a simpleton and he never tried to hide it. With all the glitters in my personal life if I needed something that was some honest emotion, he gave me that. I liked the way he looked at me. I saw some silent admiration in those eyes. It was harmless. We girls can feel when we are being objectified. He was not like that. I could be myself with this weird friend of mine, Dev.

I knew how emotional he was but liked it. Sometimes he was a pain to handle. Soon he became a bad habit for me. I knew you heard him fighting with me over the phone and you questioned me so many times as to why I let him do that. Maybe I was selfish, Sapna. With Dad's busy schedule and Mom's health, I missed any concern towards me. No one bothered if I reached home late. But Dev did. His way of expression was different. But I enjoyed his concern. I didn't want to lose it. I realized I had made a mistake. But it was too late.

Things changed when I started falling for Neel. His looks, his charms, his gentleness. He was the perfect boyfriend. I couldn't resist being drawn closer to him. Neel was the most romantic person I'd ever met. He did crazy things for me. I knew he was going to propose to me soon. I was ready with open arms. Then I saw it. I don't know how I missed it earlier. But Dev changed. My sweet friend who encouraged me on every small achievement and comforted me on failures was suddenly missing. I could hear jealousy in his voice. I ignored it initially. Most of our conversations ended with him asking me if I loved Neel or not. He was more concerned whether was I dating Neel than how was I feeling that day. I tried to make him understand but he just wouldn't listen. But I didn't want to give up on my friend. I thought it was just an infatuation on his side. I decided to maintain a distance from him temporarily. I wanted him to hate me for some time. Another wrong decision! The guy was too sensitive to handle that. I made a blunder the same day Neel proposed to me. I called him on the terrace to come with me. I showed him an ugly side of mine. My idea was to remove the "perfect image" he had for me. He moved away from me but in the worst way possible. The next thing I heard that he had an accident. Sapna, I can't describe what I went through. I don't know why but I felt I was the one responsible. I should have been joyful that I was in a new relationship with Neel. But my guilt was still there. Worst part was that stupid boy Dev wouldn't let me talk to him. I had to forget this friend of mine. I stole glances at him occasionally. He looked so disheartened. Sometimes I felt I was not doing the right thing to Neel. He didn't even know what I was going through. I wanted to take care of this shy friend of mine. But he just didn't let me! For months I couldn't talk to him. Then I heard one day that he was engaged to this girl, Isha. I was so happy for him. They looked perfect together. I felt so relieved at that moment. As if some stone was removed from my chest. My friend was finally happy. I had the best time with Neel during the next six months.

But Neel changed. He was not the same guy I fell for. Slowly he started acting like a control freak. He didn't want me to speak to any boys other than his friends. On my birthday Neel scolded me like hell. No one ever spoke to me like that. I needed someone to understand me. So I contacted my old friend, Dev. I thought he might have forgotten about me. But he was there for me with the same care, same concern which I cherished earlier. I needed someone to talk to. I guess he did too. We became a perfect support system for each other. Sometimes I wondered if Isha would like this. But I ignored that. It was a pure friendship, Sapna.

I never lied to Neel about Dev. He knew I spoke to him regularly. Neel didn't like it and we fought about Dev multiple times. He always had this idea that Dev was in love with me and he wanted to break us up. But I assured him Dev would never do anything to hurt us. He cared for me too much to do anything like that.

As we approached our final years, I saw Dev changing again. He used to talk about how Neel flirted with other girls and how he didn't deserve me. I doubted his intentions a couple of times but I ignored it. When Neel got his job offer, I was the happiest girl. But Neel was not happy. Our conversations used to end every day with a fight. He started checking on my messages and call lists. He forced me so many times to stop contacting Dev that I eventually did.

Then came the day that changed everything. Neel and I had the ugliest fight ever. I broke up with him. I didn't know where to seek a shoulder. I committed an act of madness,

Sapna. I contacted Dev and informed him about our break up. I should not have involved him. Never! But unfortunately I did. He consoled me like he always did. Neel called me in the afternoon and requested a meeting. I could have said no, but I loved him. We talked for hours. We cried and made up. He requested me to do something which he believed would strengthen our relationship. He wanted me to ask Dev not to contact me ever. I don't know what I was thinking. Maybe it was just an emotional moment for me or I just wanted all our problems to go away, but I agreed. I chose Neel over my friend. I called Dev and asked him to stay away from me. I had the belief this would be good for everyone. But I didn't have the slightest idea where it was heading.

My dearest friend Dev sent me a message where he cursed me with the ugliest words one could think of. He questioned my intentions about speaking to him every night. He called me a characterless girl. I never lost my temper so badly. But that day I got really angry. I wanted to teach him a lesson. He sent a message to Neel as well. How could he say something like that about me, the girl he had befriended for so many years? How could he insult our friendship?

I was driven by fury. Neel fuelled it. I involved Dad. I wanted him to punish Dev. I didn't realize the gravity of my actions though. Neel had some more ideas to harm him. I didn't want to be part of it. Believe me, I refused many times. But with his continuous insistence I agreed. I did something terrible, Sapna. I don't know if I can forgive myself for this ever. I called up Isha and told her how Dev sent me that offending message. The poor girl even didn't know that we talked daily. She broke down.

As time passed, my anger cooled and I realized what I actually did. Something inside me cried. How could I do something like this to my old friend? Was it only about Neel? Why did I listen to him? Why did I involve Dad? I wanted to stop Dev's punishment but I didn't have enough courage to face Dad again. I wanted to make Neel understand but he didn't. What did we achieve by making this boy lose his career and his love? Did I portray myself as a better person harming him back that way? The punishment Dev received was too harsh. His personal life and professional life both got crushed in a single moment. I wanted to say sorry, but I don't have the courage to reach out to him again. Would you believe that I can't look eye to eye with Neel now? Speaking with him, I still remember what happened that day. I don't think I can continue this relationship any longer. Those 72 hours changed everything. Dad doesn't speak to me normally. His eyes always depict disappointment. He trusted me with all my decisions but I let him down. I can't concentrate on studies anymore. I want to look for a job in Bengaluru. Can you help me? I have to get away from Kolkata, from home, from Neel, from everyone who knows me. My dear friend, can you help me to do that? I am counting on you to get me out of here.

Love,

Neera

15
A BIT LIKE ILLNESS: A LOT LIKE LOVE

"Dev! What are we doing here?" Rishi didn't sound excited about this little adventure.

"You'll see. Are you sure your girlfriend gave me the correct information?" I enquired, peering into the darkness.

"First of all, Sapna is not my girlfriend. Secondly, I think she did. But what's your plan?"

It all started 24 hours ago, when I decided I needed to check on Neera after reading her email. I tried to meet her this morning. It was not that this hostel didn't allow male guests. There was a visitor's room, but Neera's case was different. She had been moved to the sick room. Rules dictated a visitor would need the local guardian's permission to meet a patient. I had a feeling that might be Bala! Good luck with that.

As always, my crazy mind came up with an impossible idea. I got help from Rishi to reach Sapna and get Neera's number. Unfortunately, Neera's phone was switched off.

Just when I was thinking I wouldn't make it, suddenly I remembered an important piece of information from their conversation. Neera used to come down and sit in the hostel garden after dinner. I found the ray of light I was looking for.

"What happened? What shall we do now? Other than standing here like dissatisfied spirits?" Rishi raised his voice.

"Wait. Neera comes down around this time. I might get to meet her."

Rishi made a face like he had swallowed a bitter gourd. "What? You might? You donkey! You made me come here and wait with all these mosquitoes singing in my ears, based on a mere possibility? She has a fever for God's sake. I am out of here." Rishi started to walk away.

C'mon. I can't wait in this dark alone. I tried to stop Rishi.

"Rishi, wait! Sapna mentioned she met Neera last week around 10. So there's a chance. Please buddy! I have always screwed up when you left me. Don't do it this time. I can't do this alone."

Emotional blackmail worked. Rishi stopped. But his pissed off expression didn't. He looked at my hands, "What do you have in this packet? Gifts?" Before I could stop him he snatched it.

"What? Freaking unbelievable. Apples? Protein bars? And a get well soon card? You missed the cough syrup," he burst into laughter. Frankly, I was not feeling very proud of these gifts myself. I just picked up what I could at 10p.m.

"It's not funny. She's sick. These will help her."

Rishi controlled his laughter, "You miss the banana? It has calories and matches your personality too. But the point is it's already past 11. I don't think she is coming down today. If you are feeling sorry that your nutritious gifts will be wasted, give your packet to the guard to deliver."

I didn't like the idea. Did I come here just to deliver a packet?

Rishi gave me an ultimatum, "10 more minutes, Dev. I am gone after that."

Shit. Bollywood movie friends are much better. They even give their lives for each other. Nonetheless, I didn't like the idea of standing there alone. I couldn't afford being robbed. My pay was still ten days away.

"Ok," I hesitated.

"C'mon man. We need to head back."

Disappointed, I walked towards the hostel gate. Where is the damn guard? Shall I call him? I hope there are no dogs around.

"What do you want?" someone called out from behind. I jumped. That must be the guard. Why was he standing outside? Then I realized he must have been coming back from somewhere.

"No visitors after 8. Go away." I noticed his gait, a perfect zigzag. Then I got the whiff. This guy was drunk. Should I hand over my packet to a guy like this? I didn't care about the apples and stuff but I wanted Neera to get the card. How else would she know that I had come to meet her? "I... have brought stuff for someone. Can you deliver it for me?" I tried to sound as sweet as possible.

"What am I? Courier service?" So that would be a 'no' in short.

Now what? Oh, crap. I started walking back.

Maybe the guard felt sad for me, "I don't deliver gifts. You can leave it at the ground floor reception. Write the room number on it. It will be delivered."

Now that was a solution. Wait! Damn! I didn't know the room number. I just knew she was in the sick room for the last few days. I told him my problem.

The guard looked disgusted, "You young Romeos, you don't do your homework. The sick room is on the first floor. Mention that on the packet."

I thanked him multiple times. He didn't feel flattered though, "What are you waiting for? Go and put it at the reception."

Ill-mannered punk! I scrambled before I was shouted at again. I was here this morning. Then it was quite lively with visitors and residents. But at this time it was all quiet and dark.

I needed something to write Neera's name and room details. I had neither pen nor paper. I crossed the reception table to check. I could see the staircase just a stone's throw distance.

An evil idea struck my mind. The sick room is on the first floor, right? What if I could get a peek at Neera? But what if there is another guard there? If I see anyone I will not proceed further. When I was done thinking I realized I was already going up the stairs.

It seemed too easy. The whole passage on the first floor was empty. There was an arrow indicating the sick room. My confidence level increased. I just had to say Hi to Neera, hand over the packet, and be gone. I opened the door of the sick room confidently.

I could see a couple of girls sleeping. None of them looked like Neera from a distance. The third bed was empty. Maybe one of these girls *was* Neera. I slowly entered the room. No, this one was far too big. Next one, what happened to this one? She looked like an Egyptian Mummy with a dressing on her face.

No signs of Neera! This entire 'prison break' was for nothing? Maybe she was already back in her own room. I started shuffling away.

Fuck! My phone rang at the worst time possible. Must be Rishi! Impatient asshole! Before I could silence my phone or get out of the room, Biggie sat up.

"Neera? Is that you?"

I couldn't reply on Neera's behalf. I slowly moved towards the door. Suddenly the Mummy shouted, "Pushpa! It's a boy!"

Pushpa and I were equally shocked with this sensational revelation. Did she have X-Ray vision? I tried to run towards the door.

Pushpa was quite flexible despite her size. She stood up and took a posture of Kabaddi in front of me and tried to stop me from escaping. I needed some weapons. I threw a couple of apples at her. Either she loved apples or she was quite an athlete. Amazingly she caught both of them. But I gained an extra second. I threw the rest of the apples and got out of the room.

I didn't have any time to think where I was running to. I could hear the screaming already. Oh God! Lights were getting switched on all over. Would I be a mob victim today? I almost reached the end of the passage. No damn steps here. I was lost.

"Dev? I don't believe it. What are you doing here?" It was more or less becoming Neera's signature dialogue. This must be the pantry or something. The patient was quenching her thirst when I was performing those deadly Kung-Fu stunts with her roomies.

I struggled to catch my breath. I needed this girl to save my ass, "Neera, I came to see you. But I have to get out now. A couple of girls saw me..." I panted.

Neera took some time to understand the situation. The loud voices at the end of the passage helped. "C'mon! There is a staircase in the back. Switch off your phone! It's making noise," she scolded me.

Oh shit. I switched it off.

"Come this way." The back side of the pantry opened to a spiral staircase.

"Here. Go now. Let me try to stop them from coming here."

"Neera, here! It's for you." I offered her the protein bar and the card.

"What? How did you even know I was not well? A protein bar? You're so sweet." She laughed hard and touched my cheek. I felt like I got recharged with 1,000 batteries. With such a display of affection, I may even pull off the Olympic 100 meters. Time to go. Voices were closer. I started taking the steps.

I touched the ground and looked up. She was looking at me. I didn't have time up there to look at her properly. She looked thinner and her eyes looked puffy. Then she smiled at me. All my misadventures seemed totally worth it. Keep smiling like this Neera! I can even break into the Tower of London.

"Dev? Did you seriously just…" she hesitated, "come to see me?"

Girls! Why do you have to ask the obvious questions? I smiled, "Neera! Take care of your health."

"I am feeling much better now. What's your number?" I don't know how feasible it was to exchange numbers like that. I could see around four-five girls coming down to the garden with torches.

"I will call you, just please keep your cell on." I don't know if she heard me. I was already running by then.

I saw the guard on the way. He looked a few pegs wiser since I last saw him. "What happened?"

I said, "Go there! They are trying to catch a thief." I pointed to a random direction.

He started running in a completely different direction. Whatever! I opened the gate and continued my Milkha act.

When I reached Rishi, he stopped me. "What happened? By the way do you have any sense at all? Why did you switch off your mobile? I've been calling you."

Adding insult to injury? This guy almost got me killed in there. I jumped onto him and started punching him. This guy deserved a high dose of bumping right now.

⊕⊕⊕

"Devashish? What happened? You don't like something here?" Hiten looked at me as if he could see through my skull and read my thoughts.

My manager remembered my full name for the first time. Unfortunately it happened on the day I put down my papers. This morning I sent a formal email to my manager and my team leader, informing them I wanted a release from TTS after serving the sixty days notice period. Rajan didn't come and talk to me neither did Hiten call. But I noticed both of them having a number of talks between them.

Finally I was called into Hiten's room in the afternoon. I thought I had my answers ready.

"Sir, it's not about this project or TTS. I have some family problems at my hometown. I need to go back."

"Family problems? Why are you looking at this extreme solution? We all have problems Dev. Every single one of us has. Both family and work need compromises but not at the cost of the other. I am sure you can work out something. How much are they paying?"

Hiten's conversation was going in a certain direction and I was preparing to answer, but sudden mention of the money factor surprised me. "Money, Sir? I mean…"

"Yes Dev. I know what the aspirations of a young engineer

are. Is it 40% or 50% hike from here? Or is it a commitment of long term foreign travel? Tell me." Hiten looked at me shrewdly.

I hung my head. Alas! If I would have really got an offer like that! I am going to a lesser salary, mister.

"What happened, Dev? Tell me what are you looking for in this new job? I can feel something is wrong."

I don't know why, but I told Hiten all about my family problems and the offer details in ITCON. This person had been nice to me from the very first day. Yeah, he messed with my head with his 'fish madness,' but overall he helped me out.

He listened carefully, "Dev, I can judge people. That's why I am sitting here. I see a potential resource inside you. Frankly, I thought you had a great career prospect here with TTS. Better salary, foreign travel, responsible position; you can achieve it all."

He paused and started again, "Your justification of leaving this job makes me feel that you are acting too sentimental. Work and family are like water and oil. Mixing them never really works. Balancing both of them is a tricky act. Some people just surrender to the situations and end up losers. But there are a few who can balance them perfectly. They are the winners. So what do you want to be, Dev? A winner or a loser?"

I was silent, so Hiten took control again, "Dev, you can ask anybody about me. They might say a lot of things but one thing they all will agree: Hiten Shinde doesn't practice favouritism. So when I say this to you, it's purely based on my observations. You are a good technical resource Dev. But you mess up with your personal stuff."

I didn't need my manager to put an official stamp on that.

"I am doing this not only for you but for this project too. I will not accept your resignation. I will let you think about it for another one and a half months. Wait! I get that you need your release by the end of February. Don't worry. I will see you in the third week of Feb. If you still feel you want to leave, I promise I will release you in the next couple of days." Hiten looked at me.

Is it one of those evil managerial tricks? Can this man be trusted? I sighed. Why does everything with me have to be so complex?

Maybe Hiten understood my dilemma. He stood up and walked to the window. He didn't look at me when he said, "Dev, do you know someone named Bala Subhash Roy?" A shiver passed through my spine.

Hiten looked back to see my reaction, "So you know him. I don't know what you did, but you sure pissed off this chap. I got a request from someone very influential in TTS that I should release you immediately. I did some investigations and I know the source of this request was Subhash."

My head started hammering. Why didn't Hiten mention this earlier? I couldn't believe Bala would go to this extent. Arup and Rishi had tried to warn me but it looked like I underestimated the evilness of this man. He tried to play with my career. You suck Bala, you suck big time.

"Sir. Why did you not tell me about this earlier?"

He smiled, "Why? You know what I do when I hear dogs barking in the street? I close my window." He demonstrated with his hands as if he was really closing the window.

"You must be wondering why I am telling you this now. I didn't want to. But I don't think you trusted me completely about the release. So I wanted to let you know that as a manager, I have always got your back."

"Sir? Have you ever tasted Betki Paturi or Bhapa Hilsha?"

Hiten's eyes rounded, "No. What are they?"

"These are fish delicacies. You should definitely try them. If you don't get a chance, whether I am here in TTS or not, I promise you, I will take you for a treat one day."

Poor Hiten! This man is just crazy about fish. He took out his iPad and started noting the names down. Go ahead Sir. You are a way cooler human being than I ever realized. You deserve it!

16
THE FIRST TOUCH, THE LAST KISS?

"Dev, I need to talk to you. Meet me at 7 at Triangular Park near my hostel." I read the message for may be the 15th time now. Since our meeting at her hostel, Neera and I had exchanged messages multiple times.

I was the first to initiate the conversation. The first few days I just asked about her health and she replied. Then we moved to casual chatting. I know that she went back to work, she received a welcome party from her colleagues, and her parents would be coming soon to Bengaluru. But this was the first time she had called me for a meeting.

I promised myself I would keep my distance from Neera. All my resistance vanished when I heard she was ill. I can't deny the fact I love her to the level of insanity. So I justified my actions of continuously contacting her to myself by saying that I was worried about her health. Then what now? She is perfectly cured and back to her normal life. Why can't I stop contacting her? Why do I wait each evening for her messages? Why in a corner of my heart do I still believe that if she comes to know that I am leaving Bengaluru she will try and stop me?

My love has become an addiction for me. I can't live without that feeling. I started my quest to meet her again.

This must be Triangular Park. I looked at my watch. It was almost 7. Where is Neera? Triangular Park looked quite full at this time of the evening. Some elders were taking their evening walk. Some health freaks were doing their jogging rounds and there were young love birds. They were everywhere.

"Dev! Sorry I was a bit late leaving the office." Neera was in a yellow Kurti and jeans, trying to catch her breath.

"No problem. You look tired. Do you want to have something? I mean soft drinks or coffee?" I was not really feeling comfortable asking her to sit in this park among all these teenage lovers.

Neera thought about something. "No. I know a place. Come with me. I need to talk to you in private."

What is in the mind of this girl? What is so important that she needs to talk to me in private? We walked a couple of blocks and reached a place which looked like a car workshop. Some abandoned cars were visible.

"This one," Neera pointed to a white Ambassador, "…this one is my favourite. You know Dev; my dad's first car was also a white Ambassador. I have so many fond memories of that car."

Neera went ahead as if she came here before. I hesitated. God knows what could be there inside this abandoned car. What about snakes? I asked her.

She laughed it off, "C'mon. It's winter. No snakes around. Just come here and sit down. The back door should be unlocked. Wow! It is. I told you." She giggled like a child.

Neera got in there and sat down. Is this girl mad?

"Dev? Are you that boring or just acting like that?" She made a face at me.

Girl, there is a difference between being boring and hygienic.

"C'mon, hurry. I have to get back. It's not dirty. They rent it out occasionally so they keep it cleaned."

How did Neera know all this? "How do you have all these details? Do you come here with Bala?"

Neera looked down but answered, "No. Not with him. We used to come here a long time ago just after Neel came to Bengaluru."

Surprise! That means Neel and Neera were in touch even after she reached Bengaluru. I felt like an idiot. After I read Neera's email I assumed that was the end of their story. Neel is more like Fevicol, he just doesn't go away.

Other than sitting, I actually crashed into the back seat. "Wait Dev, don't push it too much. It's an old car." She smiled.

I didn't reply. Neel was an invisible ghost, still chasing me after all these years.

"Dev! I wanted to ask you something. And I need the truth."

I didn't show much interest. I was still recovering from the last revelation.

"Are you even listening to me? Look at me." She sounded restless. I obeyed her this time.

"Dev, I…I have seen Isha with someone else. What is going on? Did you lie to me about you guys?"

I was not surprised. Isha could embarrass her boyfriend a lot with her romantic displays in public. Who knows it better than me?

"Maybe…you have misunderstood…"

"Dev, tell me the truth."

What is going to change if Neera knows the truth? I am always the loser friend who just gives a protein bar to the girl. The ambassador backseat is reserved for the special someone else.

"Ok. If you want the truth, here it is. We broke up right after college. But still we are in touch and she is one of my best friends. I met her new boyfriend and he is a great guy. They are perfectly happy together," I informed her in a single breath.

Maybe it was a lot of information for her to digest. She was silent for some time, "It's because of me right? Dev, I did something terrible. I called her right after…" she could not complete the sentence but covered her face with both her hands.

I know what you did, Neera. I have read your email. But I couldn't really disclose that in front of her. I didn't want to put her and Sapna's friendship at risk.

"Dev? Will you ever forgive me? I have…" I stopped her and held her hand.

"Stop blaming yourself Neera! It's not about you. I know what you did. Trust me! Sooner or later it was going to happen. I was not the perfect choice for her. She always deserved better. Most importantly she is happy now. It makes me feel more satisfied to see her cheerful with someone else rather than being miserable with me."

I wasn't sure how much Neera understood my emotions towards Isha but she looked a bit relieved. "You should have stopped her from going. She really loved you a lot. I could see that in her eyes."

Can we change the subject please? I was getting irritated. Enough about me and Isha! What about you girl?

"Neera! You have asked me a lot of personal questions. So I will not accept silence as an answer to my question this time. Tell me what happened with Neel?" Maybe my anxiety got through too much in the last few words! She was taken aback.

She took some time, "It didn't work out Dev. My emotions died after college. I didn't feel the same way that I used to for him. When he reached Bengaluru I thought maybe we could give it a try again. I tried. But I couldn't revive those emotions anymore. I knew he was disappointed. He blamed me for everything. But it was just not right. We had to…Wait. Are you smiling?" Neera was shocked.

I just couldn't hide my joy. Finally, Neel was out of the picture! But Neera saw it. So I tried to recover, "No. Why would I? Something went into my mouth."

Neera looked with fake anger at me for some time and then she smiled too, "You are a bad boy, Dev. You never liked him, did you?"

I didn't hide my smile anymore, "No! I never liked your dancer boyfriend, that Neel Armstrong!" I grimaced.

She didn't look much bothered though, "As if your girlfriend was Julia Roberts!"

We laughed hard for some time. We were back! After so many years, Dev and Neera were actually back. I felt relieved inside. Neera suddenly stopped laughing and looked away.

"What happened?"

"Nothing Dev! I had forgotten to smile for so long. But here I am, laughing so much with you. How do you come every time and make me smile? After what I did to you?" Her voice sounded wistful.

I sighed. Where should I start, Neera, and where shall I end? Do you have any idea that I wake up with nightmares that I have given you so many bloody wounds? I want to heal them all Neera, for my own selfish reason.

I held her hand tight, "I made a terrible mistake Neera and you punished me. That's the way it should be. I have compensated for my mistake. It's not your fault. I have come out a stronger person. Stop feeling guilty about it. I can't see my friend mourning over the past every single moment. We both have recovered from it. Let's move on."

Maybe it was the emotion in my voice or just the magic of the moment. She hugged me for the first time. In a second, the broken back seat of this abandoned white Ambassador transformed into the 'Garden of Eden' for me. I thought she would release me any second but she didn't.

"Dev? Why are you so nice to me? Why do you care so much about me? I can't really do anything for you."

Just stay like this girl, holding me. I don't need anything else.

I didn't have any idea what I was actually doing. Emotions were in full control of the 'flesh and blood' Dev. I touched her hair. I had always imagined doing this. Surprisingly she didn't resist.

I played with her hair, "Why didn't you finish your higher studies? You were so passionate about that."

She spoke gently, "I wanted to. But I didn't have the courage to convince Dad anymore. He lost his belief in me." She started crying. Something inside my chest hurt. It hurts, Neera, when you cry.

I whispered in her ear. I was not sure how much she could actually hear, "I am so sorry! I have messed up your life so bad. I want to see my old Neera back. Please do it for me."

Then I did something which I did a lot of times in my imagination but never came even close to doing in reality.

I kissed her on the forehead and cheeks. She didn't move. I could feel her body was getting warmer each second. She looked into my eyes. I pulled her closer still and covered her mouth with a hungry kiss. She responded immediately, the caress of her lips softer than I could have ever imagined. I tasted tentatively with my tongue, and Neera opened her mouth with a soft, low moan.

The jarring sound of her phone got me out of the most beautiful dream I was living. Something inside told me, 'Not like this Dev. It's Neera. She is vulnerable right now. You can't take advantage of her.'

I let go of her. "Neera! It's getting too late for you," I whispered.

"Hmm…but I want to stay…" she kissed me again while speaking. She was clearly not in any hurry. But her phone rang again. This time she released me in a panic.

Before I could say anything, she got out of the car. I had no idea who called but Neera was acting really weird.

"What happened? Is it Bala?" I asked.

"Dev, I have to go now." She started running.

"Wait Neera, let me walk you …" She had already crossed the road. Damn! What an anti-climax of the most romantic evening of my life.

I slowly patted the white Ambassador. Don't worry friend, I will come back on my own terms.

"Old romance is difficult to forget Dev, isn't it? Just like the movies. It comes back to haunt you," I heard the haunting voice. This man had shocked me before with his surprising villainous entries.

But this time and place was when and where I was expecting him the least.

⊕⊕⊕

I tried to look as composed as possible. I had no idea how long Bala had been standing there. Did he witness the little chemistry that Neera and I shared? I didn't give a damn about me. But this person would not spare Neera. Suddenly I remembered what Hiten had told me. This guy had already tried to spoil my career. What else can he do? Enough of this hide and seek. Let's talk face to face, Bala.

"What are you doing here?" this time I took the liberty to ask him the question first. Bala wasn't prepared for it.

He looked surprised but recovered, "You are quite a young talent Devashish Banerjee. I like young talents. But young blood can be too hot. Sometimes it can boil you from the inside." He smiled devilishly.

Is he trying to threaten me?

Bala continued his sophisticated attempt of frightening me, "I already know lot of stuff about you. But as a big brother I want to suggest something to you. From now on you should carefully choose who you want to be friends with and who you don't. TTS is normally a stable company but you never know! Job security has always been difficult to predict. Then there is Mr Hiten Shinde, your Project Manager, he is a good friend of mine. Let me tell you he is quite strict in some policies. Salary and growth depend directly on manager, right? And what if something worse happened? Obviously, you don't want to go back to Kolkata. Friends are friends, Dev. Romance is romance. But career has the highest priority. Why put your career at risk? Stay away from these unwanted nuisances. Call me anytime if you need any more suggestions. Ok?"

I looked at him for a while and then couldn't control it anymore. I burst into laughter. This loser had collected some information about me and he thought he could just come and give me this killer threat and I would run away from Neera like a rat. Dude, forget Bollywood movies. You can't control other people's lives. You are just another manager in a software company with a few contacts. Don't try to act like *Gabbar Singh*.

"What's so funny?" Bala was dumbstruck.

"Sorry. But you are too funny. I know you put in your best efforts to collect data about me and to screw my life already. But you missed something. I lost one year in my final semester, so I couldn't sit for any companies in campus and was idle for more than a year. I started my career with a company of 5 employees. In next 3 years here I am working for one the biggest IT companies in India. Now why am I telling you all this? I don't want you to think that my life is like a fairy tale. Believe me it's not. Every bit of that struggle sucked. But there is a positive point about starting from the dust. You lose the fear of being there. What can you do at your worst, Bala? Make me jobless? I have been there. Anything else? I should get going then."

Bala searched for some more filthy words but couldn't find any. Then he sat on the ground. The fiery manager was literally sitting in the dust.

"Why Dev? Everything was going so smoothly between me and Neera till you came. Why in the whole world did you have to chase my fiancée? Why did you have to curse my life like this? My marriage?" He covered his face.

Standing there I had a strange feeling inside me. I saw Bala in exactly the same position as I was years back. Waiting for Neera to like me desperately but she chose Neel over me. Bala is a monster in human disguise. But I knew the feeling that he was currently going through.

I walked towards him and put my hand on his shoulder, "Bala, I am not forcing myself between you guys. Let Neera decide what she wants. If she picks you, I promise I will go away."

This is the moment when the villain experiences a change of heart in the movies. But I am losing my faith in Bollywood every day.

Bala looked at me for some time and then shouted, "You? A junior engineer? You decide my marriage? Do you have any idea how powerful I am? I can destroy you with a blink of my eye..."

I walked away. I was wrong. I can be a thousand bad things but Bala is in a different class of his own. I can never be like him.

17
I WAS HOLDING ON: I LET IT GO

"You're coming right?" Arup double checked.

"Of course! It's your promotion party. How can I miss it?"

"Thanks. See you there." Arup disconnected.

I knew about this event long ago. Venkat invited me to the party last week. But I wanted Arup to feel as if he was the one who surprised me. Venkat kept his promise. Though he didn't actually replace Bala with Arup, Arup was now promoted as a joint-secretary of the organization. So practically he and Bala would have the same authority. Bala must have been so pissed off. I wanted to attend this party mainly to see his reaction.

There was another reason why I desperately wanted to attend it. It had been over three weeks since I had spoken to Neera. We met last during our Ambassador episode and since then she had been quiet. I sent lots of messages and got very few replies. Even those replies were not as spontaneous as they used to be. I initially thought maybe she was feeling a bit shy about the physical closeness we shared but now it was getting on my nerves.

Rishi was hesitant coming to the party but I roped him in too. We reached the venue exactly at 8. Arup was at the gate.

"Congrats Mr. Secretary! Will you recognize us after today? Or would we have to stand in a queue to meet you?" I laughed and hugged him.

Arup smiled, "How can I forget you? You guys have something to eat. I will join you shortly."

The decorations were stupendous. No wonder. Venkat himself was coming to the party. It had to be grand. Rishi elbowed me, "Dev, isn't it too big a party? I feel suffocated man."

I tried to console him, "It's ok Rishi. We'll just have dinner and go."

We walked inside and sat down on a sofa. I looked around for Neera. Did Neera miss the party? But the chances of that were very low. Bala might have been annoyed with Arup's promotion but he couldn't show that in front of Venkat. He had to come and his family too. I waited for another 5 minutes and then got up to find Neera.

"Where are you going?" Rishi was surprised.

"I'll be back in 5 minutes." I signalled Rishi to wait. I walked around the hall. No trace of Neera. What about the dining area? Initially I couldn't see anyone. But before I could look around, someone called out my name.

"Hey Dev! Good to see that you have come. Join us," I recognized the voice, it was Venkat.

I looked back and froze. Venkat was there, accompanied by Neera and her family. I had heard from Neera earlier that her parents were coming. But I had no idea they were already there. I could see Advocate Dinesh Sinha and his wife. Then there was Neera, sitting beside her father.

Maybe I hesitated for too long, Venkat called me again, "C'mon. You can join us." How close is Venkat to them? What if her father identifies me? What if he remembers I was the one responsible for that scandalous SMS episode? Oh no, God! My story with Neera would be finished even before starting.

But I couldn't refuse Venkat. That would definitely look rude. Venkat offered me a chair. I sat down and looked at Neera. As our eyes met she looked away. I could understand this was not very comfortable for her. But I couldn't run away. I tried to control my fear.

Venkat introduced us, "Let me to do the introductions. They are Mr. and Mrs. Sinha. Dinesh is my close friend and a very famous advocate. And this is their daughter, Neera! And Dinesh, this is Dev. He is a tenant at my daughter's place. Let me tell you that he is a very bright boy, more like a family member to us." Neera's mother looked at me as if she was trying to recognize me. She saw me around eight years ago, only for 5 minutes. The chances were pretty low but still I didn't feel relaxed sitting there.

I nodded to each of them as I was introduced. I even nodded to Neera. She didn't respond.

"Dev? What do you do?" Neera's dad had quite a deep voice. No wonder, he earned his livelihood from his speeches.

"I work in TTS sir, it's a software company." I skipped the part that I'd already resigned.

"My daughter Neera is also in software." I nodded again silently.

Venkat took control of the conversation, "Unfortunately, Dev is leaving for Kolkata very soon. He has some family issues to take care of. I and my family are going to miss him badly. He is such a charming boy."

Neera was looking down earlier, but hearing this she looked up at me. Her eyes asked 'why didn't you tell me'? How could I, Neera? You were not talking to me.

Everyone stayed quiet for some time as if to maintain a minute of silence over my family conditions. I wanted to get up and get going. Before I could say 'Excuse me', something unexpected happened.

"Wow Dev. You are the man, I must say. You are very quick at making friends." I looked back and saw Bala. Damn! Nothing was going right! It was not my day at all.

Neera's dad called him, "Join us Subhash! Looks like you guys know each other."

I didn't look at Bala. I had a bad feeling about what would be coming next. His devil acts might ruin my image permanently in front of Neera's parents.

Bala took the chair next to me. He put his hand on my shoulder, "I know Dev very well. He is one of the most important members of this organization. Plus he is an old college friend of Neera! Didn't he mention that to you?"

Suddenly there was silence. Venkat recovered first, "Dev? You didn't tell us? You guys know each other?"

I looked at Neera's dad. He was looking straight at his daughter. Neera stayed silent. Should I say something? Before I could speak, Neera finally took charge, "We were not exactly friends. We were in the same college but in different sections."

It seemed Neera's dad was satisfied with this. I understood the reason why Neera didn't disclose our actual situation to her parents but somewhere inside I felt a bit of a pinch. Does she feel embarrassed introducing me to her family? Am I too insignificant to be mentioned as her friend?

I didn't feel like sitting there any longer. I stood up and looked at Venkat, "Sir! You have to excuse me. I have to go somewhere." Before Venkat could reply Bala spoke, "What's the hurry buddy? We have good news to share. At least wait for that."

Good news? I don't trust this man. His happiness will definitely cost someone very heavily. Neera's dad spoke, "Yes Dev. Please stay. You are Neera's classmate. You should be here for the announcement and the dinner."

"Announcement?"

"Dev, you will be very happy to know that Bala and Neera are getting married on the 26th of February. The ceremony will be at Bengaluru. Dinesh wants to invite all the members of this organization to attend the wedding. I hope you will make it too. When is your last day in TTS?" Venkat revealed the secret with an excited voice.

I felt dizzy for a second. Neera is actually getting married to him! How could she say yes? What about that evening? Didn't it mean anything to her? Why is this table spinning? I needed to get out before I throw up and spoil this perfect family picture.

I got up, "S...Sorry, I have to go."

"Dev? Do you want me to see you off?" Bala was back with his evil smile. Why not? He was the one who won the game. I was on the losing side as always.

I just walked out. It definitely looked rude. But I didn't care anymore.

Rishi found me near the door. "Hey? What happened?" My friend understood I was troubled. Rishi's concern broke me from inside. I felt some burning inside my eyes, "Rishi. Let's move. I need to get out of here."

"But what happened?"

"Let's go now." I didn't feel like talking about it right now.

Maybe Rishi was about to say something else but someone stopped us before that.

"Wait Dev!" I saw Bala walking towards me with a smiling face.

Maybe Rishi understood it was something about Neera. He stood between us, "Bala! It's not a good time to talk."

"Wait, Rishi! Let me handle this." I pushed my friend away. It had finally come down between us, two devils.

Rishi didn't want to, but he walked a few steps away.

"Dev! Now have you seen what can I do? What did you say? At maximum I can make you jobless. I did much worse than that. I took your girl! I am marrying your college love. She is mine..."

That moment another explosion detonated inside my head. I wanted to jump on that bastard, hold his shirt collar and punch him in the face, "What did you do to her, you son of a bitch? She would not have agreed to marry you in a sane frame of mind. You must be forcing her. Tell me right now, before I break your neck!" But I was never a warrior material. I sucked at school fights and I kept up my reputation after all these years. My action sequence completely misfired.

I tried to jump on Bala but he was way faster than me and moved away. I reached his collar but couldn't hold it. So what happened was Bala remained untouched but I fell on my face. Guys! Either take care of your fitness from early childhood or never try this at home. I was already feeling dizzy and when I stood up I could taste blood on my lips. Rishi came running to help me out.

"Did you just try to hit me? Guards! Throw this thug out…" Bala shouted.

"What is going on?" Neera was standing just at the main gate. I had to stop and look at her for a second. But only for that second! Because the next instant I remembered that her being here was all for her husband-to-be.

"Neera! You stay out of it. This ill-mannered goon needs to be taught a lesson," Bala tried to make a point.

"Let me take care of him," she said.

"What?" Bala clearly didn't like her proposal.

"Subhash, please go inside. My parents are here. I don't want any melodrama right now. Please listen to me. I will be following you, I promise."

Bala couldn't refuse that. He gave me a killing look and went in.

The guards were still awaiting their final instruction. They didn't want to miss out on this rare opportunity to throw a guy out. Neera disappointed them, "What are you guys doing here? Go away."

They left. Neera stood in front of me, "What are you? A hooligan? Did you just try to hit my fiancé?"

I remained silent. I was not sure if my little stunt could even be called an attempt to hit. It was more like a frog jump. Rishi couldn't stay quiet anymore, "Neera, it's not fair. You don't know the full story. Your fiancé was the one…"

Neera stopped him, "Rishi. I would like you to excuse us. It's between me and Dev!" Rishi made a sound of disgust and walked away.

Neera started again, "What do you want? Do you want me to look small in front of my parents? I thought you were my friend. That's what you do to your friends? How many times will you try and hurt me Dev? Why can't you tolerate my happiness?"

It was a tough question. Especially when it was asked by someone for whose smile you have risked every damn thing in your life. Nothing came out from my mouth.

Neera's anger was just burning more and more, "…you did it once, years back. I tried to forget about it and gave you another chance. But no! Here you are. You ruined my love life in the past and now you are trying to ruin my marriage. What do you want from me, Dev? Speak up."

Dev didn't speak up.

Maybe my silence was irritating Neera more, "I can't imagine what you did. How could you say to Bala that we were a couple in college?"

I looked straight into her eyes. Bala is a rotten tomato. He obviously lied to her either to find out the truth or to show me in a bad light in Neera's eyes. But Neera, you? Did you believe I would do something like this to break up your marriage? I believed you were the one who understood me.

I finally could speak, "What bothers you more Neera? Is it that I lied to Bala or Is it that a substandard boy who had a dark patch in his life is associated with you? Do you feel shame if my name gets linked with yours?"

"How can you be so shameless Dev? You're trying to put it back on me? Why did I even talk to you when I saw you after all these years? Let me live in peace. What is this new drama of leaving Bengaluru? If you want to, then go back to your hometown. That will be better for everyone."

"You got it Neera!" I turned back and started walking.

"Dev? Are you really going back to Kolkata?"

"Dev, wait. I am speaking to you."

"Oh Dev. Don't be a kid. Please stop…"

"Dev…………."

Slowly the voice faded. I kept walking. I didn't know where I was going. I needed to keep moving. I didn't have any idea how long I walked. I saw a cyber café. The guy started telling me something about the charges. I didn't listen. I logged on a computer and opened my office webmail.

I started writing an email.

To: Hiten Shinde

Dear Sir,

I have thought about your proposal and I appreciate your help, but I can't continue this job anymore. I have to go back to Kolkata. Will you be kind enough to release me as soon as possible? I have to get a release before the 26th February.

Yours faithfully,

Devasish Banerjee

⊕⊕⊕

"How do you want to spend your last evening in Bengaluru?" Hiten smiled at me.

"Nothing much, sir. I will just complete the formalities here and then I have to say good bye to a few of my friends, including Gayathri!" I smiled back.

Gayathri didn't come to the office today. I didn't have any idea how I would say goodbye to my friend Prabhu and his emotional mother.

"Good luck Dev. From this moment, we are not manager and employee any more. You can consider me your elder brother. If you need anything, call me." He shook hands.

When I came out of Hiten's office, Rajan called. They had arranged a small farewell party for me. Rajan wished me luck. I am going to miss my team.

I got out of the office. When I submitted my ID card, I felt a bit emotional. In this short tenure I had got attached to

276 ◀◁ *Error Code:: **Love***

this techno plaza Tower A. I took an auto from there for the last time.

I reached Gayathri's place to find out there were a few more surprises. Venkat had arranged for a good-bye cake. It's so difficult to leave this warmth behind and move on.

Prabhu was not moving away from me, "When are you coming back?"

I hugged him, "Very soon buddy. Before you will know!"

"Promise?" he demanded.

"Promise." I smiled. I didn't lie. Venkat finally convinced Gayathri to take his financial help and arrange Prabhu's heart surgery. Things are far from simple and it's too early to be optimistic. But I promised Gayathri that I will be there with her during the surgery.

"Okay, sis. Time to say good bye." I smiled at Gayathri.

She hugged me, "Take care of yourself and your family. Come back soon brother!" Brother? I liked 'Thambi' better.

Venkat came down to see me off, "Dev. Before you go, do you want to talk to me about something?"

"No sir. Nothing as such."

"Anything related to Sinha's daughter?" He looked into my eye.

I looked down. What does he know?

"Age brings experience Dev. Do you think Bala is the best choice for her? I introduced him to Sinha and their family in the first place. But I am not so sure any more. What do you think?" He again gave that 'lie detector' expression.

What should I say? I better stay away from all this. "I don't know Sir. It's her decision." I sighed.

He thought about something, "Alright son. See you very soon. Remember that offer is still valid. You can call me anytime." He smiled.

Venkat's car dropped me at Rishi's place. I planned to go to the airport directly from there. I could see Rishi standing on the terrace.

"Are you back early today?" I asked.

"Kind of! I took a half day. What happened to your phone? Why is it always switched off? Your mom is trying to call you," my friend/local guardian scolded me.

I had my own reasons. Why did Mom have to talk to me so desperately today? I will be home tomorrow morning. "When is your flight tomorrow?" Rishi asked.

"At 5 in the morning," I groaned. I was not excited about catching a flight then. But I had to look for the cheapest one.

Rishi looked shocked, "What? Do you realise that you have to start from here in a few hours? The airport is far away and you won't get a cab that late."

"I know. I'll go around midnight. I'll wait in the airport."

"Ok. But call home now." I looked at him suspiciously. Why does he keep on bringing it up?

I switched on the mobile. Lot of messages indicating missed call alerts beeped. There was one from Isha!

"Divs, let's meet up this weekend. Prashant and I have a movie plan. You should join us."

I hadn't told Isha about my plan of leaving Bengaluru. I have to inform her, but not now. I don't have any strength left to face any further disputes.

I replied, "Not this week Ish! Busy nowadays. You guys enjoy yourselves!" I dialed Mom.

"Where were you? I have been trying to call you for over a week," Mom shouted right from the first.

"My cell had a problem. What's so urgent? We can talk face to face tomorrow morning. Is everything okay? Your health? Dad?"

She hesitated, "Yes. Everything is fine. But I wanted to ask why are you coming back to Kolkata? Rishi was telling me that it is not good for your career."

Oh! So this was it. Rishi couldn't convince me not to go back so he tried to take Mom into confidence. I got irked.

"Mom! I know what I am doing. Why are you listening to Rishi? I have already left my last job. I have to come back anyway. Won't it make you happy if I come and stay near you? Why are you trying to stop me?"

Mom sighed, "Nothing will make me happier if you stay closer. But I don't want it to happen at the cost of your career. Your father and I both understand that career and job requirements have changed from our time. It's not exactly possible for a person to commit to a single place or location. Just come to us when we need you the most, that's all we ask for. Nothing else! So don't do anything stupid just thinking about us."

Too late for the wisdom, Mom. I wanted the conversation to be over soon, "As I said I am already done with this city. Forget about it and please make some of your fish curry."

"Babu? Whatever happens, learn to face it. Don't be an escapist. I don't know why you want to go away from that city so badly, but think again about it. Will getting away from there give you the peace of mind you are actually looking for? Is it the solution to all your problems? If yes, then I will be waiting for you tomorrow." Mom disconnected.

I remained silent. These lines of intelligence look pretty good on paper but doesn't really help much in reality.

I started my final packing. My phone rang. Damn it. I should have switched it off again. I looked at the caller, Arup. I picked it up. "What happened, Arup?" I tried to sound perfectly normal.

"What happened to you? I've been trying to reach you for days now. Your phone is always switched off," Arup complained.

"There was some technical snag. Anyway, what's up?" I wanted to hang up as quickly as possible.

"I...I heard you are leaving Bengaluru," Arup said cautiously.

"Yes. I have a flight to catch in a few hours. So I am busy packing. If you don't mind I will call you from Kolkata..." Arup didn't let me finish.

"Dev, they were fighting so badly..." Arup said as if he was revealing the climax of a thriller novel.

"What are you talking about?" Why can't this man come to the point directly even once?

"Bala and your friend! They had a bad fight. I saw it. Bala was shouting like hell. She was crying…"

I was quiet for a second. No, Arup! I don't want to get into this anymore, "Why are you telling me all this? I said I am leaving this city. If you don't have anything else to say I will hang up now."

Maybe Arup was too surprised at my dry behaviour, "Oh. Sorry! I thought you would want to know. Your friend was…"

Something clicked in my mind. Is it one of those evil stunts by Bala? Is he involving Arup to make fun of me for the final time? I raised my voice, "I don't know, Arup, who told you to inform me about this but let them know I don't give a damn about anyone anymore. Let me leave in peace."

"No Dev. You are misunderstanding …." I didn't let him finish. I disconnected and switched off my phone immediately.

I turned around and saw Rishi standing there.

⊕⊕⊕

"What happened? You look edgy."

Not now Rishi. Arup's little play got my blood pressure pumping. I don't want to spread the fire. Give me some space.

But Rishi never learned to give space to his friends. He spoke again, "You are not doing right Dev. Not right for her and not for you."

So now Rishi will teach me about my love life? "Rishi! I still have some packing to do. You have already done your part by trying to stop me from leaving Bengaluru and conspiring with my mom. I don't want any other active contributions from you in my personal life for at least the next 24 hours."

Rishi kept quiet but he didn't leave. I was almost done with my packing so I moved to shift the luggage to the door. My backpack, which I had given earlier to Rishi, felt unusually light. I opened it and it was empty.

"Rishi? Where are my journals?" I was shocked with my own pitch of voice.

Rishi didn't reply and started to walk away. I ran towards him and held him from the back.

"Where are you going? I asked you something," I shouted.

"Are you out of your freaking mind? You're behaving like an animal." Rishi tried to calm me down.

I pushed his hand away, "Answer me first. I'll give you one second. Give them back," my voice smouldered fire.

Maybe Rishi didn't expect me to behave that way so he got a bit defensive, "Dev! They're not with me. Believe me…"

"Where are they? Answer me!" Rishi literally looked afraid witnessing this savage form of mine.

"Dev! I gave them to Neera. Trust me I wanted only good for you…and you told me those didn't matter to you any more…so…"

I slapped him hard on his face. "You scoundrel! You…" I couldn't speak anymore. I sat on the ground.

"Dev? You hit me?"

"Do you have any idea what you did?" I covered my face with my hands.

"What's wrong with her reading your journals? It's about time that she knows about your feelings. Why can't she read it?" Rishi tried to argue.

"You moron! She already chose Bala. She rejected me, Rishi. But what you did will only ruin her life again. Just now Arup called. He saw Bala and Neera fighting. Don't you understand? It must be because of the journals. Her parents are here. She is still trying to get her dad's trust back. Can you imagine what will happen if her father finds out that she used to speak every night with the ill-famed 'SMS boy' in college? She told me that I messed up her love life in college and now I was trying to mess up her marriage life. She wanted me to go away. Why did you do something like this?" I was breathless with anger and emotion. So I stopped to take a deep breath.

Rishi looked down. My voice broke as I continued speaking, "Do you know that I have nightmares in which her life is scarred permanently because of me. I thought maybe if I go away at least she could live peacefully. But No! You gifted me the same remorse back for the rest of my life!"

Rishi sat close to me. "I didn't realize Dev. Please forgive me."

I couldn't reply. I stood up and walked away.

It was almost 9:30. I should get a cab soon. But I didn't know what to do. My brain stopped functioning. It could have been a memorable adieu for me. I would have said an emotional goodbye to my best friend and left this city which had given me a gift in the form of a perfect mixture of happiness, friendship, enmity and pain called life. But as always something happened in the final moment which changed everything. I just didn't know what to do next.

I left the house and started walking in a random direction.

18
THE FORMULA OF LOVE - THERE'S NONE!

"Is this hotel Rani Palace? Why don't you go inside the gate?" I asked the auto driver.

"That's the one. It's a five star hotel. They won't allow three-wheelers inside. You have to walk," the driver looked irritated with my foolish question.

I paid him and crossed the road. According to Arup, Neera's parents were staying at this hotel. Neera had also moved in with them till the marriage. What exactly was I doing here? No idea what to do next? Just going along as it comes? Bingo! That's Dev for you.

I stood at the gate. Both the guards looked at me. Obviously they were habituated to guests coming here in fancy cars. This underdressed young boy standing outside their gate around 11:30 at night didn't impress them.

"What do you want?" one of them asked me.

Mister, if only I knew. I needed to get my journals back. I needed to see if Neera was alright after her fight with Bala. But how? "I want to meet someone."

"It's late. Who do you want to meet?" Clearly he did not trust me.

"I want to meet Ms. Neera Sinha," I said in a hesitant voice. Oh no. What if they called her dad?

"You know the room number?"

"No. I don't."

"Then call her and get the room number and come back in the morning. What kind of people come here nowadays?"

I hung my head and started walking back. What to do next? I was so involved in my thoughts I didn't notice a car just in front of me. A loud honk brought me back to my senses. I almost stumbled at the sudden loud sound. The car was trying to enter the hotel and I was obstructing the way.

I gave way. But it stopped very close to me. The window came down. Oh No! Me and my cursed luck! It was Dinesh Sinha, Neera's dad! I didn't even imagine in my dreams that he would recognize me. But he did. No wonder he is a successful advocate.

"Dev right? What are you doing here?" he asked me from the car.

I stammered badly, "S...s...sir, I came to meet someone. But the guards didn't allow me to enter. No problem, I will just go."

He thought for a second, "Wait. Come in. These guys are idiots. You can check at the reception. Come on."

Taking a lift from Neera's dad? When I am trying to break in to meet Neera? Wow! I have to congratulate the All Mighty. He just doesn't stop supplying enough thrills in my life.

Hesitantly, I sat on the back seat with him.

"Who do you want to meet? Any friend of yours or a relative?" he asked.

"Friend, sir." I kept it brief. You should speak as little as possible in front of an advocate. They can sense lies.

"Good. Isn't it late to meet anyone?" he smiled at me.

Hope it's not too late mister, "I need to collect something from her…I mean him. I will collect it and just go." I justified my actions to him.

He spoke again, "Venkat is an old friend of mine. He speaks very highly about you. He believes you will go places. Keep it up Dev."

I sighed; Venkat's remarks are mostly emotional because he likes me a lot. Here I am in reality! Literally going to unexpected places and screwing up my life. We reached the hotel main entrance and I got out. I said thanks to him.

"No problem Dev. Why don't you keep in touch with my daughter, Neera, more? I don't know what that girl is doing with her career. She has been working as a junior engineer for so long. She could do with some career tips from you."

Either Venkat exaggerated my capabilities or this man undervalued his daughter too much. For God's sake, she was the topper and she has one year more job experience than I do.

I didn't like him thinking about Neera in that way, "Sir. We were the average to good students; Neera was the one with the extraordinary capabilities. I believe she can excel at anything. She just needs to have focus and necessary support.

That's all. Emotional support and trust can do wonders. I believe it strongly." I said that from my heart. I wanted him to trust his daughter more. We don't realize it but parents and family can make you excel or can limit your potential to a large level. Neera lost her self-confidence for the exact reason that her father thought she was not good enough.

Dinesh Sinha thought for few seconds, "Thanks Dev. I would like to talk to you more someday. Keep in touch." He went away.

Now what? Obviously I couldn't go directly to her room. She could be with her family. I just had a decent encounter with her father. I switched my phone on. But damn! I deleted her number long ago.

It was almost 12. I didn't think there was any chance I would get to see her in the hotel lobby. What to do Dev? Think of something. Quick!

"Aren't you the same boy?" Oh no! Who the hell recognized me now? I might get a heart attack at any time. I looked back. What? Is Neera's whole family following me? It was the mother in the wheelchair.

"What did you say, Ma'am?" What is she doing at this time so close to midnight? Has she gone completely insane?

"You are the boy. I remember you. You were holding Neera's picture right?" Wow! What a photographic memory! Even my weight gain didn't stop her from solving this eight year old puzzle.

"I …I …Ma'am…"

"You have hurt my daughter badly. Don't do that again." My mouth remained open. Is she psychic or something?

She understood looking at my dumbstruck expression, "Neera doesn't hide anything from me. Are you here to meet her?"

Of course I am. But does her mom want to help me or hand me over to the police? I took a risk. I nodded.

She smiled, "She is in the garden. That way!"

Is this some kind of joke or what? If her mother knows all about me why the hell would she want me to meet her daughter when she is getting married in 4 days? What is Neera doing in the garden at midnight? I sensed something was terribly wrong here.

With enough anxiety and hesitation, I walked towards the direction she pointed. When I reached the garden, I got struck by another bolt of lightning.

Am I dreaming again? Did the mad mother knock me unconscious? I tried to pinch myself. Shit! It hurt badly this time. So this was not a dream. Unbelievable! It was the same garden. More beautiful than I actually remembered. There were the bird cages and the artificial fountain. Shit! There was the swing and I could see the girl sitting there too. Just like the dream with her back towards me.

I took some time to control my fear. It's just a dream Dev, I told myself. You are here to talk to Neera. Just do it and get away. I walked towards her and stood very close to the swing. I don't think she felt my presence. She didn't move.

Suddenly I started shivering. What if I see her the same way I did in the dreams? For a second I felt I had no strength at all. I couldn't go any further. That nightmare scared the shit out of me on countless nights. I didn't have enough courage to go and face it for real. Never! Run away, Dev.

I turned around and started to walk away quickly.

I had to stop as the mystery girl called me.

"Dev? Where are you going? Don't you want to wish me on my birthday?"

I looked at the watch. It was the 23rd February, midnight.

Is it a sign or something? How do I end up connecting with Neera every time in the most unexpected circumstances on this particular day?

⊕⊕⊕

With a nervous mind I looked back. She was wearing a night dress almost similar to what I remembered. But No! Neera didn't look exactly as bloody as she was in the dream. I sighed. It was just a dream.

I looked at her for some time. She looked like when I saw her for the first time eight years back. That pony-tailed Section A girl with the glowing face and shy smile.

"What are you doing here alone so late? It's midnight!" I was still trying to digest the whole situation.

She looked down for some time and then spoke softly, "It's over Dev. My marriage is off," she raised her hand. I looked at what she was holding. Holy shit! It was my journal.

I moved from the most romantic to a freaked out state within a blink of an eye.

I said in a crazed tone, "Look Neera. These are fictional. Don't believe them. It's more like a story. I am sorry if you faced any problems because of these. If you want I can speak to Bala and admit that everything is imaginary..."

She looked straight into my eyes, "So it's all a lie? A made up story? But then why are the incidents so close to reality? What's the truth, Dev?"

I couldn't lie with her eyes fixed on me, I looked away. Sorry Neera! I have already scarred your life enough. I can't ruin it again.

"Yes. Everything is a lie! I liked you earlier in college but I am over you now," Oh God! Why does it hurt so much inside?

She couldn't speak for minutes. When I looked at her I could see tears flowing nonstop, "Dev? Why does it have to be always about you? Whenever you wanted you talked with me for hours, whenever you wanted you just stopped talking. When I expected you to stay away from me you came back in my life forcefully. And now when I don't want you to go, you are going away. When you wanted, you loved me insanely and now you say that you are over me? Why can't I get to decide any of it?"

What's happening? Girl, why aren't you happy that I am going away? I am doing it for you. That's what you asked for.

"Don't worry Neera! I think it's not over yet. Let me speak to Bala. I will clear things with him. Just don't let your life get spoiled because of an insignificant guy's bullshit journal. Arup told me that you guys fought. I know it's bad, but not necessarily the end..." I spoke breathlessly.

She almost shouted before I could stop, "Oh shut up Dev. You don't have to speak with anyone. It's me who asked Arup to call you. The wedding was already called off. I didn't have any fight ..."

"Wh...what? But...why? I mean you wanted me to believe that you guys fought? Why?"

She bit the words out, "Because you didn't pick up my calls. Your cell was switched off. How else would I stop you from leaving this city? After reading this diary or whatever... I thought you couldn't just go away if you knew I am suffering. I was expecting you would come and see me...."

Things were seriously getting over the top of my dumb head. I was feeling more stupid as each moment was passing. Why would she expect me to come and save her? What am I? Spiderman?

"Why? I don't get any of it. You are the one who told me to get the hell out of your life. And now you are trying to stop me from leaving? Are you insane?"

Neera confirmed her lunatic status with the next set of statements.

"Look at me. I am out of my freaking mind. I always cared for you, idiot, and you kept on hurting me. But when you came to meet me at the hostel that night, something changed. I just couldn't stop thinking about you. But I freaked out, Dev. I was getting married to someone, my parents were coming to decide my wedding date, and here I was falling for you. I didn't know what to do...I...I..." maybe she uttered something else too. It was not audible.

Why do girls speak emotionally and don't use simple English? 'Kiss me' or 'Get Lost' why can't you mention any of these extremes and just end the scene? Why go round and round? Don't you know we boys are fat heads? We only hear what we want to. We make 1,000 meanings out of these little '50-50 Love-Concern' speeches.

"Neera…wait…"

"No you wait. Do you have any idea how it feels to decide on your marriage date while thinking about someone else? No you don't! When I saw you fight with Subhash, I was so worried. I know you can go to any lengths when pushed in anger. I had tested that once years back. I wanted you to go away Dev, because I didn't want Subhash or anyone else to harm you. I couldn't see you making another mistake in front of my eyes. But you never listened to me before. You kept chasing me for years whether I liked it or not. But this time suddenly you had to listen to me and go away. Why?"

I looked at her, she was crying profusely. I couldn't take it anymore. Whatever happened between us but I can't see this girl in pain. I never could.

"It's ok Neera! Don't punish yourself. I am not blaming you for what you did. Your decision was correct. You would only get hurt if I stay near you. So it's better for both of us…"

Neera looked up with tearful eyes, "That's what you understand after all this? That's what you have to say to me after I tried desperately to stop you from going and waited here till midnight just to express my feelings to you? You are right Dev. You never understand what love is …"

I was playing the 'tough guy' for quite some time but I couldn't anymore. Neera's last remark injected uncontrollable emotions through an invisible needle inside my veins and brain cells. The years of pain and agony just erupted.

"How would I, Neera? How would I understand what love is? Love is a sophisticated term for people like you. It's not for animals like me. Dev has temper issues. Dev is jealous. Dev is weak. That's why you chose Neel, right? I don't know how to show affection to a girl. Damn it! I don't even know how to speak to a girl properly. I am not a monk; I feel intolerable jealousy and insecurity inside me if someone touches you. I know if someone insults you I want to break that bastard's head though I don't have skills to fight even a 10-year-old. I know I have to see you when you are unwell even if I have to combat your sumo roomie to do that. What can I do? My expression of emotion is like that. I am not a perfect person! I can never be …"

I paused to control my crazy nerves which could burst any freaking second.

She clearly didn't expect those extreme reactions from me. As she took a couple of steps towards me, I stopped her. I was not done yet.

"No. Wait there. Your so called 'Love' is about heroes, right? That's what a girl looks for. Charming! Wealthy! Handsome! Big heart! Dictionary meaning of a perfect man! Just jumped out from the movie screen! I am the *bad* guy with all the weaknesses and imperfections in the world whom the girl loves to reject. I only end up making mistakes and hurting her again and again. The universal truth is the baddie never gets the girl in the end. I have learnt to live with it, Neera!

Enough of chasing this impossible dream! Just let me go away, please!"

She came very close to me. After the outburst I didn't have any strength left. I tried to push her away but only could whisper, "Go away ..."

She didn't listen. She touched my face, "It's ok. Calm down now. It's not a movie Dev. It's life. The important thing is how to learn from your mistakes and get over them. You have done it successfully for years now. Nothing is unreal. The funny thing is life doesn't follow any such set of rules. It never did. Do you say this is real?"

She kissed me on the lips. It felt like 10,000 volts of electric shock passed through my veins. I stood awestruck.

She adjusted my hair with her hand, "I know Dev is not perfect. He is always driven by extreme emotions. He doesn't think rationally. I knew that from the moment I befriended him. But I like him that way. If he was too balanced and calculative would he have taken the risk to check on me at the hostel? Would he have left his job just to honour my words? Would he have stood by me all this time when I needed him though it broke all his relationships apart? Would he be talking to me right now when he needed to leave this city? No he wouldn't. I am aware of his limitations. Still I cared for him and now I don't know when and why but slowly I have loved all this imperfection. Never ever say anything harsh about him again."

She stopped for a second and then cried out, "I love you, Dev. Please don't go away."

She was already in tears and I, myself, was not in my most macho mode. I broke down. She embraced me. We held each other for a long time.

"Let it all go, Dev!" she was still trying to calm me down. I held her tighter.

While holding her I could say only one thing, "I love you Neera! I always did..." I don't know if it was audible but the next moment I could feel her tears flowing through my chest.

Give it back to me all right now, girl! All the wounds, all the worry and all the pain I gave you over the years. You had enough. I promise you from this moment you will only smile.

✠✠✠

We were sitting together on that infamous swing from my dreams. With our occasional show of affection it was slowly becoming my favourite romantic place.

I sent Rishi a message. I didn't want the poor guy to feel bad anymore. He sent thumbs up in reply. He also did an unexpected favour by speaking with my mom. My friend is the best.

"How did you get rid of Bala? Didn't he create any problems?" I was having difficulty believing that Bala accepted rejection gracefully.

"Don't ask me. It was so damn embarrassing. When I knew I couldn't marry him I had to tell him to his face. Oh Dev! You've made me do such things..." She punched me softly and smiled, "But truly it was a real pain. Initially he didn't react much, but then I learned he was trying to take my parents into confidence and force the wedding. Luckily, Venkat uncle saved me. Dad trusts him more than anyone. He said a few things about Subhash to Dad. Then Dad himself called off the wedding."

I don't know how to say thanks to Venkat. He paid me back a gift of a lifetime and more. He kept on helping me from the sidelines. God should make more people like him.

"Dev," Neera kept her head on my chest, "…we have to talk to Dad about us. You know it will not be easy. But we will manage it."

I sighed, "I know. My past is going to come between us."

She looked at me, "No. It won't. You trust me right? I will convince Dad."

"I trust you. But I think another person can also help us out in this." I know your Venkat uncle, Neera! I am hoping he can put in some good words for me.

"What about your family?" Neera's face looked a bit tense.

"Oh! Don't even worry about it. My mom chose that insane girl for me who threw sand balls at my face. Clearly their expectation level is not that high. You will not only meet that but you may cross their maximum expectancy bar. They will be ecstatic to see their loser son scoring a girl like you." I laughed.

"Shut up! Don't exaggerate!" but her smile said she liked the thought.

"Oh shit!"

"What?" She looked nervous.

"Neera! I am currently jobless. I left my job at TTS and now I am not going to Kolkata. So I will need a new job."

"Do you want to go to Kolkata for a few days?"

"I am not sure. I can't stay away from you now. Maybe I can talk to my old manager in TTS." I thought of Hiten! He might help me out as I knew they hadn't recruited anyone yet.

"Don't worry! I am sure you will find a solution. I trust you." She kissed me on the cheeks.

That was enough invitation; I kissed her longer, "Happy Birthday Neera!"

"Dev? Whatever happens, promise that you won't leave me."

"Never!" I have no idea how long we were there. Eventually she slept in my arms.

I can't predict what awaits us tomorrow. I don't care as long as Neera is with me. I don't really know how badly my past mistakes are going to haunt me.

But it was never about the past or the future. Was it?

The story of our life is always about one perfect moment. That moment is something we strive for. A yes, a nod or an eye blink can make you run a 1,000 miles if it gets you to that. We rejoice, fight, laugh and cry but through everything we still want to live that moment again and again. Whether you gain or miss it, you will try for yet another 100 years and make the same commitments and mistakes to get that one moment back.

Lucky me! Right now I am living my moment.

Srishti's all time bestsellers

- A Dilli-Mumbai Love Story
- A Feeling Beyond Words
- A half baked love story
- A Life that you knew..
- Animal Farm
- A Thing Beyond Forever
- An Unequal harmony
- Because You Loved Me..
- Beep You! You BeepHole
- Belong
- Be Ready for Child Birth
- Best of Rabindranath Tagore
- Boundless Saga of Love
- By the River Pampa I...
- Complete/Convenient
- Corporate Atyaachaar
- Dancing with Maharaja
- Everything you Desire
- Forever in these Pages
- Here Sat A Key Maker
- I am Broke....! Love me
- If God went to B-School
- In Course of True Love
- I too had a love story..
- It's all About Love...
- Journey of two Hearts
- Life is Always Aimless
- Life is What you Make it
- Love Power Politics!!

- My Beloved's MBA Plans...
- My Love Never Faked...
- Never say Goodbye...
- Nothing Lasts Forever
- Ohh! Gods are online..
- Oops! 'I' fell in Love!
- Reflections on the Self
- Shodh
- Something in your Eyes
- Spicy Bites of Biryani
- 34 Bubblegums and Candies
- That Kiss in the Rain..
- The Equation of my Love
- The Funda of Mix-ology
- The Homing Pigeons...
- The Legends of Amrapali
- The Little Prince
- The Secrets of the Dark
- The story of my life
- The Storm in My Mind
- The Quest for Nothing!
- The Thing Between U & Me
- Those Small Lil Things
- Three Times Loser....
- What to eat & what not to eat
- When Strangers Meet
- Where the Rainbow Ends
- When you became my life